ABRACADABRA AND ALCHEMY

MISS SASHA'S SCHOOL OF MAGICK: BOOK ONE

APRIL AASHEIM

DARK ROOT PRESS

For my Mother

When I was a kid I openly laughed at your spells; your crystal balls; your astrology books.

But, secretly, I was fascinated by you.

How fitting that you left us in October, when the Veil was thin.

You are my Miss Sasha.

And I am forever grateful to have been your daughter.

Your lessons will not be forgotten.

Shari Runkle—

March 5, 1946—October 1, 2021

PROLOGUE

THE MID 1990'S

Dark Root, Oregon
Miss Sasha's School of Magick
Dusk

There were many signs of the impending darkness, yet Sasha chose to disregard them all. The omens were small at first: ravens in the cornfields, snakes emerging from their burrows mid-winter, and trees dropping their leaves earlier every year.

Over time, the warnings magnified, and even Sasha found them impossible to dismiss. The rains turned sour and withered the gardens, the clouds shaped themselves into dragons, and there was the scent of brimstone lingering in the air, disappearing whenever she inhaled deeply, like the remnants of a dream.

The world was changing—much quicker than the witch anticipated. The wheel had turned, and a new era was budding. But would it come in a trickle...or a wave?

**

Sasha lifted her chin, trying to catch the sulphuric scent wafting in through the second-story window, attempting to discern its origin. *Sniff. Sniff.* She turned her head right, then left, nearly locking on to it—and then it was gone.

"Frickle-frack," she grumbled, shutting the window hard. Sasha preferred other words, but she promised Dora she'd work on setting a good example for the girls--especially Maggie, who blurted out curse words when she was angry, as indifferently as she slept when she was tired. Words had power, and one had to be careful with them. Especially curse words.

Sasha left the window, wringing her hands like a silly old woman. The smell had intensified in the last weeks and she couldn't quite get a fix on it. It hung over the school like mist on a mountain top.

She, herself, used brimstone in her craft, mostly for protection spells and counter magick. But the element was also used in exorcisms, binding spells, necromancy, and other dark arts. It was used in alchemy, too, though there were no true alchemists still alive that she knew of, except perhaps herself. She wondered if her former apprentice, Armand, and his mistress, Larinda, had something to do with it? She had sensed they were dabbling, but had they really turned to practicing forbidden magick? And so close to the school? She decided to keep an extra eye on them both, though their appearances had been scarce since they were removed from *The Council.*

"Let them try their tricks," Sasha said, clapping her hands together firmly, like two chalkboard erasers that needed cleaning. Armand might be a powerful warlock, and Larinda a witch of her own family line, but Sasha was far better trained, and far more disciplined.

But there was an even more troubling option than the warlock and his concubine--one she hadn't wanted to entertain before—though now felt compelled to address: Hellhounds. Demonic beasts summoned up from the bowels of the earth, with the bodies of dogs and wolves, and imbued with the darkest of human souls. Their arrival was said to herald *The Final Trial.* Sasha shivered, pulling her shawl around her bony shoulders. Hellhounds were not to be trifled with. Not even by a witch as accomplished as herself.

Leaving the window, Sasha walked the vast library room, strolling past hundreds of books and scrolls that called out to her with their magick. Writings on spells, myths, legends, arcane languages, maps, math, geometry, and religion. Knowledge that was meant to be forgotten, but had found its way into her possession. The last accounts of their kind, for most.

She went to the large stone altar in the middle of the room, where a golden book the length of her forearm lay open. "Hellhounds," she said to the book, careful not to touch it. The tome was sentient and temperamental as a feral tomcat to those it distrusted. And as such, she treated it like a beloved pet rather than a book. The broad pages flipped of their own accord, generating a breeze that ruffled her sleeves, before stopping at a section titled: *Beasts of the Netherworld.*

"Mom!" Ruth Anne, her eldest daughter, peeped her head inside the library. Sasha turned quickly, attempting to block her view of the book, and the ghastly, demon-eyed creatures staring back from the pages. "Aunt Dora says the tea leaf readings are about to begin if you want to watch."

"I'll be there shortly," Sasha said, straightening up and adjusting the collar of her fitted black gown. "Dora doesn't need me for that."

"A'ight," Ruth Anne said, craning her neck to see what Sasha was hiding. She was the least magickally talented of the girls, preferring academics over practice. "When do we get to use your library?" she asked, scanning the shelves that lined every wall.

"Soon," Sasha promised. "You girls have a library of your own to read from, until then."

Ruth Anne sighed and left, having been given the same answer as every other time she asked. But these books were precious, and the girls were still too young. Besides, Ruth Anne's fingers were forever sticky with gum and candy bars. If these writings were lost, their unique knowledge might never be recovered.

Closing the arched wooden door behind her, and locking it thrice, Sasha descended the circular staircase to the main floor, where an enormous cauldron bubbled over a blazing fireplace hearth. The pot reeked of onions, cabbage, and rabbit meat—Dora's special stew. Sasha covered her nose and hurried past, quite disliking the smell. At least it wasn't Dora's 'famous' kidney soup—the ammonia smell of which made even Sulphur preferable.

Crossing the stone floor, each step an echo, she worked past the curio cabinets exhibiting curiosities from around the world: pickled animals in jars, animatronics from the Victorian era, cursed dolls, and grinning marionettes. When she reached the main classroom, with its long tables, chalkboards, and Bunsen burners, Sasha stood quietly in the doorway, watching as Dora gave her lesson on reading tea leaves.

"Now, swirl the cups, girls," Dora instructed, walking around the table with her arms clasped behind her back, peering over the shoulders of Ruth Anne, Merry, and Eve, as they worked their tea leaves. "A little swifter! Merry." "Yer not throwin' a football, Ruth Anne." "Eve, that was perfect. Ya have the knack fer teas," Dora smiled.

Where is Maggie? Sasha wondered. That girl. Never where she should be, especially during lessons. How was she ever going to take over *The Council* one day, if she didn't learn to get control of her magick?

"Now, e'eryone look in yer cup, an' tell me what ya see."

"A hawk?" Ruth Anne asked, lifting her eyebrows uncertainly. "It has wings."

Merry looked inside Ruth Anne's teacup. "It could be an angel," she said.

"Why would Ruth Anne get an angel?" Eve asked, still dreamily swirling her own cup. "She never does her chores or eats her vegetables. I bet it's actually a devil."

"Don' ya talk like that about yer sister!" Dora scolded, tapping

Eve's shoulder with her wand. "Words have power and just sayin' the *D*-word, may bring him here."

"You're afraid of the devil?" Eve asked, looking up at her aunt with her dark round eyes. Merry and Ruth Anne looked up, as well, their teacups motionless in their hands. "You're not afraid of anything."

"Bah! I'm afraid o' plenty! Jus' been aroun' so long I don' care as much. But I know this much--there's good in the world, an' there's also evil. An' when ya name that evil, ya let it in." She drew an invisible sigil in the air with her finger, one Sasha recognized as a protective sign.

The girls returned to their leaves. Merry saw a ladybug. Eve saw a heart. And Ruth Anne decided her winged creation was an airplane, and that soon she'd be going away on an adventure, though she'd never been further than Linsburg, Dark Root's neighboring town.

"I'm back!" Maggie ran in from the hall, past Sasha's hip, zipping up her hand-me-down jeans as she went. She was a lanky girl, with wild red hair and mismatched socks. And there was a hole in her t-shirt that Sasha was certain hadn't been there when they left the house that morning.

"What took ya so long?" Dora asked, as Maggie wriggled into her seat beside Eve.

"There were weird sounds in the bathroom."

"Old pipes," Dora said.

Eve raised her hand. "Can we be excused?"

"Nay! No one is excused 'til Maggie's done with her leaves. We work together, girls. We're stronger that way."

Sasha crossed her arms, watching with more interest. Maggie was undoubtedly the most talented of her four daughters, but her magick lacked all focus and discipline.

"Swirl," Dora encouraged, standing behind her.

Maggie's brow furrowed as she shook her teacup, in the same furious manner that she emptied her piggy bank.

"Now tell us what ya see." Everyone leaned in.

Maggie lifted the cup straight up to her nose. She squinted one eye, then the other. "Nothing," she sighed, tugging on the end of her hair. "Nothing ever works for me."

"Try again," Dora said. "Soften your eyes—pretend yer falling asleep. Then tell me what ya see."

Maggie squirmed--finding it hard to sit still, let alone pretend to fall asleep. After several false starts, her eyelids drifted to half-mast. "I see... letters. Words. Only, they're not like any letters or words I know."

Sasha stood up straighter, taking a step inside the room. It was very rare to see actual words in a reading.

"Ya only have a couple o' leaves," Dora said, scratching her head and ruffling her gray curls. "How many letters can there be?"

"So many..." Maggie peered deep into the porcelain cup as if it were bottomless. The room was dead quiet, everyone watching with held breath. Maggie's head swayed side to side. "It's a string of sounds--ohhmenirsirsinomananumlooshoo—"

The hairs on the back of Sasha's neck rose beneath her collar as Maggie whistled out the sound, foreboding as a banshee's call. She knew those sounds—but from where?

Silvery lightning flashed outside the east-facing windows, illuminating the iron gates of the school property. Sasha's crystal bracelet flashed an amber ring of protective light around her--a warning of supernatural danger. She stepped from the shadows, crisscrossing her hands as she hurried towards the table. "Maggie!" She thundered. "Stop! *Now!*"

The force of Sasha's order pushed Maggie backward, away from the table, knocking her onto the floor. In a flash, Merry was by her side, tending to her sister, as Sasha smashed Maggie's teacup against the wall.

But it was too late. Sasha understood what the words meant. This cycle of time had run its course, and Maggie's words had sealed it. How had this happened?

"It's storming!" Eve pointed at the sudden downpour hammering down onto an open windowsill.

A large raven landed at the opening, with moon-yellow eyes and iridescent black feathers that easily repelled the raindrops beating against them. "Caw!" Its eyes rested on Maggie.

"Get out! Get out you dark minion!" Sasha grabbed the hearth broom and swatted at the bird. The raven ignored Sasha, cocking its head and studying her, before turning its attention back to Maggie. "Leave her alone!" Sasha commanded, thrusting out her hands and hurling the raven back into the rain.

She hastily closed the window and locked the latch, feeling light-headed from harnessing so much magick, so quickly.

"She okay?" Sasha asked, joining the others gathered around Maggie, who was shaking from head to toe.

"I'm calming her down now, Mama," Merry said, applying her healing hands to her sister's shoulders, then helping her to stand, like a wobbly-legged calf.

Sasha attempted to appear calm herself. *Those words coming out of Maggie's mouth!* Where had she heard them? They were not something Maggie could make up herself.

"Ruth Anne, grab your rain slickers. I need you to take the girls back to Sister House." Sasha pulled Ruth Anne up by her collar and pointed her towards the door. "Take only the enchanted path, and lock the doors and all the windows once you get home."

"Why? What's wrong?" Ruth Anne asked, already handing out the slicks.

"Nothing. I just fear the storm will get worse and Dora and I don't want you girls to get sick."

"We can wait it out with you."

"No. Go now. Dora and I also have to go over tomorrow's lesson. We'll be there shortly." Sasha licked her lips, knowing Ruth Anne doubted the explanation. "Don't stop for anything. And if you smell sulphur, run."

Ruth Anne's eyes widened behind her enormous glasses, but she nodded.

"I'm scared," Eve said, sliding her fingers through her black hair.

"It's just rain, Eve," Merry said calmly. "And you're very brave."

The girls headed for the door, except for Maggie, who stalled mid-step. Her eyes rolled back and her head flopped to the side. Sasha worried she'd collapse. Instead, she lifted her hand, pointing straight at Sasha. When she spoke, it was in a toddler-like, lyrical voice:

"The wheel of karma spins and spins,
around the way and back again.
Just when the lessons have been learned,
another spinner takes her turn."

Dora and Sasha exchanged looks. It was a poem Sasha's mother, Juliana, had often recited, a woman who had been dead for decades, and whom Maggie had never met. Sasha had never heard the poem since, nor spoken it, that she remembered.

Merry took Maggie's hand, instantly breaking the spell, and Maggie snapped back.

"Go, now," Sasha said, herding them out the door. The floors seemed to be tilting, making it difficult to keep balance.

The girls ran out through the iron gate and down to the forest path leading back to Sister House. They would be fine on the protected trail, but the school itself was not as fortified.

"What is it?" Dora asked, their eyes trailing the girls. "An earthquake?"

"I'm not certain. Can you look at your tea leaves?" Sasha asked, closing the door against the pouring rain.

Dora nodded and poured a cup, drinking the tea down swiftly before swirling her mug. When she looked inside, her eyes widened and her fingers let go. The cup shattered on the stone floor.

Sasha clutched her heart, awaiting Dora's verdict...

"A demon loose! More 'en one, too! It can' be! There's no demons in Dark Root! We have the domes, and *The Council*!"

"Has it already happened? Or is it yet to come?"

Dora shrugged. Time didn't work on the other side the way it did in this world. The past, present, and future often overlapped.

The entire school rumbled, as if breaking apart, and it wasn't from the storm or an earthquake. Taking Dora by the hand, Sasha pulled her into the hallway and onto a very narrow staircase that bypassed the second floor entirely, leading directly to the attic. This room was off-limits to the girls, and Sasha and Dora rarely came up themselves--the magick of the space was so potent, and the energy so dense.

"Demons prefer basements," Dora objected, who had bad knees and arthritis in her hips. But Sasha didn't have time to explain her hunch. She kept pulling Dora up the stairs, as the tight walls around them quaked so hard she feared the building might collapse.

The door at the top of the short landing was secured with a deadbolt, and Sasha took a deep breath before removing the ankh key from around her neck and twisting it into the lock. The women braced themselves as if entering an accursed tomb. There were artifacts inside this room older than even mummies.

As she suspected, the rumbling came from inside the attic, booming like a hundred hammers, beating on all four walls. Sasha's bracelet flashed as she swept past the threshold, surrounding herself and Dora in a protective light circle.

There were flashes of color inside the room, illuminating the exposed ceiling joints. Electric blues and greens zipped about, vanishing when she turned on the light switch. The pounding was so deafening that Dora covered her ears.

"It's coming from the mirror," Sasha said, working her way towards the back corner of the room, through a maze of cardboard boxes and old furniture pieces. There were many magick mirrors in the world, and they all held their own secrets, but this one was particularly vile. Only Sasha knew its true origins and purpose. The obsidian glass warbled and warped, as flashes of light danced with swirls of dark mist upon its surface, and ghostly handprints appeared from the other side.

"Maggie somehow broke the seal," Sasha said, as they watched the mirror begin to stretch itself apart. "The demons will soon be free... and so too the *Ring of Resurrection*."

"It's been hidden inside this mirror? All this time?" Dora asked, her mouth agape. Sasha nodded, readying her wand while Dora did the same. "That would mean that six of the seven rings have returned! An' if *The Ring of Malchezdiach* is recovered..." Dora swallowed loud enough for Sasha to hear.

"The *Final Trial* begins." Sasha finished for her. She twisted the band on her finger: The *Ring of Life*—one of the famed seven—then closed her fist over it and tucked the ankh back into her gown.

A large fragment from the center of the mirror exploded outward, flying just over their heads. "Darkness comes!" Dora cried, as a swirling black mist with red flashing eyes shot out from the jagged hole left by the missing piece. A *darkling*. A lesser demon, but still far more powerful than any human, and even most witches. And there were more of them, fighting their way out.

"Draw a chalk circle around the mirror and place a hexagram within it. Then, add any protective sigil you can remember, from any school of magick, along the outside border! We must contain them!"

Dora removed the classroom chalk from the pocket of her housedress and began drawing the circle, as Sasha exhausted her magick holding back the *darklings* funneling out of the hole. They hissed at this new barrier, lashing out at the women, their touch as cold as winter ice.

"Faster, Dora!" Sasha called, swatting at the disembodied creatures with her wand. One coiled itself around her arm, scorching her wrist, but she managed to keep hold of the wand. Before Dora could finish the ward, it slipped through the broken circle, disappearing into the rafters.

"We'll deal with that one later," Sasha said, turning back to the swarm before her as Dora closed the circle. The darklings threw themselves against their prison walls, again and again, shrieking as if in pain. "The circle won't hold long. And I fear we have something much worse coming through."

The hole in the mirror expanded, until the glass was gone, leaving only a vacuum in its place. An apparition stepped through--a shadow resembling a man. Even in his shapelessness, Sasha detected his smile. On one phantom finger, she saw the flicker of a golden ring —*THE* golden ring, and was momentarily overcome by its stout magick. Her ring tightened on her own finger, responding to its long-lost sibling.

The darklings greeted the shadow man, twisting around him and lapping at his ring like a pack of hounds at feeding time. The creature shook them off, his eyes falling on Sasha's hand, his mouth opening wide as he leapt forward to seize it, only to be stopped cold by the chalk circle.

"The sigil won' hold him," Dora said, backing away and readying her own wand. "He's too strong. What is he?"

"A minion of *The Dark One*, his soul too twisted by his countless evil lives to ever find redemption, bound within this mirror centuries ago, where he could do no further harm. Not one to be trifled with," she said, as the shadow soundlessly roared at his new restrains.

If he got loose—and somehow took possession of her ring—then nothing they'd worked for would matter. Though weakened by her expenditure of magick, and the darkling's' heart-stopping touches, Sasha summoned all of her power. She drew from the elements around her: the stonework, the hearth fire, the pouring rain, and the howling wind. And the aether that saturated all of Dark Root. Once full, nearly to the point of tipping over, she said, "Dora, get me a bottle. Quick!"

Using her third eye, Sasha projected her mind back to the golden book in her library, mentally flipping through pages until she found one on binding demons. It was an archaic language, words known only now to demons, and said to have been scribed by Solomon himself.

"Fista mora asperatus. Pomera Forgan Amura Tu!"

Sasha repeated the incantation three times, her voice loudening with each recitation.

The lesser demons shrunk back away from her, but still hovered near the *Shadow Man* and his *Ring of Resurrection*. Sasha waved her hand, flashing them her own ring. The demons drifted cautiously towards her again, both hungry and curious, hissing with desire

What are ya doin'?" Dora asked as Sasha stepped up to the chalk border, nose to nose with a darkling.

"Praying I'm right about this." She slipped off her ring, kissed the seal depicting a tree encircled by two snakes, and threw it into the void. The demons darted after it without hesitation, blindly following it back into the mirror. Dora then quickly placed the missing piece of glass back into place. The glass reformed itself, and the mirror sealed shut.

The Shadow Man howled at the loss of his minions, his dark eyes turning on Sasha. His energy was cold. Angry. And cruel.

"Bottle, now!" Dora handed Sasha the corked bottle, their eyes never leaving the beasts. She had bound spirits before, but never an entity this powerful. "Take my hand and say these words with me. '*Fista mora asperatus. Pomera Forgan Amura Tu...*' It will take both of us to cage this thing."

"Fista mora asperatus. Pomera Forgan Amura Tu..."
"Fista mora asperatus. Pomera Forgan Amura Tu!"
"Fista mora asperatus. Pomera Forgan Amura Tu!!"

The lone attic window shattered. Boxes lifted from the floor and took flight, swirling about like Dora's tea leaves. The *Shadow Man* raised his hands as the spell took hold, his mouth open wide, watching himself morph into a column of red flame. The flame was then sucked down into the bottle; the ring, too large for the container, dropped heavily to the ground.

Sasha promptly capped the bottle.

The boxes crashed to the ground. The school stopped quaking.

"Is it o'er?" Dora mopped her forehead with the hem of her housedress, looking from the mirror to the bottle and back again. And then at Sasha's empty finger, and the *Ring of Resurrection*, lying on the floor. "Ya better cleanse that before ya put it on," Dora warned of the ring. "It's tainted."

"I'm not putting it on." Sasha picked it up with the tip of her wand, letting it slide halfway down the rod. "I'll hide both this bottle and the ring. They must never be allowed to conjoin, nor be spoken of, again. That ring is a powerful elixir, and the demons we trapped today aren't likely to forget it. And they aren't alone. There are others who hunger for it--to taste the breath of life once again."

"But ya threw away *your own ring,"* Dora said. "The tree needs it!"

"We'll make do with other magick, until I find a solution. As for the school, we'll remove what we can from the building, and then close it permanently."

She pressed her lips together, her anxiety growing, though she wouldn't admit this to Dora, who worried enough already. They had opened the school to train the girls for the *Final Trial.* But even with their superb divination skills, neither witch had guessed the end would come so soon.

But fate takes no heed of preparation; it was wise to always have a backup plan.

"We'll cast a spell over the school grounds, and cloak this area in vines," Sasha announced.

"So drastic?" Dora asked, already collecting up boxes.

"There's a rogue demon on the loose, who will undoubtedly be drawn to this place, and bring others back with him. We either hide the school or burn it down. We've collected too much knowledge to have it be lost again forever. Whatever comes, we will not be plunged back into the days of ignorance."

"What about the girls?" Dora asked, her arms full as she headed for the stairs.

"I'll cast a forget spell over them. The ring wasn't the only thing the darklings seek. They want the girls, while they are still young enough to siphon from, and mold."

"An' *the Stone*?" Dora asked. "Surely, that will be a beacon fer the darklings."

"It will be hidden, too. Even from myself."

CHAPTER 1
MAGGIE
TWENTY-FIVE YEARS LATER

"Honk! Honk!" Ruth Anne hollered at us from her Jeep, rolling up to the curb beside the gravel lot. The top was down, despite the forecast of rain. Then again, there was always a chance of rain in Dark Root--cloudy with a chance of gloom. But Ruth Anne was impervious to the weather, enduring even the most extreme seasons with hardly a change of attire--much like the sturdy, evergreen pines surrounding us.

"Busted," I whispered to my younger sister, Eve. We were nearing the front of the line at the new Java Juicer coffee truck—a line we'd been standing in for half an hour. The pumpkin spice latte scent was so close now I could almost bite the air and taste it. "She's not going to be happy about this," I added, as our oldest sister turned off the engine and marched our way.

"Calm down. We're just buying coffee, Maggie," Eve reminded me, though I detected a trace of guilt in her eyes as we moved up in line—but only a trace.

"I see you both. Don't pretend you didn't see me." Ruth Anne's boots crunched the newly fallen leaves on the sidewalk. "My own sisters---traitors!"

I smiled widely as I turned to greet her, decked out in her camouflage pants and a yellow t-shirt reading: *Haunted Dark Root Tours*, and beneath that: *The Most Haunted Town in the Pacific Northwest.* The spirits brought tourism to Dark Root, though I wasn't convinced the ghost-to-person ratio was higher in Dark Root than in any other small town. Then again, spirits seemed to find me, no matter where I traveled. "Hey, Ruth Anne." I waved. "Just getting a latte before I begin my *very* long day."

"Seriously?" Ruth Anne scratched her ear, which in turn wriggled her glasses. She then puckered her lips and lifted one finger. Eve and I exchanged quick glances, knowing we were about to be lectured. "For Gouda's sake, Maggie, your husband owns a diner. A diner that sells coffee." She pointed to *Dip Stix Café'*, just across the street. "And Eve, you and Paul are trying to start a coffee house of your own. Ladies, I don't mean to preach, but the local economy is how we keep this town running. Why are you supporting outside vendors? And a chain coffee company, at that?"

"We get lots of outside vendors in this town," Eve shrugged, resigning herself as she stepped out of the line.

"Yes, but only seasonal vendors for the festivals. This truck will likely be here to stay, so long as we keep giving it our hard-earned dollars."

"We just wanted to try something different," I said, reluctantly joining Eve in surrender. "It's the same thing here, day in and day out. And if you'd read the sign," I said, standing aside and pointing to the sandwich board propped against the side of the truck, "You'd see that coffee is free today, to celebrate their grand opening."

"And that's how they get you!" Ruth Anne narrowed her brown eyes behind her large square frames. "Soon, you'll be spending every morning waiting in line for a seven-dollar coffee, just like these other zombies." A woman from the line shot Ruth Anne a sour look. "Sorry. I meant those zombies. Not you, of course."

"It's got chocolate in it," I said.

"I'll buy you a bottle of Hershey's syrup." Ruth Anne replied.

Eve rolled her eyes, grinding the heel of her black leather boot into the gravel. "We get it, Ruth Anne. No fancy coffee. We'll just drink it out of a tin can, cooked over a campfire, just like you. Any other joys you want to kill this morning?"

Ruth Anne twisted her knuckles into the side of her scalp, looking like a robot about to malfunction. She nodded to the endless line still waiting for their free drinks. "It's not just the outside vendors. Our entire town is changing. How many people do you actually know in this line?"

"Like three," I admitted, scanning a line of about twenty. That did seem odd. I had spent most of my life in Dark Root and knew most everyone. "Tourists?" I ventured, surveying the vacant eyes of the caffeine-deprived as they shuffled forward in slippers and house-coats. Not tourists. Tourists dressed better. "They can't all live here?"

"Over the summer, a bunch of the old houses were sold. According to my research, Dark Root's population has almost doubled this year."

"So, our population's up to fifty now?" I teased.

"Why Dark Root?" Eve asked. "There's not even a real grocery store in this town—just Merry's hokey roadside vegetable stands."

"All we have to offer is ghosts," I agreed. *Both real and imagined.*

"That might be part of the charm." Ruth Anne rubbed her hands together as if warming them by a fire. "There was an article in *Spooked Magazine* about Dark Root last year. Our town was featured for its year-round 'Witchy Vibe'."

"*Spooked Magazine*?" I asked, quickly retrieving my phone from the back pocket of my jeans. The internet connection was spotty in Dark Root, on even the nicest days. But a person could get lucky for a minute or two if they held their phone to the sky and didn't move it more than an inch in any direction. Sure enough, an article about Dark Root appeared in the gothic style magazine, with pictures of pumpkin patches, a quaint downtown, the old cemetery, and our ancestral home—*Sister House.* I couldn't read much, as I was quickly disconnected, but I did catch the authors name: R. A. Maddock.

"Ruth Anne! You wrote that article!" I pulled her by the elbow, to the side of the truck, where a picnic table had been erected overnight. "You might be older than me, but I'm still head of *The Council*, and you should have discussed this with me."

"It was just an article, Maggie," Ruth Anne said, jiggling her car keys in her pocket. "I can't help if I'm a word wizard. Besides, I needed the fifty bucks it paid."

I shook my head. Ruth Anne seemed oblivious to the wheels she set in motion. With so many newcomers--not simply tourists who ate, shopped, and moved on, but actual residents--some of our secrets were bound to get out. "Outsiders moving to Dark Root puts us all in jeopardy."

"Overreacting a bit there, Mags?" Ruth Anne said, drawing a circle in the rocks with the toe of her boot. "It was one article. I'm a writer. That's what I do."

Eve leaned against the corner of the picnic table, drawing her icy-pink cashmere sweater closer around her. "Normally, I'd very much agree that Maggie usually overreacts to just about everything, but we can't have dozens of new people moving in without warning. We have children to look out for now."

"Says the woman who sent her daughter on a picnic with a box of Kraft Macaroni and Cheese."

"Step-daughter. And she didn't tell me it needed to be cooked."

"Don't derail this conversation," I said to Ruth Anne, though she did have a point about Eve's maternal skills. "This town has a 'witchy vibe' because we are witches! But what happens when people start seeing through the illusion of tourism and discover what we are? We'll be freaks, at best. Hunted, at worst."

"Hunted? We're not living in the ye-olden days anymore, Mags. The Spanish Inquisition has been dissolved."

"Sasha thought that we needed to be protected. She spent her final years hiding us from the world." I shook my head, feeling my anger rise. I wasn't sure why, exactly. It was just a few new people coming to town. How many more old houses were there to sell? But it felt like Ruth Anne had opened a gate—and with it—our security.

I stomped between Ruth Anne and the picnic table, trying to ignore the prickling sensation building in my palms, as annoyance and magick intermingled. If people truly saw us for what we were, what would happen? It was fine for us to be odd, eccentric, or even outright magickal during October, but no one wanted a witch around come Easter.

Ruth Anne removed her baseball cap, speaking through clenched teeth. "People aren't just moving here because of one little article. Merry's the mayor. Blame her for making this town too charming."

We turned in unison towards Main Street. With its colorful shops, popcorn carts, Victorian streetlamps, rustic benches, and mouth-watering aromas, Dark Root *was* rather enchanting. If you liked that sort of thing.

"This looks nothing like the dump I remember from our childhood," I lamented, as two boys dashed around us in a game of tag. "Remember when we were the only kids living here? We had the run of the place then."

We all sighed, recalling the days when we skipped along sidewalks and leapt into street puddles, without the fear of getting hit by a car. Our afternoons were spent wandering in and out of shops because we knew all the owners. And the enchanted paths meant we were free to explore the woods. There was a sense of adventure in our childhood that I feared our own children would never know.

"Of course, we were also bored out of our minds," Eve said.

"Some things never change," I said, thinking of the routine ahead of me that day: get the kids to school, run my shop, cook dinner, clean the kitchen, tuck kids into bed... Perhaps I shouldn't worry about being outed as a witch. It had been months since we'd done anything by a full moon. Or any moon, for that matter.

"Who knows, maybe our weirdness will eventually scare them all off." Ruth Anne ventured.

"Doubtful. Weirdness is trending," said Eve, who was the only one among us who ever knew what trended outside the town.

A man's head popped out of the Java Juicer window. "Caramel mocha with whipped cream and colored sprinkles."

"They have colored sprinkles," I grumbled, then felt guilty as I looked back at *Dip Stix Cafe*. I checked the time on my phone. "Alas, dear Sister," I said to Ruth Anne. "We must beg your leave now, sadder and less caffeinated than whence we arrived," I bowed, slinging my beaded handbag over my shoulder as my eyes locked with those of a woman in yoga pants, sipping a steaming latte.

We walked together to Ruth Anne's Jeep. She tossed her baseball cap onto the dash and grabbed something from the back seat—something furry and stinking.

"Are you still taking that online taxidermy class?" Eve demanded, backing away from the wooly thing Ruth Anne was pushing onto her head.

"It's not roadkill--it's a hat." An old-fashioned raccoon hat, complete with open eyes and a bushy tail. "Although, it does kinda smells like roadkill," she admitted, pushing the tail out of her eyes.

"Davie Crocket called and he wants his..." I began, then got too close and accidentally smelled the thing. "Nope. He says you can keep it."

"It belonged to Sophie's great-grandfather, and she wanted me to have it. I'm trying to get used to it before she comes back."

"That's love," I said.

"Need a ride?" Ruth Anne asked.

"Nope, we can walk it." I pointed in the direction of a walking trail leading into the thick woods that encircled our small town.

"First day of school," Eve said when Ruth Anne's brain did not compute where my pointy finger was leading.

"Already? Geez. Where did the summer go?"

"Cuddled up with your girlfriend in that horror-movie cabin of yours," Eve said, dryly.

"Fiancé," Ruth Anne corrected. "And it's rustic-chic."

"No ring, no engagement," Eve said, nodding to Ruth Anne's barren fingers.

Ruth Anne swallowed, keeping step with us as we crossed the street, towards our family business, which I now owned and ran: *Miss Sasha's Magick Shoppe.* "We'll do the ring-shopping thing when Sophie gets back in December. By the way, where are all your kiddos?"

"June Bug walked the herd up to the schoolhouse earlier," I said. June Bug was our sister Merry's daughter, and the oldest of our children.

"June Bug's a trooper," Ruth Anne nodded, walking with us.

"She was bribed," Eve said. "But it was the best three dollars I'll spend all day. Honestly ladies, this parenting thing is tougher than I thought it would be. It's always *comb this, wash that, cook something.* I was grateful for the break. Though, a fancy coffee would have been nice, too."

I gave Eve a sideways look but held my tongue. Eve had one step-daughter in the fourth grade, who dressed herself, did her chores without nagging, and made her own eggs. I had three wonderful, but exhausting children. My youngest son, Montana, peed into a heating vent that very morning, leaving our house smelling like burning ammonia. Sometimes, I daydreamed of a *Freaky Friday* moment, where I got to trade places with my bombshell sister and her fake boobs and self-sufficient child for just one day. My fantasy always soured the moment I imagined Eve in my place, lying in bed with my husband Shane, even if she was in my body.

The curtains were drawn inside *Miss Sasha's Magick Shoppe,* but I could see a flicker of light within. Jillian was inside setting up.

"I sense you still need to talk about something," I said to Ruth Anne, who shuffled from one foot to the other.

"I need your wisdom."

"Our wisdom?" Eve asked, skeptically.

"Yes."

"We should write down this day, to memorialize it for all time," I said.

Ruth Anne was the smartest of us all; she also knew it. But her face was serious now, and I stopped joking.

"Is it hard? To be a parent?" she asked. "Not just, 'I need a break' hard, but really hard?"

"Why ask us? Why not Merry?" I asked, positioning the folds of my long skirt so that a grape juice stain didn't show. "She's the one raising the golden child."

Ruth Anne scoffed. "Because being a parent comes naturally to Merry. So, I thought I'd ask you two, instead."

"We're flattered," I said, shouldering up to Eve in the doorway of my shop, as I pulled a dried Cheerio from my hair. "Yes, Ruth Anne, it's hard. Every day it's hard, in different ways."

"I agree," said Eve, inspecting her manicured nails. "Sometimes I don't have the time to apply primer before my foundation. And my face just feels so...not dewy."

"Damn, I thought so." Ruth Anne straightened her raccoon hat, forcing me to meet the creature's long-dead eyes. "Sophie's pushing me to have a kid. I don't want to be a mom. I never wanted to be a mom. That's not on my vision board."

"Maybe you can be the dad?" Eve reasoned. "Since Sophie will no doubt be carrying it. Unless you adopt."

"It's not the title—it's the parenting. I'm used to being a carefree honeybee, you know? Off pollinating whenever I choose." She flapped her arms in a demonstration. "I've always been 'the cool aunt', not the primary caregiver. The only reason my cat's not sitting on my head right now instead of this raccoon, is because he at least meows to remind me when he's hungry. Babies can't meow!" She walked in tight circles, her footsteps matching the cadence of her worries. "And once we have a kiddo, I'll be losing a lot of my me-time."

"You'll also be losing your sleep, solo bathroom breaks, house keys, day drinking..." I said.

"Not to mention your car radio station, TV channels, romantic dates, and sex with sounds," Eve added.

A gust of wind swept across the corner, fluttering the colorful new banner lacing the streets:

The Fall Foliage Festival!
(Sponsored by Merry's Mentionables).

Great. Another festival Merry added to the town calendar. I wondered when this one started, or when it ended, or if it mattered.

"But you love being a parent, right?" Ruth Anne asked us, wringing the tail of her raccoon.

"I definitely love the kids," I said, honestly. "But sometimes the responsibility feels like it's just too much. There are days, even weeks, when Shane and I barely get to say hello to one another before its bedtime. And then we're both too tired to... Anyway, I take it day by day, Cheerio by Cheerio. I'm not perfect like Merry, but I make it work." I looked to Eve for confirmation, but she was distracted by a snag in her sweater. "You two aren't even married, yet. Why the rush?"

"Sophie wants to hurry things along. She's worried about my age."

"You will be one of the older dads at school," Eve said, having solved her sweater situation. "Forty's just a couple of years away."

"A few."

"What's the diff?"

"There's a big *diff* when you're talking about fertility."

"Ruth Anne..." my eyes went down to her would-be womb. "You're not thinking..."

Ruth Anne rocked back on her heels. "Not my idea. But, Sophie wants me to carry the baby."

For one lingering moment, no one spoke, nor even blinked. Then Eve and I laughed so hard that we had to clutch each other for support.

"Is it that funny?" Ruth Anne asked, turning red.

"Yes! It's that funny! The thought of you being pregnant is even more hysterical than Eve being pregnant," I said

"I'm never getting pregnant." Eve looked down at her chest. "I didn't spend all that money on these ladies to be sucked dry in six months."

"Forget I mentioned it," Ruth Anne said, knowing we wouldn't. In fact, the conversation would probably provide many laughs for us over the coming weeks. She looked at her watch. "I better go. I have a meeting with the chamber of commerce."

"Also known as Shane." My husband *was* the entire chamber of commerce. "Tell him I said hi, and that we're out of toilet paper."

"Roger that." Ruth Ann waved goodbye with her pinky, then dashed directly across the street to *Dip Stix*, avoiding two oncoming cars, with one agile twirl.

"All those years of Nintendo finally paid off," Eve observed, as Ruth Anne reached the café door unscathed.

"I need to pop inside real fast," I said, peering through the window into my store. It was dark inside the store now. Jillian must have left out the back, for her morning break. I had to be quick.

I unlocked the door and went inside, hoping Eve wouldn't follow. She did. "Hurry, Maggie," she said. "If I'm late to Nova's first day of school, Merry will give me that look she's always giving me."

"You can blame me. She asked me to bring her some cleaning supplies," I said, flipping the light switch and smiling as the shop came alive. No matter how frazzled or frustrated, being inside *Miss Sasha's Magick Shoppe* always calmed me. It was the one place I felt like myself these days.

"Smells good in here," Eve said, sniffing at the air as if surprised.

"Merry brought over cinnamon pinecones," I said, pointing to the bowls placed carefully throughout the store. "She mixed the scented oils by hand."

"Of course she did," Eve said, unimpressed. Eve did not have to make her oils--she simply wished for a scent and it lingered in the area for hours, sometimes days. It was a small but impressive ability, especially in the right circumstances.

"Remember when we hated working here?" I asked, reminiscing over our teenaged years. I wandered through the store, touching a display of dangling quartz crystals as I passed, enjoying the moment of quiet nostalgia. My adopted mother--Miss Sasha, as she was known to the town--had opened the store half a century earlier. Her shop attracted people from all over, with its collections of oddities from around the world: books both rare and new, herbs, enchantments, runes, and mood rings. Everything associated with magick, the mystical, or the supernatural was sold or traded at *Miss Sasha's Magick Shoppe,* at one time or another. Though the layout had changed many times over the decades, the founding spirit of the shop remained intact.

"I'm glad I lived in New York for those years," Eve said, perusing a glass cabinet featuring indigenous fetishes. "It gave me perspective." What that perspective was, she didn't articulate, but there was a shimmer in her eyes, unnoticed by the rest of her face. "Your book display looks a bit empty," she said, wandering to the reading area, consisting of two bean bag chairs, a love seat, and a small kid's table off to the side. The magazine rack was admittedly sparse, and many of the regular books we offered were sold out. "Jillian forget to place the order?"

"I'm sure she placed the order," I said, heading through the arched doorway leading to the backroom, beneath a sign reading: *There are no Coincidences.* There was a tall stack of mismatched boxes lined up against the walls, most labeled with Jillian's handwriting, all of them partially opened. I looked through a few, expecting to find the missing books and magazines, without success. "But even if she didn't place the order, it's not the end of the world," I called back through the doorway.

I didn't like having to defend Jillian, who was conscientious most of the time. But, I had noticed her slipping a bit lately.

"Well, that's good, because these magazines are all from June."

Eve had done the orders before Jillian started helping out. "Maggie, if you need me to come in and assist, I can." She peeped her head into the back room. "I mean, if this store fails, we're all screwed right?" Her head disappeared back out of the doorway. "After all, this town was built around *Miss Sasha's Magick Shoppe."*

"An empty magazine rack is not going to make or break us," I said, loading a basket with paper towels, sponges, a can of Mr. Scrubbs, and a half-empty bottle of dish soap. I looked again at the numerous boxes, wondering why they remained unpacked.

Maybe I'm putting too much on Jillian? She is getting older, after all.

With my basket filled, I steeled myself to leave the back room, always more difficult than entering it. There was a magnetic pull emanating from inside this room now, unfelt by everyone else. But I sensed it--strong as the moon's tug on the ocean tides.

I felt the awakening of magick under my skin, surging up and down my arms, into my fingertips. My eyes drew upwards, towards the picture hanging over the archway, to a portrait of Juliana Benbridge, our grandmother, and Dark Root's first witch. But Juliana's hollow gaze and stiff shoulders weren't what called to me--it was the secret cubby behind it, and the much deeper secret I kept hidden inside.

"If you're worried about being late, you can go ahead," I called to Eve, hoping for a moment of privacy. "Tell Merry I'll be right there."

"She just texted. Merry's not taking the kids inside the school until she makes some sort of outdoor presentation," Eve called back. "We have some time."

I bit my tongue, quickly exploring my options. I could climb the stepladder, open the cubby, then take what was mine. Hide it in my skirt pocket, or the bucket of cleaning supplies.

The compulsion was growing, wobbling my knees. "Fight it," I said under my breath, bracing myself in the doorway. Its magick was strong, but I had to be stronger. I reminded myself it wouldn't be that easy to break in anyway. There were barriers put in place to prevent me from taking the artifact, barriers I had installed myself.

I pondered hiding it somewhere else, somewhere where there was less temptation. But I couldn't bring myself to do it. I needed to know where it was, at all times. Even if I couldn't touch it, knowing it was nearby brought some comfort.

"Ready," I said, emerging, and Eve opened the front door.

I looked back over my shoulder as we walked the path to the schoolhouse. Shane said it would take time to detoxify, but after 214 days, I felt its call now, stronger than ever.

CHAPTER 2

MERRY

Merry Maddock stood in the early September drizzle, just as proud and optimistic as if the day was filled with sunshine. The pale yellow schoolhouse, with its shingled steeple and its shiny brass bell, stood eagerly behind her--a metaphor for Merry herself. It was the original structure of an old county schoolhouse, with all its dings and history, though its imperfections were now masked in new molding and fresh paint.

"First day handbooks," Merry said cheerfully, handing out her hand-crafted booklets to the parents and children as they made their way up the walk. Many of the adults gripped paper cups labeled *Java Juicer*, while their children carried colorful lunch boxes depicting superheroes and pop stars.

"Hello, Miss Merry," a little girl said, skipping her way.

"Hello, Suzanna," Merry said, then quickly checked her clipboard when the girl frowned. "I mean Susie. Looks like you'll be having a birthday soon. We'll have a class party when you turn six!"

Susie grinned as her parents stepped up behind her. They were new to Dark Root, as were most of the enrolled children. "Looks a bit tight," said the father, stretching his neck to take in the small school.

“It’s cute though,” the mother said. “Charming. Everything in this town is so charming.”

“Well, I’m glad you think so,” Merry said, sensing that by *charming*, she meant small. Merry felt herself blush. The classroom would certainly be tight, at full capacity and then some. But she would make do. She always did. She had to.

“Over there is the playground,” Merry said, redirecting them to an un-mowed field with a few new play structures and three trees with tire swings. She blushed again, perceiving their scrutiny.

“Quaint!” said the mother.

“We had to get rid of the old equipment because it wasn’t...safe,” Merry explained, looking at the playground with new eyes. It did seem rather empty, but the steel monkey bars and hot metal slide of her childhood no longer fit the standards of the day. “But I have fundraisers planned, and by spring we should have a new sandbox, a swing set, and some sports equipment. Big plans,” Merry reassured, scrawling a note in her ledger that read: *Come up with playground fundraisers.*

As Susie and her parents joined the other families milling around in the playground, Merry studied her roster. Most of the kids had arrived, but not all the parents--most notably, those she was related to. It was several more minutes before Maggie and Eve appeared on the path through the trees. Eve’s heels were so tall that she sunk an inch into the earth with every step, though somehow she managed to persevere gracefully.

“It’s about time you lazybones showed up.” Merry passed them each a handbook, which Maggie promptly stuffed inside her purse and Eve tossed into the recycling bin beside the walk.

“Sorry about being late,” Maggie said, handing Merry the basket of cleaning supplies she’d requested. “We had a coffee incident.”

“A lack of coffee incident,” Eve said.

“There’s decaf inside the break room,” Merry said, knowing they wouldn’t drink it. She spun towards the yellow schoolhouse. “What do you think? I just put in the flower boxes yesterday,” she said, directing their attention to a small garden on the side of the building. "It's a nice vibrant blue, don't you think? And Shane painted the door that rich red. Primary colors! Perfect, right?"

"It is nice," Maggie agreed, her eyes wandering towards the packed playground. "But I'm worried about class size. As you know, my kids need...*extra* attention."

Merry laughed and gave her a wink. "Don't you worry. Auntie Merry will see to it they are well taken care of." Merry hugged the roster to her chest, to let them know everything was all under control.

Maggie looked doubtful, which Merry understood completely. Their children had abilities that few others possessed, and the isolation of Dark Root had protected them well. But now outsiders were moving into their remote haven. It wasn't going to be so easy to keep their children's gifts hidden, but Merry was resolved to try, all the same.

I've invested too much time and energy in restoring this to change directions now. Months spent demolishing old floors. Setting stained glass into windows. Stripping paint. Repainting. New shingles. And the bell! Did anyone know how difficult it was to secure an original schoolhouse bell from the 1920s? And then have it shipped to Dark Root? Merry did. She'd even gone the extra mile, literally, attending an auction two counties over, where she secured several wood desks matching those in the pictures she found of the original classroom. She also unearthed some leaded glass ink wells, but those were just for show—though she did entertain thoughts of starting a calligraphy group, if enough kids showed interest.

"Your renovation projects might have been a little too successful," Eve said, flipping her long black hair behind her shoulders, Cher style.

"What does that mean?" Merry asked.

"She means we don't all share your love of progress," Maggie said. "Dark Root is losing its darkness."

Merry laughed, brushing the comment aside. She loved her

sisters, but they didn't always look on the bright side of things. "I'll never let Dark Root lose its historical charm, but I think it's okay to pretty it up a bit."

"I liked it ugly and charmless," Maggie said.

"Give it a chance, please?" Merry playfully batted her eyelashes. Maggie could appear indifferent, but she had a sharp mind and a soft heart... though the latter was only visible once you got beyond all the sarcasm and deflecting.

"I don't think I have a choice," Maggie said. "Unless I want to homeschool my three children myself, which would be disastrous for all parties involved."

"Hi, Mommmmmm!" Maggie's six-year-old son, Montana, called as he zoomed by, arms out like an airplane, narrowly missing them before veering away. "Gonna help Luna collect rollie bugs."

"Me too!" Maggie's nine-year-old stepson, Marshall, called as he zipped by. "Luna's paying us in marbles!"

"Where does she keep finding all these marbles?" Maggie asked her sisters. "I don't buy her any, but they just keep appearing."

Merry shrugged, looking at Maggie's youngest child, Luna, sitting in the grass beneath an elm tree. Luna was an odd child. Perhaps *unique* was a better word. A quiet little bird who kept to herself and had her own private language.

"Hey!" Eve's stepdaughter, Nova, jogged up, her braids and glasses bouncing with each step. Eve gave her a quick side-squeeze.

"Are those Swarovski crystal earrings?" Merry asked, bending to look closer. Nova pulled back her braids to showcase an ear.

"Well, I wasn't allowed to buy her the diamonds," Eve explained, frowning. "Paul says I'm spoiling her. But you're not spoiled, are you?" she asked Nova.

"Nope! Eve, can we go for ice cream after school?" Nova asked, bouncing in her purple rain boots.

"Of course. If you have to suffer in school every day, it's important to reward yourself." Eve tweaked Nova's nose, sending her bounding off to join her cousins.

"Isn't she perfect?" Eve asked, watching Nova skip off. "She reminds me so much of myself at that age—smart, funny, fashionable--that I can't help but love her. Sometimes I like to daydream that her real mother was only a surrogate, so I wouldn't wreck my body."

Merry and Maggie exchanged looks. "You don't have to buy her love," Maggie said. "They have to love you. It's in the contract."

"Says the woman who's jealous of Santa, because he gets all the credit."

"I just want one toy to be from *Mom*—is that too much to ask?" Maggie blew her hair out of her face, scanning the playground. "Where's June Bug? This goes through Middle School, right?"

Merry nodded slowly, her motives for restoring the old school not entirely altruistic. The school reopening was initially designed as an elementary, but that meant June Bug would be bussed to Linsburg. And despite Linsburg's claim of being *The Happiest Town in the Pacific Northwest,* Merry knew better. The older families of Linsburg held a deep-seated distrust of Dark Root, going back to the town's founding days, festering with each new generation.

Looking at her fitness-tracker wristwatch, Merry frowned. Her daughter was scheduled to ring the opening bell in twelve minutes. "June Bug forgot something at home. She'll be back soon." She explained to Maggie and Eve. As predicted, her daughter indeed appeared, walking the trail with a broad-shouldered, floppy-haired boy.

Who is that? Merry wondered.

She checked her roster. Trevor Addison. *Noooo.* Was that really Trevor Addison? He was the same age as June Bug but must've shot up over the summer while staying with his grandparents in Alaska.

"Hi, Mom!" June Bug chirped, waving as she passed.

"Hey, Sweet Pea!" Merry called back brightly, her fingers kneading her long flaxen ponytail.

"Hi, Mrs. Maddock," Trevor grinned as he walked by. Not a boy's grin. A man's grin. *What did they feed him in Alaska?* Trevor turned to June Bug. "I can't believe your mom's a teacher."

"Substitute teacher." June Bug corrected. "She doesn't have her degree yet."

"First day of school is off to a great start!" Merry turned back to her sisters, forcing a smile and bracing for their interrogation.

"You're teaching, too?" Maggie asked, crossing her arms.

Merry clenched her teeth, leaning in. "The teacher I hired quit last weekend."

"Why?" Eve asked.

"She heard a rumor that our kids were...*different.* She even used the *W* word on the voicemail she left. Apparently, it spooked her."

"Who is she?" Maggie said. "I may be enlightened, but I can take a day off." Her face reddened to the color of her unruly mane. Maggie's temper was legendary, and though she'd mostly outgrown her *Wilder* ways, they sometimes resurfaced, despite her shaky claim of achieving enlightenment.

Merry touched her sister's arm to calm her. "Namaste there, Maggie. I'll find someone else. But teachers need a college degree, which is hard to come by around here. I'll fill in until I hire someone."

"What about Ruth Anne? She went to college," Maggie said. "And she's great with kids."

Merry tapped her pen against her clipboard. Ruth Anne *had* gone to college, but her degrees were in parapsychology, journalism, and Jungian symbolism. Ruth Anne also had several irons in several fires at the moment, including planning a wedding, making her book deadline, and running her *Haunted Dark Root Tour Company*. "Maybe she could fill in sometimes," Merry agreed, licking the pink gloss from her lips.

Maggie shifted her weight from one foot to the other, slinging her purse over the opposite shoulder. "Merry, you're an empath. You should be protecting your energy, not expending it. Why are you taking so much on?"

"I know you think you need to protect me, even from myself, but I'm a big girl. I'll be just fine."

"I'm just asking you to take a step back and look at it. Besides being the mayor, a mother, and running this school, you also own an antique store..."

"A collectibles shop," Merry said.

"You teach karate."

"Only on Saturdays."

"You pick up dog poop."

"It's called pet-sitting. And I love working with animals."

"Still teaching those bendy classes?"

"Yoga? Yes..." Merry was starting to see Maggie's point. Perhaps she did have a lot on her plate.

"Anything else?"

"I, uh... may have gotten my realtor's license." Merry looked away to avoid eye contact, watching as June Bug raised the flag up the flagpole, while Trevor hovered near her with his man-grin. "There's a lot of interest in Dark Root property right now. And someone was going to sell those old houses, most likely an outsider, who wouldn't understand our town's unique history." She looked briefly away. "I also took an online house-flipping course. I plan to refurbish the old homes before I list them, and bring our town back to its former glory."

Maggie took a step back, shaking her head, not in judgement, but disbelief. "I can't even get two matching socks on any two matching feet in my own house, and you're out terra-forming our town. What am I doing with my life?"

"You have three young children, a husband, and an old house to keep up with. I'm single, currently living with my elderly aunt--who dates more than I do--and one adolescent daughter, who doesn't need me much anymore." Merry's throat began to close, and she swallowed before it could. She didn't just like to keep busy—she *needed* to keep busy. Life was about moving forward, not backward. Too much time alone led to ruminating—and regrets.

She turned her attention towards the walkway, where a rail-thin man in an indigo pinstripe suit and a fancy hat, made his way. He resembled a bird, with his long slender neck, aquiline nose, and plumed fedora, and seemed strangely out of time, even for Dark Root. She smiled pleasantly as he passed, though Merry couldn't see if he returned the smile beneath his thick mustache.

"Do you remember Peter Dune, from our childhood?" Merry whispered.

"No," Maggie said.

"I think I'd remember that face," Eve said.

"He has a sister named Isabella."

"I hope she fared better in the looks department," Eve said.

"Twins," Merry said. "Identical."

"Poor thing," Eve said.

"I haven't seen Isabella yet, so I can't comment. She lives in Boston. But I am curious." Merry giggled. A female version of Peter Stanton would be rather comical. "I'm sure they've changed since childhood." She didn't mention that she didn't remember them either, despite Peter's insistence they had math class together. "They inherited The Old Dune House from their grandmother. I'm working with him to fix it up for resale."

"The Dune House?" Eve wrinkled her nose. "Who would buy that place?"

"That's a creepy house, even by Dark Root standards," Maggie agreed. "Good luck with that rehab."

"It has good bones," Merry countered, wishing they would show a touch of enthusiasm. Or at least support. "It just needs a little love."

In truth, the project worried Merry. The Dune place was painted a dreadful purple-black color, with crumbling columns and a sunken porch. It had three disintegrating chimneys of varying heights, six broken windows, and it was certainly not up to any safety standards. Peter's grandmother had lived there for decades, her back as crooked as the columns. Merry had vague memories of the old woman, hissing at the girls whenever they wandered into her clearing, far more frightening than any of the real witches Merry knew.

"The more I look at him, the more familiar he seems," Merry said, watching Peter fuss with his umbrella near the schoolhouse door.

"I don't trust anyone from the pacific northwest who uses an umbrella," Maggie said.

"He's been gone a while. I tried to look for them in my yearbooks, but I have no idea where my yearbooks went," Merry said.

"Did we even have yearbooks?" Maggie asked, scratching her head. "I feel like we did...There's this big patch of my childhood that's missing. I didn't even remember Shane when we first met up again. I chalked it up to all the pot I smoked when I lived in California."

"I can't remember a thing from our childhood," Eve said with a shrug. "It must have been either very dull or very traumatic."

Merry smiled tightly. She didn't remember much of her school days, either. Her ex-husband, a psychiatrist, told her memory loss was common when you were raised by a mentally ill parent. But Sasha wasn't mentally ill--she was a witch. Did the same rules apply? "My theory is we had such an interesting childhood, being raised by witches, that mundane things like elementary school just faded to the backs of our memories. I'm sure they'll return, now that we're shining a light on them." Though Eve and Maggie looked dubious, Merry clung to her theory, refusing to believe that her early years were so bad she wiped most of them from her memory.

Maggie's three children ran towards the sisters, screaming gleefully as they charged, and Merry pasted on her 'auntie' smile. "You kids all ready for the first day?" she asked, bending forward to pinch Luna's nose.

"Yes!" Luna nodded, her silvery hair waving about her delicate face, her eyes sparkling. "Looooooook--" Luna took her time with the word. She was mostly nonverbal, though the other kids claimed she spoke just fine when adults weren't around. Luna opened her small hand to show her prize. "Rollie buuuuug!" she exclaimed with a laughing snort.

"Very nice," Merry said, smiling with a memory of her own daughter, whose critter collections had earned her the nickname 'June Bug'. "How many do you have now?"

Marshall opened up a brown paper lunch sack and Luna delicately placed the black bug inside, where a dozen of its friends waited for him.

"Want me to take that?" Maggie asked Luna, reaching for the sack.

"No!" Luna shook her head, bunching her small hands into fists. "Mine rollie bugggs!"

"Now where's our marbles?" Montana asked Luna, pulling a leaf from his unruly auburn hair.

Luna reached into the pockets of her Oshkosh overalls and produced two handfuls of marbles, funneling them into the waiting palms of her older brothers. Then, they all ran off again in search of more.

The brass bell rang nine times and Merry checked her watch. June Bug was only four minutes late. She'd take it.

Merry joined Peter Dune and her daughter by the red door. Families began assembling at the base of the stairs, and around the flagpole. Merry felt the first full drop of rain plunk on her head and realized she wouldn't get to do the full opening ceremony she had planned outside. Not to worry. She could move everything inside just as easily.

"Please, everyone come in and I'll show you around," Merry called to the crowd, now covering their heads with their 'welcome packets'. "The class is divided by age—youngest up front, oldest in the back. After a short presentation on what to expect from the year ahead, please enjoy a complimentary breakfast of vegan cookies, soy milk, glutton-free muffins, and decaffeinated coffee. Now, if you'll follow me."

Merry turned towards the door, beaming with pride as she

gripped the handle—a portal to a lifetime of friendship and learning. Having few memories of her schooldays made her even more resolved to do a good job. She'd hire new teachers, plant a garden, start a yearbook...

Where are my yearbooks?...

"Ah! Ah! Ahhhh!" A high-pitched scream rang out behind her.

That's Luna!

Everyone turned to see her niece, sobbing and pointing to the ground at her feet, her paper sack ripped, and her bugs escaping. Whenever anyone got close, Luna released a heart-stopping shriek and put out her hands, to keep them from stepping on her pets.

"It's okay, Looney-Bird," Maggie said, working her way towards her daughter. Luna could spin out of control quickly if she wasn't readily consoled. "We'll get them back."

"Rol-lies!" Luna wailed, as her brothers dropped to the ground, returning the bugs to the torn sack, as best they could.

Maggie kissed Luna's tear-stained face as Marshall handed his sister the ripped sack. Merry smiled--for all Maggie's posturing, she was a good mother, especially when it counted.

"There's one on me!" The girl named Susie screamed, frantically shaking her hand, where a black bug clung to her wrist. "Get it off! Kill it!"

Luna stopped crying. *Instantly.* That's what Merry remembered the clearest. Luna was in full sob—and then, in a blink, went dead quiet. Maybe no one else noticed, as their attention was now on Susie, but Merry noticed. Luna's diamond eyes flashed, locking on to Susie. Merry felt the intensity of Luna's energy, even at a distance.

"No!!!" Luna pointed a finger at the girl; not a mere word, but a commandment.

Merry felt an unusual rippling sensation: three brief pulses—one after another--an invisible wave. It emanated from Luna, sweeping out in a wide circle, engulfing the entire schoolyard. Merry had always been sensitive to energy and magick, and this moment was heavy with both.

The wave passed quickly, leaving Merry disorientated. The others seemed disorientated, too. They murmured, looking about, rubbing their eyes. Trevor clutched his stomach, as if suddenly sick. Peter Dune looked up at his umbrella, still lifted in his hand, but no longer open.

Strangest of all, Susie was now standing with her mother, a good ten feet away from where she'd been only a breath ago. There was no sign of the rollie bug on her wrist.

It started raining. Not just occasional drops, but a downpour.

Peter snapped open his umbrella again, shielding them both—but Merry rushed down the steps, letting the rain plaster her ponytail against her back, as she ordered everyone inside.

She pulled Maggie and Eve aside, who appeared just as shaken as she was. "What just happened?" Merry asked.

"And where's Luna?" Maggie asked.

Eve pointed behind them.

They all turned to see Luna, sitting on the edge of a flower bed, soaking wet, but smiling. She put her finger to her lips as Maggie went to scoop her up. "Rollieees," Luna said to them, opening her jacket to reveal a paper bag. A bag that was no longer torn.

CHAPTER 3
DORA

It was early September, still two weeks until Mabon, but it certainly felt much colder than the calendar date implied. And wetter, too. There'd been a noticeable chill in the air since mid-August, hastening sweater season and putting a frost on Dora Maddock's prize-winning pumpkins.

Dora held her spade tight as she hunched over her garden, wearing only a floral housedress and slippers that were too tight for her swollen ankles. One eye closed, Dora inspected her pumpkins. Though it was dusk, she saw better in the moonlight. Dora sighed heavily, then licked a finger and lifted it to the north wind, catching the scent of ripened apples from the orchard as she tuned in. It was only going to get colder. Not just in Dark Root, but everywhere. If she hadn't sensed it intuitively, she felt it in her knees.

"Bah!"

She patted the soil down around her small pumpkins to warm them, sending each wishes of health and abundance, as she lovingly tended the garden. *Guess I won' be winnin' this year*, she told herself. She'd always ribboned in the annual pumpkin growing competition, though admittedly she sometimes resorted to magick for an assist. It was difficult to resist applying her magick this year, too, just to give them a little nudge. But Merry had lectured that using magick wasn't fair to the other contestants. Dora counter-argued that this was Dark Root--if you were going to ride with the big witches, you'd better have a pretty big broom.

She rooted out a weed with her small spade, wondering why she even cared. She had more blue ribbons than she had years left, and one more wasn't going to make or break anyone. The changing weather should be at the top of her mind, not winning some silly local contest. She dug down into her psyche. Who was she trying to impress?

"Just myself," she said, as she cast the image of Herman, the owner of *The Imaginarium*, from her mind. But it was not so easy to rid him from her thoughts, with those deep amber eyes, that stared into her soul. She had recognized his eyes, long before she recognized his body. They had known each other previously—many years ago—and possibly lifetimes, too. They might have even been in love once, if a man like Herman could love a woman. His expositions on love were airy and lofty, prone to poetic and philosophic idealism rather than physicality. *Heart was folly,* he liked to say, *but mind delivered reason.*

But she was a woman of blood and bone —a woman before she was even a witch. She needed less orations on the nature of love and more of the real thing. A lingering touch. Holding hands. Perhaps even a kiss. She didn't dare let her mind wander beyond the kiss--not with her age and bad hips. But some bodily contact would be nice.

Which brought on another thought: Maybe Herman didn't take their relationship to the next level because of his own physical decline? She was old, but he was older.

Perhaps she could slip an herb inside his tea one day—

"Bah!" she said, cracking a smile at the absurdity. The Council believed in free will—and slipping him an aphrodisiac without his consent would certainly be considered a violation. *So... what if I got his consent?*

"Auntie!" It was Merry's voice. Dora stood and dusted her knees, surprised to see all four of her nieces coming out the back door of Harvest Home, crossing the lawn towards her. They were dressed in sweaters, scarves, and boots. "Why don't you have a jacket on, Auntie?" Merry asked, removing her sweater and draping it over Dora's shoulders. "You'll catch your death of cold."

"Nay! When it's my time ta go, it won't be from a silly ol' cold," Dora promised, looking up at her nieces. Merry was the shortest of the four, and Dora was shorter than Merry, and shrinking more each year. "If yer really worried 'bout my health, ya wouldn' be sneakin' up on me like that," she chided, hugging them one at a time.

"You're going to outlive us all," Maggie teased, unleashing her curly red hair from the knitted cap on her head. "You're immortal."

"Used ta be. Used ta be a lot of things."

Merry gave her a confused look and Dora realized she probably sounded like a dawdling old woman. The girls had been watching her too closely lately, and Dora worried they might call in a home health care worker, or a personal shopper, or something as equally awful to *come help out.* Dora had been independent her entire life and wasn't about to start taking help now. Her body might be slipping a bit, but she wasn't losing her mind--which she knew the girls sometimes discussed. She was just preoccupied with... other things. She stood up tall, to show she still had her wits and strength. "Made an apple pie today. An' homemade cream, ta match. It's waitin' in the kitchen."

"You spoil us," said Ruth Anne, rubbing her hands in anticipation. "And I have no problem with that."

"Your pumpkins look...small," Eve commented, frowning at the meager garden. "Did you already pick the good ones?"

"Nay. Ain't no good ones this year," Dora said. "But we'll make do. My apple harvest was good, though. Early, but good." She sighed, knowing how disappointed the shop owners were going to be when she couldn't deliver on her acclaimed pumpkin pies. "I've been resistin' magick, but my fingers are itchin' ta use it, as the season wears on." She rubbed them together, feeling the prickle in her thumbs.

"Why not?" Eve said, patting Dora's shoulder. She smelled like peppermint and rain, and Dora couldn't tell if it was magick or the real thing. "We only live this life once. Enjoy yourself."

"I agree," Maggie said, sitting on the weathered concrete bench embossed with the inscription: *Believe.* "There's no harm. It's just pumpkins."

"But it wouldn't be fair!" Merry said, tightening her scarf. "At least for the contest. Though... maybe it would be okay if you tweaked the pie pumpkins. But just a little."

"Cheatin's cheatin'," Dora said, wiping her hands together as if that was that. Merry always meant well, but she didn't need her niece explaining what was right and what was wrong. Dora understood ethics. She might not always like them, but she understood them.

"Aunt Dora's right," Ruth Anne said, her glasses all fogged up. "If she's stealing someone else's ribbon by using magick, we could say she's also stealing someone's livelihood by using magick to make her pies. *Dip Stix* and the pie house commission those magickally enhanced pies because they're bigger, crustier, and frankly, more delicious. But..." Ruth Anne held up a finger, clearly on a roll, though Dora knew what she was going to say. She raised one bushy eyebrow, waiting for it. "But if Auntie stopped using magick to make them, they might be—"

"Ordinary?" Dora said, crossing her arms.

"Well, yeah. In a good way. There's no such thing as ordinary pie."

"My pies are good, e'en without magick." Dora huffed. She took great pride in her culinary skills, and she used magick only in the way some chefs used paprika or steak sauce: to enhance it, not cover it up.

Merry, sensing a larger debate, stepped in. "Auntie, you do whatever you want. You're a grown woman. I support your decision and won't say another word about it."

"Ta be honest, I'm scared ta use magick," Dora admitted, setting her basket of pumpkins on the bench beside Maggie. "Dark Root's rife with magick these days," she said, sniffing the air, sorting the scents of aether from the apples. "But it smells different. Ya can almost taste it... like metal on the tongue. I think it might be tainted."

"What do you mean?" Eve looked at her lithe fingers, which could spin magick fine as spider silk.

"It's unreliable," Aunt Dora said, plopping down on the other end of the bench. "None o' my spells come out quite right. An' the mole removal cream I made fer Herman gave him e'en more moles! I've ne'er been so embarrassed. Luckily, the next batch worked."

But it had been a harrowing few hours, Dora recalled, as Herman applied the cream on his wrist, then wiped it away to reveal two more bumps. And her bragging beforehand at how skilled she was at such things.

"Maybe you forgot an ingredient," Merry said.

"Or he didn't follow the instructions exactly," Ruth Anne added.

"Potions *are* very particular," Eve nodded.

"I'm still stuck on the part about you seeing Herman's moles," Maggie said, with a shiver.

Ruth Anne removed her glasses, running her thumb along the ridge of her brow. She squinted her eyes as she paced along the neat garden rows while the others watched her, trouble shadowing her face. "I haven't said anything, but I've noticed some oddities in the way the aether is working, too."

"She means magick," Eve explained, though everyone knew the term. It was an element, like fire or air. An element more abundant in some parts of the world than others, and an element that only few could harness—at least consciously.

"My equipment has been picking up some strange electromagnetic frequencies, technical abnormalities, etcetera. Sometimes it just goes bonkers or breaks for no reason." She stopped pacing and returned her glasses to her face, looking over her shoulder, at the woods beyond the house and garden. "My *Haunted Dark Root* tours seem to be getting a bit more haunted lately. Take the old Dune place—"

"What about the Dune place?" Maggie asked, suddenly interested and leaning forward.

"I've driven by it twice and saw lights in the windows each time. And I swore I saw the silhouette of a dancing couple, too."

Merry clapped her hands. "Whew! Not a haunting, thank the gods! I'd have to include that in the property listing. You saw the heirs to the house, Ruth Anne. That was Peter and Isabella Dune. Their *eccentric* old grandmother used to live there," Merry said, choosing her words carefully.

"But you said it was just Peter in town right now," Maggie said. "Isabella's back in Boston."

Merry waved her hand. "She must have come for a visit. I don't keep up on everything in this town."

"Yes, you do," said Eve.

Dora licked her lips, her eyes shifting left and right. The Old Dune Place? That house had been empty for nearly twenty years. And she didn't remember Lady Dune having any heirs.

"Check this out," Ruth Anne said, playing a video on her phone.

Two shadowy figures waltzed in the windows. The moving images lasted only a few seconds before disappearing. No...dissolving. But not before Dora recognized their faces clearly, as if they were still alive today. "Put that thing away!" she snapped, pushing the phone out of her view.

"Don't be afraid, Auntie," Merry said, reassuringly. "It was probably just a projection of an old movie or – "

"T'was no projection. I recognize those faces, e'en decades later! The Murloughs! The couple was murdered, way back." She blinked her piercing blue eyes, trying to penetrate the veil of time through the thickening fog. "Must be their ghosts. But why now?" Her fingers squeezed a swatch of her housedress tightly.

"No, no, no." Merry scissored her hands. "There are no ghosts there. Ghosts are good for Ruth Anne's business, but bad for mine. Absolutely no ghosts allowed."

"I never heard of a murder there," Ruth Anne said, removing a notebook and pen from inside her jacket. "Who were the Murloughs, and who murdered them?"

Dora felt her chest constrict when she breathed. It was years ago, yet only a fold in time, as if she could step through a door and be right back there. "The Murloughs were the original owners. They built that home long before the Dune's ever moved in. Their bodies were found in the upstairs library, drained of blood, but not a mark on 'em."

"That's horrific," Ruth Anne said, grinning, scribbling down notes as fast as her hand would move.

"That's not all. They had four children, an' all four disappeared without a trace. The sheriff secretly asked fer mine and Sasha's help —hopin' we could help locate the kids with our..." She wriggled her fingers. "We went into their rooms, lookin' fer things that would help us connect, but there weren't a single toy nor a single photo left. Nor anything in their bedrooms. When we went back ta tell the sheriff, he seemed ta have forgotten he'd asked us.

"Were the kids ever found?" Ruth Anne asked as the girls all huddled in.

"Not that I know of. But there were so few people in Dark Root in those days that the story was quickly forgotten. I had my theories, but Sasha and I were busy with larger things by then, leavin' no time to go chasin' ghosts."

CHAPTER 4
MAGGIE

Aunt Dora's tale of the Murlough family sent a chill through our circle. My sisters and I huddled on the garden bench around her, as if she were a crackling fire on a cold night, and our only source of warmth. Aunt Dora dabbed at her eyes and leveled her spade at imaginary spirits for minutes after. At least, I hoped they were imaginary. There were no orbs or lights that I could detect, and my bracelet didn't react with any warning.

"Did you know the children?" I asked, having never heard the tale before.

"Nay. T'was a long time ago. E'en so, I've been aroun' fer a longer time, an' I was already grown. But we saw 'em around sometimes, on our deliveries. Mrs. Murlough sought out Sasha fer rare books an' oddities—long before Sasha opened the store. I heard the Murloughs owned quite the collection when they were...uh..."

"Sucked dry?" Ruth Anne asked.

"Ruth Anne! Don't upset Auntie even more," Merry said.

"You got a better way to say it?"

I moved the basket that separated me from Aunt Dora, and slid up beside her. She was agitated as an old hen, rattling on beneath her breath. The smell of rain was thick in the air, and I knew the brief reprieve would not last long. When the first swollen drop fell into our circle, Merry popped open an umbrella and shooed us towards the house through the back kitchen door. "I need to ask Auntie about a recipe," Merry said, which was code for, 'I will calm her down.'

We marched into the house like obedient children, as the three of us were notably short on comforting skills. If you wanted something researched, you went to Ruth Anne; something brewed, you saw Eve; and if you needed to talk to ghosts, unlock doors without keys, or blow out a power grid, I was your witch. But the healing arts, both emotional and physical, we left to Merry.

After discarding our muddied boots, we entered our aunt's cozy kitchen. We all shared a fondness for Harvest Home, having spent as much of our childhoods here as at Sister House. Sasha was often cross or forgetful, but Aunt Dora was always welcoming, with a piping kettle of tea and fresh-out-of-the-oven baked goodies.

Tonight seemed no exception, as the scent of apple pie and chamomile quickly replaced pine and rain. The pie sat on the stove, brown and bursting. I couldn't resist fishing out a warm apple chunk and stuffing it into the side of my mouth when I thought my sisters weren't looking.

"And that is why you can't lose that last eight pounds," Eve said, glancing at my hips as I tried to cool the apple in my cheek by blowing inward. "Discipline, Maggie. Life is all about discipline."

"These are the little things that keep me going," I replied, defiantly plucking out another piece of apple. "And if that adds *five* extra pounds on me, who cares?" I asked, slowly sucking in my lower belly.

But Eve struck a nerve. A regular at my shop had recently asked if Shane and I were 'expecting.' *Someday* I'd be more disciplined, I promised myself, but those little bites of dopamine were what carried me through until that magical day. "Besides, it's natural to gain weight in colder months."

Eve and Ruth Anne half-smiled at each other. Eve had never gained a pound in her life. Ever. Her secret was a combination of iron discipline, gray magick, and her body's fear of defying her. Ruth Anne was of normal build most of the time--not too big or small in any one area, but she appeared to have lost a few pounds recently. Her clothes were always oversized, and it was hard to tell in her camo pants and trench coat, but her face was thinner.

"I gotta pee," Ruth Anne said, rushing into the next room.

"Her bladder is half the size of her coffee thermos," Eve said, setting an old brass kettle onto the new gas stove. She pulled back the flap of the blue-checked curtains over the sink, revealing Aunt Dora and Merry through the rain. They were having an animated conversation on the bench, the umbrella managing to keep them adequately dry. "Aunt Dora seems off these days," Eve said, wiping off the glass for a better view. "She's too old for 'the change,' isn't she?"

I shrugged. No one knew Aunt Dora's true age. Not even Aunt Dora. "What comes after menopause?" I asked.

"Forever-pause?" Eve guessed.

Ruth Anne chuckled as she returned from her bathroom trip, drying her hands on her pants and heading straight for the pantry. She came out with a tower of snacks, stacked so high in her arms that she almost ran into the table. As she unloaded the crackers, cookies, mustards, and jams, she found what looked to be a baby food jar filled with cigarette ash, tucked inside a box of Ritz.

"Maybe she's secretly smoking," Ruth Anne said, returning the little jar and the cracker sleeve to the pantry.

"Or trying to stop," I offered. "That would explain her agitation. Honestly, I didn't see any faces in those silhouettes. Did you guys?"

Ruth Anne and Eve shook their heads. "I wasn't gonna say anything in front of Aunt Dora," Ruth Anne said. "I just looked at those photos again, in the bathroom, just to be sure I hadn't missed anything. Just shadows to me."

"Gross," Eve said, looking at the offending phone, now sitting on the kitchen table.

"I washed my hands," Ruth Anne defended, not saying that she also dried them on her pants.

"What I don't understand," I said, laying cheese slices alongside Ruth Anne's crackers on a wood tray, "is how we never knew about the murders. It's not like we were sheltered kids. We grew up on stories of demons and spirits, and lived in a house where things literally went bump in the night."

"Ghosts are one thing. But murder and disappearing children are another story," Eve said. "That would have threatened our sense of safety."

"The Dune place always gave me the heebie-jeebies, and it takes a lot to give the *Haunted Dark Root* lady the heebie-jeebies." Ruth Anne pushed buttons on her phone, holding it up in various angles, seeking reception. "Or is that heebie-Jeepies?" She chuckled at her own joke.

"Think Aunt Dora's mind is slipping?" I asked, worrying. "I just feel like we would have heard a rumor..."

"Maggie, come see this," Eve said, beckoning me over to look at the image in Ruth Anne's phone. It was a grainy picture of a newspaper article dated December 3, 1938 from *The Linsburg Sun*. The headline was written in bold black letters that took up half the page:

Dark Root Couple Murdered!
Children all Missing!
Supernatural Forces Blamed!

The article went on to say that some very respected Linsburg citizens had it on *good authority* that the Murloughs were witches, who had made a dark deal with the devil for their powers. And now the devil had come to take his due.

Ruth Anne shook her head. "Not great journalism here, but fascinating stuff. It's crazy, the things people believe."

"Is it, Ms. Ghost Hunter?" I asked.

"Touché." Ruth Anne readjusted her glasses as she scrolled

through the pages. "Geez, these poor people. The article says the couple was drained of blood, though there was no blood found anywhere in the house or even on their clothing. A spilled bottle of moonshine was found in the library with them, but nothing else out of the ordinary." She rubbed her eyes and lowered the phone. "They also say there was a pentagram, painted on the floor of the library the night the bodies were discovered, but had mysteriously disappeared the following day."

Linsburg had a long history of animosity towards Dark Root, rooted in decades of fear and superstition that grew over the ages, though no one knew when it quite started. Some say a Linsburg cow went missing and never returned, supposedly bewitched. Others, that a 'man of morals and means' left his wife and fortune to be with a Dark Root girl, also clearly bewitched. And then there was the darkest rumor: that our grandmother, Juliana, had lured a lover over from the neighboring town, had used him for her...carnal desires... and when she was done with him, he leapt to his death from a cliff. Most definitely bewitched. According to the Linsburg old-timers, everything about Dark Root had some connection to witches. Not that it was without merit.

"I would think that if witchcraft was really involved, Sasha and Dora would have figured it out," I said.

"Maggie's got a point," Eve nodded, taking the cheese tray through the doorway and into the living room.

"There were no further stories in the paper. No follow-ups on the murdered couple or their missing kiddos." Ruth Anne's brows knit with bewilderment. "And Dark Root never even reported on it. That is quite strange, don't you think?"

"To be fair, Dark Root never had much of a newspaper. From what I've heard, it never managed to operate for more than 6 months at a time." Eve returned for napkins, silverware, teacups, and dessert plates, expertly balancing all these on her forearms and hands--evidence of her many years in restaurant work.

"Har-har," Ruth Anne said. Now and again, she attempted to

bring back the *Dark Root Press,* but within a few months, she'd get bored or distracted. A few missing issues turned into a few missing months. "I'm working on getting another edition out soon, but except for Merry's school opening up, the only news on my radar are Aunt Dora's small pumpkins and the new *Java Juicer* truck. Not exactly riveting stuff."

It was true. There was not much going on in Dark Root. Merry's festivals came so often they wouldn't even qualify as news. And Ruth Anne didn't dare print anything involving magick—except near Samhain.

Through the window I saw the rain had mostly stopped, and Merry and Aunt Dora were making their way slowly back to the house, Merry's arm wrapped around Dora's shoulders.

"When did the Dunes move in?" I asked, plucking another apple from the pie once Eve left the room again.

"Good Question." Ruth Anne returned to her phone. "The house was sold a few months after the murder, when no heirs were found, to the Dune Family. Shortly after that... Gah! Nooo!" She moved her phone about, hunting for the signal, slapping it against her thigh to bring it back to life. *Mayor Merry* had been promising our town broadband for a year now--had even campaigned on it, but two tin-cans-on-a-string later and our service was no better than it had ever been.

"Merry's working with Old Lady Dune's grandson to restore the house and sell it," I said, recalling Ruth Anne's sighting of ghostly silhouettes dancing in the windows. "It's not unusual for spirits to manifest when their home is about to be sold. Perhaps the Murloughs have reappeared to protest the sale?"

"Are you Mag-splaining ghosts to me?" Ruth Anne teased. "Though that is a passable theory. Maybe I should run some tests out there?"

"Or maybe you should mind your own business," Eve called from the living room, clear as if she were in the kitchen with us. "Let the old ghosts and the new occupants work it out between themselves."

"I think you're just trying to avoid writing that book." I followed Ruth Anne into the living room, where Eve was already curled up in the corner of the orange pleather couch Aunt Dora had *won* at auction, as she was the only person who bid on the hideous thing.

"Yeah, maybe." Ruth Anne scratched the back of her neck. Her eyes shifted back and forth, revealing that *maybe* she was avoiding a lot of things. "Nice work, Eve," Ruth Anne said, to change the subject.

The coffee table was neatly arranged, with cookies, plates, teacups, and old doilies knitted a century ago. Ruth Anne sat in the middle of the couch, where she could easily fill and refill her plate, dipping slightly into its center where the cushions didn't quite meet. I sat on a floor pillow at the end of the table, closest to the hearth.

The room was pleasant, as always, though I admittedly missed its previous charm. The décor was mostly from the Victorian and Edwardian eras, with mid-century pieces thrown in, all the way up through the 1970s. These were the furnishings I grew up with. Though I was glad Aunt Dora didn't live in the past, as some older people did, I wasn't overly fond of some of the newer decor. A giant flat-screen TV dominated the wall that once displayed various paintings of flowers. Now, life-size telenovelas played out all day long.

"Thank ya, dear," Aunt Dora said, appearing with Merry in the doorway. The pair was rosy-cheeked and smiling, walking arm in arm, not a drop of rain between them. "Ya always make me feel better." Dora patted Merry's hand, lovingly.

"I'm glad I can return the favor," Merry said, escorting Auntie to her recliner before finding herself a floor pillow, across the coffee table from Ruth Anne.

I looked around the living room, at the flaking wallpaper, the burning fireplace, and the purple velvet pillows that clashed with the orange pleather couch, and smiled. A smile so heavy it was nearly a sigh. The room was as heartening as the thistle and honey tea we sipped. Perhaps that's why I opposed the *new' stuff*--there was comfort in the old, the familiar. And today of all days, I needed familiarity.

"Sorry 'bout my reaction," Aunt Dora said, wrapping both hands around her teacup. "Somethin' just feels amiss. Can' put my finger on it, but I'm feared to e'en read the tea leaves. I'm fearin' things are turnin' sour. T'is the way o' the wheel, though." She shrugged and took a long sip.

"Oh, Auntie," Merry said, dipping a biscotti cookie into her tea. "Things will be fine. They always are. You just have to keep your spirits high."

"Sounds a bit dismissive," I caught myself saying. I loved Merry, and her positivity was mostly appreciated, but sometimes there were issues that a smile and sunshine couldn't ward back.

Merry tilted her head, looking at me. "Did I miss something?"

"There is definitely something amiss." I didn't know what, but things had felt strange lately. Like an invisible hand had come into our world and gently moved stuff around. Just a little. Just enough to throw us off. "Things feel...scrambled."

"Yes!" Eve said, and we all turned towards her way. Eve rarely weighed in on the heavier topics, and rarely so enthusiastically. "I've been feeling...*off,* too." She blinked several times then shook it away. "I've been experiencing déjà vu, all the time. I can't even walk into a room without thinking: didn't I just walk into this room? Like this very scene here," she motioned to all of us, "with us here around the coffee table, having this very conversation... it feels like it's happened before." There was not a hint of deceptiveness in her dark eyes. It was as earnest as I've ever seen Eve look.

"Why haven't you said anything?" I asked.

"I thought I did."

We all laughed, even Eve.

"I'm having weird personal experiences, too." Ruth Anne admitted, setting her half-empty plate on her knees. "Last night I found myself standing by my stove, but I can't remember how I got there."

"That's called being old," Eve said.

"I can't remember how I got back to bed, either," Ruth Anne added.

"That's called being drunk," I said, nodding to the silver flask protruding from her pocket.

"You could be right." Ruth Anne grinned, and pushed the flask deeper down, out of view.

My own hands instinctively reached into my own pockets, searching for... something I no longer carried on me.

"Now that it's been brought up..." Merry audibly exhaled and our heads spun her way. She clasped her hands together before her, as if to restrain them, and spoke quickly before she lost her nerve. "I'm having memories that aren't mine. Almost like dream segments, but I'm wide awake. They seem so real but I can't make sense of them. Scenes... images, no real rhyme or reason."

"Me, too!" I said. "I thought I was just suffering from sleep deprivation." I squeezed my eyes shut, trying to call up the last vision, which happened only a few hours before we all met up. "Earlier today, I saw myself standing in a classroom, but not any class that I can remember. It was bigger. Much bigger— "

"With long tables and two hearths!" Merry launched herself up to standing, nearly dropping her plate.

"A big... white building..." Eve tapped her spoon against the rim of her teacup, each tap ringing out a new word. "Gargoyle fountains. Two stories. No—three?" She tilted the cup as she tilted her head.

"With black iron gates!" Ruth Anne snapped her fingers.

"And a greenhouse out back!" Merry said, nodding.

"Pictures and candles everywhere," Eve continued with our collective memory.

"And books." Ruth Anne's glasses fogged over and she wiped them on her jacket sleeve. "So many books. It was no Alexandria, but it was quite the collection."

"And a long corridor that branched off to many other rooms," I said. I had wandered down the hall towards those rooms in my 'waking dreams'. The hallway echoed when I walked, my sneakers slapping against the pine floor. "Hello?" I had called, but there was never an answer. There were answers, however, inside the rooms. I could almost feel the rough-hewn stained wood doors.

"It was in Dark Root, wasn't it?" Eve said. "I thought Nova's teen drama shows were overwhelming my brain."

We were all standing now, except Aunt Dora, who had lowered her recliner to a flattened position and feigned snoring, her plate wobbling on her heaving stomach.

"Auntie," Merry said, coming up beside Dora and tapping her wrist. "We know you're awake. And we want answers. Why are we all remembering a school that doesn't exist?"

Aunt Dora licked her lips, fluttered open her eyes, and reluctantly returned to her normal seated position. She set her feet flat on the floor and looked straight ahead. We huddled in. There was something shifting in her keen blue eyes--a look so far away, it seemed another lifetime.

"I can' remember much either, but I know o' what ya girls are speakin'." She massaged her knotted hands. Her chest expanded, then released, and she spoke slowly and thoughtfully, her accent nearly disappearing as she focused her words. "There was an actual school, once. It was meant ta train ya girls in the ways of magick. Sasha started it, an' then she closed it, hidden with a spell. I don' remember why." She frowned, her eyes looking into her cupped hands resting on her lap. "Memories were wiped clean—e'en my own. From then on, ya girls just went to public school, and we trained ya as best we could from the house."

CHAPTER 5
MAGGIE

For laughs, nostalgia, or possibly masochism, my sisters and I decided to walk to the 'Old Dune House' that night, as it was known locally. Only, now we knew it wasn't the Dune House, but the Murlough House. A house that had once witnessed a double murder, and the disappearance of four children.

We took the long way there, down an overgrown pathway—one of the few backroads in this area not protected by one of our ward spells, like those around Harvest Home and Sister House. Sasha and The Council originally put the protective spells up years ago, throughout the woods. But she had neglected the area around Dune House, as far as I could remember, but never gave a reason. Fortunately, Merry was magickally attuned to the local flora and the brambles parted gently, allowing us through, as long as Merry kept the lead.

"Did Peter and Isabelle actually live here with their grandmother?" I asked Merry, still not remembering them. "What about their parents?"

Merry shrugged, pausing in mid-step to allow a dogwood branch to uncoil before her. "Peter only said they went to school with us, but never mentioned his parents. He's about our age, closer to Ruth Anne's, I believe."

"I have zero memories of the dude," Ruth Anne said, jumping over a large stone in the overgrown path, rather than walking around it. She wore a light backpack, bearing some of her ghost hunting equipment, and held a flashlight in her hand, which she spun in wide arcs whenever we heard a noise.

"I don't remember anyone in school but us, and even those memories are vague," Eve said, looking dreamily up at the moon. Eve was a disciple of Nyx, the Goddess of Night—a title given to her upon completing a six-week, online certification course. She had a natural affiliation for the night, and managed the trail gracefully, even in her heeled boots. "Like, no one. Not even myself, really.

"Maybe they attended the missing ghost school with us," I teased.

"I'll ask them," Merry said, not a trace of humor in her voice.

"You're really going to ask about Sasha's school?" I asked, ducking beneath a vine that snaked from one side of the trail to the other.

It was dark and dense in this part of the woods, and Ruth Anne tended to wander off with her flashlight, but Merry radiated light. Literally. It seemed to glow from under her skin, like a candle burning beneath a lamp--unnoticeable in full daylight, but in the darkness, she was nearly florescent. I was always a bit envious of Merry, though my ego, and my love for my sister, would never allow me to openly admit it. Of all our talents, Merry's seemed the most useful. Not that I really wanted her healing, her empathy, or even her light. I enjoyed roaming around shadowy corners alone, and I had little interest in differentiating one plant from another. Eventually, they all became salad anyway.

Merry hummed as she pondered my question. "It does sound crazy, doesn't it? If they don't remember another school here, they'll think we're crazy. And if they do remember, they'll want to know where it went." Merry paused, looking left then right, and I could tell she was a bit lost. The foliage had thickened, and even with her inner light, darkness was closing in. She removed a pendulum from her pocket--a black onyx stone on a short chain. Aunt Dora's pendulum, lovingly named Oliver. She swirled it slowly three times, silently asking Oliver for direction. It tugged to the left, like an eager pup ready for a walk. "Slow down," she scolded, as the parting brush couldn't keep up with the pendulum's pull.

"I think talking to them about it would be a bad idea." Ruth Anne said, catching up. She had been snapping pictures with her phone along the way, careful not to capture me in any of them. When someone took my picture without my express permission, cameras often suddenly stopped working--a bit of my *wilder* magick that I didn't mind keeping. "They probably stayed one semester with their grandmother, and moved on."

"I agree. With all the new people moving to Dark Root, maintaining our privacy will be even harder," said Eve. "Let's not invite more probing."

The woods finally gave way to a neatly-clipped clearing, recently tamed by a riding lawn mower, evidenced by the orderly rows seesawing the landscape. A long stone pathway threatened by sprouting weeds led to the front porch of Dune House, at the far edge of the meadow. The exterior's dark purple paint blackened in the growing darkness. With its three chimneys and slightly crooked architecture, the house looked more like a spooky paper cutout than an actual home. The crumbling porch columns stood watch from either side of the front stairs, like four ghost soldiers guarding the house. The driveway ended unceremoniously beside the home, an afterthought, without even so much as a carport.

We approached slowly, holding hands as if we'd been walking the yellow brick road and had finally come upon Oz. A dark and dreary Oz. There were no lights on, and the two large windows and huge door cast the illusion of a face. Whatever memories had been erased from our childhood, the recollection of a hissing Lady Dune seemed to have seared itself into our minds, heightened by the darkness and the feeling of being watched.

Ruth Anne moved ahead of us, snapping pictures of the house and property from all angles. "That's where I saw the figures when I drove up here." She pointed to the windows. On this early evening, they were disappointingly spirit-free. And I didn't feel anything supernatural either, nor did my bracelet spark. Ruth Anne shuffled from side to side in front of the door, like she had to urgently use the bathroom. "Doesn't look like anyone's home. We should go in."

"You can't pee in there Ruth Anne," Merry said when we joined her. "The toilets don't flush yet."

"What? I don't need to... Never mind. I'll hold it," she promised. "You have the keys, right?"

"Back at my office. Why do you want to go inside so badly?" She asked, eyeing Ruth Anne suspiciously.

"Clues. I mean, those kids were never recovered. Maybe we can find something that no one else did. I've got my equipment and you all have your..." She wriggled all ten fingers. "You know I can't shut off my journalistic nature. Forever inquisitive!" She rubbed her hands, no doubt thinking of her next novel or magazine story.

"Is this one going to end up in Spooked Magazine, too?" Eve asked, narrowing her eyes.

"I see where you're headed with this. And if it helps, I promise I'll run any future stories I write about this town by you guys, before I send them off."

"Seems reasonable," I said, looking for a loophole and not finding any.

"Can't you do this in the daytime?" Merry asked, looking up at the sky. The air was ripe with the smell of rain again. "I'm measuring the upstairs bedrooms for carpet this weekend and Peter will be staying in Linsburg. I can sneak you in then."

"You know it's easier to reach spirits at night. And I have Maggie here—ghosts love her. C'mon Merry, don't you want to help those children?"

"It's not like they're going anywhere," Eve said. "But, Maggie is a magnet..."

We all looked at Merry, giving her our puppy-dog eyes, in hopes of her permission. It felt adventurous to sneak inside a locked house, to where a murder was supposedly committed years ago. So irresponsible, and juvenile. So unlike our normal routines these days. We felt as giddy as children again. Except for Merry, who had never been a kid, even when she was a kid.

"Fine. But if we get arrested for trespassing, you're posting bail," she said to Ruth Anne, though there were no police in Dark Root to arrest anyone. Merry turned to me. "Maggie, you're up."

"Ooh, Merry's letting me play with magick." I grinned, rubbing my palms together, prompting Merry to stick out her tongue. I touched the brass knob, feeling the predicted tingle in my fingertips that occurred whenever I harnessed the element. In one breath, I pulled *aether* down from the moon and up from the earth, allowing the vibrations to fill me. The door swung wide open. "Ta-da!" I said, stepping to the side with an exaggerated bow.

"Bravo, Maggie," Ruth Anne golf-clapped as she darted into the house ahead of us.

"I'll wait outside. Keep a lookout," Merry said, stuffing her hands into her pockets as she rocked on her heels. "And Ruth Anne—don't you dare pee in there!"

"Think she'd crack under interrogation?" Eve asked, as we left Merry at the door and followed after Ruth Anne.

"Like teacups in an earthquake," I said.

Ruth Anne was a blur, taking pics and dashing about the first floor, before sprinting up the spiraling staircase two steps at a time, her backpack bouncing on her back, leaving zero doubt she was seeking out a bathroom.

Eve and I wandered the ground level, which was nearly devoid of energy. It felt stagnant. Stale. Unlived in. But clean enough, after having been abandoned so long. There were only a few pieces of furniture--a grand piano and a long table with only three chairs.

"This place smells like damp socks," Eve said. She waved her pinky finger in tiny circles and the moldy scent gave way to the crisp aroma of winter snow. "Better," she nodded, "though I was going for spring rain."

I went into the kitchen alone. The appliances were very old, yet shining and clean. And the floor recently swept. The three *Java Juicer* cups on the counter labeled MM told me this was Merry's handiwork. But otherwise, the room appeared to have been unused for years.

"Find anything?" Eve called to me.

"Nope. You?"

"Spiders. But not as many as I expected."

Ruth Anne was looking for clues, but I wasn't interested in finding evidence for crimes that occurred well before our lifetimes, to people we didn't even know. I was privately hoping to find clues to the missing school. Not only would the school be a backup for my children--if Merry's schoolhouse experiment didn't work--but it might fill in the missing puzzle pieces of my life.

Sasha had bespelled it, which must have taken considerable magick, and with it, a piece of her. But why? She was a sharp woman and surely knew we'd discover its existence one day. I found it too coincidental that we'd begun recovering memories around the same time that Peter Dune, an alleged former classmate, reappeared in Dark Root. One of the first rules of magick was that there were no coincidences; there was a grand design to everything.

Perhaps it was better not remembering, as Eve suggested, but they were my experiences, and I wanted them back.

Could there really be something here that will lead us to the school?

The Dune House was large, even by Dark Root standards, which was renowned for its sprawling Victorian and Edwardian homes. With pine wood floors and peeling floral wallpaper, it was probably built in the early 1900s. A sheet of green-yellow vinyl flooring in the dining room, and cowboy wallpaper in the downstairs den, showed attempts at renovation, but the house otherwise appeared original.

It felt vast and hollow, like a forgotten mausoleum, as my footsteps echoed on the wooden floorboards. It felt heavy, too, the air dense around me as I wandered room to room. If Peter was currently staying here, he left no energetic footprint behind.

I began to have a sense of familiarity with the house, an unrelenting déjà vu, knowing without knowing, where the corridors led and which rooms they opened to--*That's a bedroom. That's the powder room. There's the playroom*--though I had no recognition of the room's occupants. After fully exploring the first floor, I headed upstairs, becoming somewhat disoriented at the winding stairwell and the thin shaky handrail that spiraled up into shadow.

"Ruth Anne?" I called ahead of me, rummaging through my purse with one hand for my phone, to use as light. A flash of deeper darkness appeared at the top of the staircase and quickly disappeared. "Ruth Anne?" I dared, louder this time.

The staircase ascended to a hallway, where portraits of an odd family with high foreheads, long necks, and whimsical clothes were arranged symmetrically along both walls. Each family member bore resemblance to Peter, in one way or another. Though none were of Peter himself, nor any recent enough to have included his sister. It would have been comical, but in the darkness, as my light unmasked them one at a time, it was unnerving. I felt their eyes follow me, watching with sneering contempt as I opened and shut doors along the way, working towards a pale halo of light at the end of the hall.

The light filtered around the cracks of a grand door. The master bedroom, I guessed, having not seen one yet. I entered into a circular room of rich woodwork shelving, lined with books. *Not a bedroom. The library.*

Judging by the outside architecture, the room should not be domed, nor the walls so tall. The book collection was astounding, more than I had ever seen in one place. They obscured the curved walls, yielding just enough surface to allow two doors on opposite ends, and four identical windows, equidistant apart.

Has Ruth Anne seen this room yet? would find her, I promised the room and myself, but first, I wanted to explore it alone. It was such a beautiful room, reminiscent of a ballroom in a Disney movie, though much smaller, and with books staring down from the balconies instead of the royal court.

I walked towards the center, to where bands of starlight intersected from opposing windows, touching the crystal chandelier above me and setting it aglow. It was the source of the light haloing the door.

I spun in place with my arms wide open, feeling light on my feet and girlish again as my skirt swirled about me. The books became blurred figures before me, my admirers, clapping as I danced. I was pulled into the arms of a phantom nobleman, who swept me around and around. There was magick in this room, so strong that I nearly forgot where I was, returning to reality only after tripping over a sliding ladder fastened to the bookshelf. I snapped my head in the directions of the doors, half-expecting to see my sisters standing in the frames, laughing at me.

Walking along the walls, I examined the bottom row of books; some with titles I could not pronounce, some with no titles at all. Most I had never heard of. As I made my way, the room's temperature began to drop. Not quickly, but noticeably. The tip of my nose grew cold. A whisper of a voice now swirled through the room, following the path I had danced.

"*Magdalene...*"

"Who's there?" I asked, turning in place, trying to follow the whisper.

I had come to understand through working with spirits, that they were often as fearful of us as we were of them. If I moved too suddenly or spoke too loudly, it might break the link. "Who are you?" I whispered, my breath coming out as smoke.

"Magdalene!" The whisper echoed all around me, reverberating along the walls, knocking books in and out of their places like piano keys played by an invisible hand. "MAGDALENE!"

I knew the voice now. "Juliana?" I asked of my grandmother, and

Dark Root's founding witch. Her spirit had contacted me before but had been quiet lately. "Juliana, if it's you, give me a sign."

The room went even colder.

That didn't mean it was Juliana. There were trickster spirits, and dark spirits, too; entities who amused themselves by misleading the living about their true natures. But my crystal bracelet remained dim, and I knew, at least, I was not in any immediate danger.

"Please speak again, Juliana. I'm listening."

The entire room spun around me, quick as a carnival ride, and I dug my heels into the floor for support. When the spinning stopped, the room appeared vaguely different, with everything slightly out of place. *Were there candles burning in the chandelier before?*

It was so cold now. Even colder than a mausoleum. The doors seemed so very far away, and my feet too heavy to move. *Juliana?*

The glass chandelier twirled, very slowly. All of its tiny parts cast silhouettes from the candlelight, and the starlight, unto the floor, mixing and blending them together. Shadow images of children--running, jumping, playing--danced all about me. I could hear them laughing, singing, their voices ringing in my ears.

A slim silhouette boy cowered, then covered his eyes.

"No, Robert! NO!" A disembodied voice cried out.

Two shadow girls turned their heads, sobbing. "I told him...I told him not to look!"

The dance ended, freezing the silhouettes in place, and when I finally blinked, they disappeared completely. The temperature quickly returned to normal and I could move freely again.

Were those the Murlough children? Who was Robert? And what did he look at? There was nothing in this room but books.

I could have explained it away, a byproduct of the herbal tea Eve had brewed, but the chandelier was still lit, with four small candles burning bright.

I turned towards the door, wanting to find Ruth Anne and tell her of my visions, when an orb appeared, shimmering and floating, as it bounced along the candle flames. The orb drifted from the chandelier, towards one of the higher shelves, illuminating the spine of a thick book, and then snuffed out.

I rolled the ladder in the direction of the book and climbed halfway up. The book looked to be both very old and very heavy, and my heart thumped as I read the title: *The School of Magick.*

"No fricken way..."

I teetered on the ladder as I carefully removed it from its place.

As the gap behind the book was revealed, a moonbeam lanced through the opposite window and struck squarely on the emptied space. Leaning forward, one eye pressed close to the revealed opening, I clearly saw a white mossy building at the end of a long tube--like a periscope. The building was far off, but not so far that I couldn't catch flashes of an iron gate before it.

The school?! I looked again, fevered by the thrill of discovery. *I've seen this building!* In those bits of memory that came and went, so frustrating over these last few months. "I just can't believe..."

"Can't believe what?"

The voice startled me into dropping the book, deftly caught by Ruth Anne at the bottom of the ladder.

"Stop creeping around like that!" I scolded as I climbed down, noting the candles had all gone out.

"Sorry. I thought you heard me. Amazing room, huh? I'll have to see if I can befriend the Dunes and get some reading time in here." She lifted and lowered the book in her hands, as if humbled by its existence. "What were you looking at?"

I had so much to tell her but I wasn't sure where to start. "Read the title," I said.

"The School of Magick? Whoa. How did you find this among all these?"

"It found me."

"Gotcha," she said, but frowned when she opened the book. "Except the pages are blank. Maybe it was a book that had been written but—"

"Was erased too?" I asked, seeing where she was going.

'Yep."

"No sign of moon runes either. Or any other invisible ink," I said. I could sense these things, it was a product of my time spent deciphering Juliana's diaries, which were written in moon runes, a written magick language appearing only at night. "See that moonbeam?"

Ruth Anne looked up, nodding. It was less visible from the floor than the top of the ladder, but still there. "Go look at the spot where the book was," I said, handing her the book as she ascended the ladder.

Ruth Anne put her eye to the opening for several long moments before pulling away. She opened her mouth wide as a toad's, and then looked again.

"That building can't exist," she said, pulling her camera from her pocket and aiming it into the shaft. "I know every inch of that area. Every square inch."

"Maybe it just looks farther away, like side mirrors on a car."

"There is nothing east of here but trees and more trees. Maybe it's a hologram? Projected somehow from this house."

"Maybe," I agreed, having just witnessed the strange visions of the children. Maybe this entire house was one big projector? "Or maybe it's the only way to see the location of the school, because of the spell Sasha cast over it?"

"I'm not sure spells work like that. But then again, we still know very little about the ways of magick. And we're only now gaining the technology to see glimpses of the supernatural. As for your theory, why would Sasha put the secret to finding the school here? It's not our house. No one's been here for years."

"Exactly. She knew it wouldn't be disturbed. And she knew we'd find our way here. She *could* see the future."

Ruth Anne put her eye back to the opening again. "Ah, crap!"

"What?"

She opened and closed her eyes slowly. "We may never know the answers. The school disappeared."

CHAPTER 6
MAGGIE

My sisters and I gathered the following morning at *Dip Stix Café*, huddling in our usual corner booth. Marshall, Montana, and Luna ran through their father's restaurant like sticky-handed goblins on a syrup raid, while June Bug and Nova sat at the nearby kid's table, discussing lip balm, tennis shoes, and Disney villains.

The cheerful café was decorated with vintage movie posters, checkered table tops with chrome borders, and a glass bakery counter, giving it the feel of a diner from a bygone era. It was only half-full this morning, odd for a weekday. Looking out the front window, most of Main Street was visible from our booth. I waved out at two of *Dip Stix* regulars, Margaret and Beatrice, hiding behind their shopping bags as they hurried past to *Java Juicer*, instead.

"They'll get tired of the new place eventually," Ruth Anne said, catching the look in my eyes. "People are creatures of habit. We all need a good adventure from time to time, but eventually, we always slip back into our comfy pants."

I laughed. She was probably right. Maybe it was a good thing that my husband's diner was losing a few customers. This would give him a chance to break in his new employees, perhaps spend a little more time with the kids. Maybe even have some time for me at night. But that was truly wishful thinking. Since having children, we communicated mostly through post-it notes and hand gestures, on the way here or there. For us to both get to bed at the same time, not completely exhausted, might be too much to ask for, even for a witch.

"Aunt Dora's late," Merry said, looking at her fitness watch and drumming her fingers along the checkered table. "She promised she'd be here by 7:45. She knows I have to get to the school."

"Aunt Dora's always late these days," Eve said, eyeing the plastic menu she helped write.

"She's with Herman." I nodded to my aunt, standing outside *The Imaginarium* with the shop owner, a few blocks down, on the opposite side of Main. It was a newer shop that specialized in selling gadgets and odd toys, owned by a strange old man with an inclination for magick. But what type of magick was anyone's guess. "I think Auntie has a crush," I said, squinting my eyes for a better look.

"I think it's wonderful," Merry said, sipping her water.

"Is it?" I felt my lips turning down. I didn't like Dora carrying on with Herman. She spent way too much time with him, and no one knew a thing about who he was or what he did before coming to Dark Root. "I don't entirely trust him," I said.

"You don't trust anyone new," Merry said. "And I thought you liked him."

"As a neighbor, he's fine. And he does draw people to our stores. But dating our aunt...?"

"We know Aunt Dora isn't getting her groove on with Herman yet," Eve said. "Or she'd be a lot more relaxed."

"Eww...ewwww!" Ruth Anne said, covering her ears. "Don't make me think about Aunt Dora like that. Ewww!"

Eve regarded our eldest sister. "How long until Sophie comes back? You could use a shot of relaxation, too."

"I say we move on from this entire conversation," I said, trying to scour the images from my mind.

"Agreed," said Merry, raising her cup.

"Ugh." Everyone looked where I was looking. Erin, the pinup-girl owner of the neighboring store, *Charmed*, appeared outside her entrance. She sauntered by our window in a tight skirt that hugged her double-barreled bottom, moving on heels that set her hips winding. She stopped further ahead, giving a little wave and smiling through the other window and into *Dip Stix*, at someone in particular. I turned my head quickly, catching Shane smiling dopily back.

The hanging light fixture above our booth flickered and buzzed a warning. My sisters smirked, though Merry tried to hide hers. When I experienced sudden rushes of emotion, I tended to burn out light bulbs or start-up engines. I was learning to control it, through meditation and practice, but when I was blindsided, my *wilder* magick kicked in without my permission.

"Must be a storm coming," said the young busboy dropping off three hot teas and my Diet Coke.

"Hurricane Maggie," Eve said, when the teenager left. She ran her finger along the rim of her cup, tapping it three times after. She was sweetening it—magick she used to 'keep her figure.' "Poor Shane has no idea he's in trouble, the dope."

"Oh, he will soon enough," I said, as Erin waved a ta-ta goodbye, and floated over to *Java Juicer*, stopping traffic when she crossed the street.

"Don't fight with him now, Maggie," Ruth Anne said, as we all watched Shane approach the kid's table and ruffle Montana's hair. "Not before he's made our breakfasts. I've got a full schedule. This might be the only meal I eat all day."

"I'm not mad at him," I said, which I knew was a lie the moment I spoke it. The light knew it too and flickered in response. I took a deep breath and tried again. I was an adept secret keeper, but a terrible liar. "I don't mean to be mad at him," I corrected. "He was just smiling. I get that."

It's *who* he was smiling at. And that dumb look on his face while he was doing it. And how long he kept it plastered on.

Erin had taken an interest in Shane and I wasn't sure what to do about it. I knew Shane loved me, and I had little worry that he would really fall for a pretty face and swaying hips, but Erin didn't just have beauty going for her. She had magick. Pheromone magick, specifically, and unless I wanted to nullify it, I had to live with it. Eve was aware of this too, and wouldn't let her fiancé, Paul, anywhere near her.

I tilted my head, studying my husband as he talked to the kids. We had been together a long time now and I sometimes forgot how handsome he was in the morning, fresh-shaved and twinkle-eyed, ready for the day ahead. But today there was no shine in his eyes—they looked weary and drawn. He grinned as he came to our table, rubbing his hands together as he greeted us. "Good morning, ladies," he said, bending to kiss me, which he didn't quite land because I moved to grab a menu.

"How's training coming?" Merry asked, too alert for this time of day.

"Training is...coming. Not exactly smoothly, but they'll be independent in no time. I'm sure." He wiped his hands on his jeans, then looked to Eve, who had worked at *Dip Stix* over the years, off and on. "You sure I can't entice you to come back now that Nova's in school?" His head boomeranged at a crash coming from the kitchen. "Name the terms. Anything you want."

Eve shrugged. "You know I always loved working here, but Paul needs me at his new place."

"I miss Paul, too. Great cook and even better company. Okay. I had to ask." He looked around the table, taking orders. "Merry, a yogurt parfait, no granola? Eve, an egg-white omelet without cheese? Ruth Anne, bacon and eggs, white toast and hash browns. Soft butter and jelly. And Maggie—what will you be having, my dear?"

I was the only one who ever changed up my order. "I don't know. Surprise me."

"Are you sure? The last time I did that, we got Luna." He glanced over at his daughter, sitting between her two brothers and quietly drinking orange juice. "I'll bring a bran muffin for Dora, too, when she gets here," he said, hurrying back to the kitchen.

A family that I recognized from school yesterday entered, the child the one who tried to kill Luna's rollie bugs. "That's the little girl," the mother said to the father as they passed Luna's table, none too quietly. "You're right. There's something different about her."

The booth light flashed brightly and my sisters shot me a 'please be cool' look—I was garnering too much attention. "They're talking about my kid," I whispered. Then to Merry. "I told you they were going to single our family out."

"We don't know what they mean about that? Maybe it's her cute little nose."

"Or the fact she might have rearranged time yesterday," I said.

The glass door chimed, bringing with it a gust of wind and our Aunt Dora. She was a flurry of gray curls and bits of leaves, wearing a red knitted scarf wrapped three times about her neck, matching the color of her cheeks.

"She does look happy," Eve said.

"There she is!" Merry chirped, as Aunt Dora's stiff cotton house-dress rustled our way. Ruth Anne pulled her a chair at the end, borrowed from the next table.

"My girls!" Aunt Dora pinched Ruth Anne's cheek, then dropped her purse onto her lap as she plopped into her chair. "Sorry, I'm late. Got tied up a bit."

We all exchanged wide-eyed looks.

"Tied up? Is that what you kids are calling it now?" I said as the busboy delivered Auntie's bran muffin and another hot tea. Dora pushed the bran muffin towards Merry, who pushed it back.

"Do I smell romance in the air?" Eve asked, batting her lashes.

"Bah! What yer smellin' is my arthritis cream." Aunt Dora lowered her bushy brows, squinting her blue-black eyes. "Herman an' I are ol' friends. That's all. Knew each other back in the war."

"Which war?" Ruth Anne asked.

"All of 'em."

"That sounds like talk for another day," Merry said, turning towards Dora, invoking her serious face. "But today, we called you here because Maggie wants to ask you something. Don't you, Maggie?"

I rolled my eyes at Merry as the new waitress set a pecan waffle down before me. I didn't need the setup. Merry had taken on the role of family caretaker, acting in any capacity she thought was needed: The smoother-over-er. The softener-of-bad-news. The keeper-of-scrapbooks. I usually didn't mind--it meant less work for me--but it could also be quite annoying at times.

"Aunt Dora, have you remembered anything else about the old school after we left last night?" I asked. "I think I saw it... or a glimpse of it.

"*We* saw it," Ruth Anne said, swirling her toast into steak sauce before taking a large bite. "Maggie and I both saw it."

"Yes," I nodded. "A white building that looked straight out of a horror movie. It was covered in plants and surrounded by a wrought iron fence."

"How?"

"Through binoculars," Ruth Anne said quickly, either not wanting to get into the technicalities of the moonbeam shaft, or not ready to confess our home invasion just yet.

"Ruth Anne mapped out the area where it should be, but there's nothing out there. Did you remember anything about the spell Sasha cast on it?"

Aunt Dora sighed, flicking her muffin back to Merry like an air hockey puck. She hunched forward, carefully lifting a crystal snow globe from her purse.

"A memory globe?" I asked. Prior to Merry, Aunt Dora had been the custodian of our family's history, and she stored many important memories inside these globes.

"Aye. Take it. My hands are all sweaty an' it's charged." She handed me the glass ball and pedestal, and I sat it on the table between us all.

"Are these memories from the school?" I asked, leaning in.

"Jus' one, so fer." She squinted. "Saw it in the tapestry. Nearly killed my eyes, but it was there, clear as day."

Tapestry?

Eve, who'd been playing a phone game, looked up. "The tapestry from the trunk in your bedroom?"

Aunt Dora snorted. "Ya know about it?"

Eve tilted her head. Her pale skin and tar-black hair conjured up the image of a raven goddess. "I discovered it when I was a kid. We were playing hide and seek, and I found the tapestry when I hid inside the trunk. It was so beautiful, with all that gold thread. There were hundreds of pictures on it, and each seemed to move, like separate scenes, depending on the angle I was looking at them." Her glittering eyes dimmed. "When I heard Ruth Anne's clodhoppers racing down the hallway, I put it away. But over the years, I visited it sometimes."

"Must be some tapestry," Ruth Anne said, turning to Dora. "Did the pictures really move?"

"Aye. Pictures woven by the Fates. Scenes o' important events, meant ta be remembered. I shoulda hid it better. It was on my ta-do list." She pulled the globe closer to herself, and tapped it with her short fingernails. "I transferred the scene from the tapestry into the globe. It's a lost art, an' now I remember why. It took a lot out o' me." She swiped at her brow, her eyes trailing toward *The Imaginarium*, where Herman was still outside, now sweeping the sidewalk.

"What did you see?" I asked, peering closer, but seeing nothing myself. I had experience with these globes. And the news wasn't always welcome.

She hooked the globe back in her hands, returning it to her purse. "If ya look too hard, ya'll suck all the images out o' it! It's not complete yet. I need ta work on it s'more." She zipped her purse.

"But, I saw enough ta know the school was real, and it jogged a few memories.

"Sasha opened it ta teach ya things—things not meant fer ordinary children. Things meant ta be guarded until the time was right. Seeds planted in the springtime, harvested in the fall.

"There are many secrets hidden in an' aroun Dark Root. Some out in the open, and some buried deep. Sasha and I were responsible fer hidin' things. An' Juliana hid things before us, too. But the most important thing we hid was ya girls—and that school was a beacon for the darklings lookin' fer ya. Sasha sensed we might be found, and ya'd be endangered."

"But we're grownups now," I said, to reassure her.

"Ruth Anne's practically middle age," Eve said.

"Hey!" Ruth Anne said, elbowing Eve.

"It's no coincidence that this is all happening as our own kids are returning to school," I said, ignoring the others. "Maybe we're supposed to reopen it and train them in private. A place they will be safe." I hadn't planned on saying all that, but as I spoke, it made more sense, especially after the comment about my Luna being different.

"Maggie, I think you're overreacting," Merry said. "We had one little incident on the first day of school. It will be forgotten by lunchtime today."

Aunt Dora took a long sip of her tea, her eyes glossing over. "Sasha cast the forget spell o'er everyone, including herself. She e'en had ya forget much of what ya'd learned, fer fear the darklings would use it against ya. It was powerful magick—and I suspect, born in shadow. It took a lot out of her, including hope. We ne'er spoke o' it again."

"So that's why we all have botched memories," I said.

"I can't remember any of sixth grade," Ruth Anne said glumly. "Did I ever watch Silver Spoons?"

"The less e'eryone knew, the better." Aunt Dora clicked her nails against her cup. "The darkness set in far earlier than Sasha projected, ushered in by someone she loved. It left her a bit blindsided, but she handled it. She always did."

I knew the person Aunt Dora was referring to, the one who ushered in the darkness. Armand, Sasha's apprentice, and a powerful witch turned warlock. He was also my father.

The metal clang of a chair crashing to the ground tore us from our conversation, followed by a sharp cry. Marshall was lying on the floor, covering his head and sobbing.

I stepped over Ruth Anne and raced towards Marshall, scooping him into my arms. "It's okay..." I reassured him, dabbing his bloodied lip with a napkin.

"It wasn't me!" Montana said from his seat at the table, preempting the accusation that was coming. "He was just sitting there and fell over."

Luna nodded. "Boom," she said, clapping her hands together.

Marshall cried louder, and I was aware that everyone was looking at us. Some even videoing the meltdown with their phones. Merry joined me on the floor, feeding him calming energy by connecting his palm to hers.

"Shane!" I called, tapping Marshall's cheek as his eyes rolled back into his head. He was mumbling something. The same thing, over and over. Holding him, I couldn't tell if he was in physical pain or not.

Shane raced from the kitchen, spatula in hand.

"I think he's having a seizure," I said.

At his father's touch, Marshall immediately stopped shaking.

"You okay, buddy?" Shane asked, pushing Marshall's damp hair from his face.

His son's eyes closed slowly, then reopened with a snap, like a Viewmaster changing images. "Mo-hi-ma-ta-ra-se-dey-far-mo..." he muttered. Then again. "Mo-hi-ma-ta-ra-se-dey-far-mo..." And again. Louder each time, until he was nearly screaming.

"What's happening?" I asked Shane, who shook his head, not knowing either.

Reaching an impossibly high pitch--*"Mo-hi-ma-ta-ra-se-dey-far-mo!!!"* Marshall lost consciousness in his father's arms.

"I'm taking him to the hospital. Stay here with the kids." Shane directed, racing Marshal to his truck before I could object, heading for the hospital in Linsburg.

Still trying to piece together what had just happened, I looked around. There were several people still recording. Seeing them, I was instantly angry. Enraged.

My mind flared and then drew in, pulling--from everyone and everything. In the blink of my eye, every phone and device in the restaurant died. Every battery drained. And every memory chip emptied.

CHAPTER 7
SHANE

Shane Doler forced his eyes wide open, fighting off the sleepiness that constantly plagued him these days as he sped along the forested highway, heading to Linsburg General. Marshall was propped up against him in the cab of his truck. The boy nodded off and on, awake and asleep. His eyes rolled back into his head periodically, accompanied by spurts of undecipherable syllables.

Perhaps he should have had Maggie come along. The other kids would be fine with Merry. But in the moment, he hadn't even considered it. Maggie sometimes accused him of being too privately protective of Marshall, and maybe she was right.

He rolled down the window a crack to keep himself awake, feeling the cold autumn air against his cheek. He hadn't been sleeping well. His dreams kept him awake. As a Dream Walker, he could normally steer them them; but lately, they controlled him. First came the rolling clouds. Then darkness. Always darkness. Then floods. Running. Panic. Fire. Fire everywhere around him. The remainder of the dreams would be his urgent attempts to protect his family. To hold it all back, somehow. And in that craziness, there was another face who stepped out of the darkness, or out of the floods, or out of the fire—one with titian hair and turquoise eyes. *Erin.*

Was she a warning? Or salvation?

Perhaps the most troubling aspect of the dreams was that he was completely at their mercy, both to the events that transpired and his own actions in response. He was used to bending and weaving his nighttime adventures--crafting tranquil environments, or scenes of adventure to explore, or sometimes a *romantic* interlude with Maggie, when life got too busy during their waking hours.

But these new dreams were disturbing, having no real plot, just gloom and desperation. Erin's unbidden appearance was frustrating, complicating his feelings. They never touched in these dreams. Never kissed, nor made love. In fact, they never even spoke. But he could see her eyes staring at him through the darkness—sometimes her hair turned ember red, sometimes a rich dark brown that he could spool himself in. She would step out of the fires or the rising waters, her eyes shifting from sea green to velvet blue. It was always Erin. He felt her. Sensed her. And she him.

And there was not a damned soul he could tell about it, making him feel even more alone. Maggie certainly wouldn't take any of it well--and how could he blame her?

Smelling the air, Shane rolled the window all the way down. He detected smoke. Squinting his eyes, he thought he could make out plumes of smoke coming off the trees near the base of Eagle mountain, though it could have been fog, too. He rolled up the window, hoping he was wrong.

"Marshall, buddy. We're almost here." He tapped his son's wrist as he took the Linsburg exit.

Marshall stirred, rolling his head to one side, clomping his mouth together as he fought to wake up. In a few minutes, he was bright-eyed, looking about.

"How are you feeling?" Shane asked, looking him over.

"Fine, I guess. Where are we?" he asked, sitting up straight and combing his hand through his thick brown hair.

"You had an episode, back at *Dip Stix*. I'm taking you to the doctor to make sure everything is okay?"

"I had an episode?" It was clear by Marshall's expression he didn't remember it. Maybe that was for the best. "Am I going to die?"

"No! God, no." Shane pulled the seatbelt away from his chest, as if it were suddenly too constraining, and snapped it back. "Why would you say that?"

"Because of that look on your face."

Shane checked his expression in the rearview mirror. He did look grim. "I was just worried. But now that you're awake, I know things will be okay. They'll just take a look and make sure, okay buddy?" He clasped Marshall's knee, giving it a little shake. "Then maybe we'll get some shakes on the way home? Our little secret." He put his finger to his lips and Marshall grinned wide, bobbing his head.

They drove through Linsburg, passing old houses crammed in between newer builds. Their Main Street was thriving, but looked a bit worn and shoddy. Still, there was the smell of rich pine hanging over the town that made it feel welcome, even if it was a bit disheveled.

"Dad, can I tell you something?"

"Yes. You can tell me anything," Shane said, ruffling Marshall's hair, which his son immediately smoothed back into place.

"Sometimes I miss when it was just us," Marshall said, tugging on his fingers. "Or me and you and my real mom. I like Mommy Maggie but..." He sucked in hard, his chest expanding fully before releasing. "I just miss it."

Shane's heart ached for the boy. He knew that feeling, too. "I understand," Shane said, as they pulled into the packed hospital parking lot. "I lost my parents young and I miss them every day. Your mother was a good woman, Marshall. *Is* a good woman. And we'll see her again. But until then, you have me, and your siblings, and Maggie. And waaaay too many aunts."

Marshall laughed at this. "I do like it here," he said, his hand clasping the door handle. "I just hope I'm okay."

Shane paced the lobby, counting all the occupied seats in the reception area. There must be some nasty bug going around, he thought, seeing all the graven faces staring back at him. He kept his distance as best he could, turning his head when he got too close to anyone, while he waited for news on his son.

"Mr. Doler?" A short dark-skinned nurse approached him. The pleasant smile on her face was a good sign--no one ever delivered grave news with a smile. "Your son is fine. All the tests came out negative. We can see nothing wrong with him."

"No concussion? Brain injuries? We thought he might be having a seizure."

The nurse looked at her notes. "Nope. The doctor says he's very healthy. She had a talk with Marshall and thinks it might be new school year jitters. Stress-related. The anxiety can be intense for some kids, especially those who... let's say, tend to bottle things up."

Shane nodded. Marshall never commented on how he was doing, unless asked directly, and even then he had to keep digging. Just like his father. But the nurse's words made sense. New school year, new stressors. "Thanks," he said, shaking her hand.

"They'll bring him out shortly," she said, disappearing down the hall.

Within minutes another nurse appeared, an older woman with tired eyes. "He's a champ," she said, handing Marshall a sucker, which he happily accepted. "He can name the capital of every state."

"And every president, in order," Marshall said, puffing up.

"Really?" Shane asked, tilting his head.

"Yep. Backwards, too."

Shane smiled but felt like a terrible father. How had he never known that?

As they neared Dark Root, Shane pulled to the side of the road. "Let's finish our shakes and discard the evidence." He brushed a wisp of Marshall's wavy hair to the side. "I love you," he said.

"I know," Marshall answered, slurping down the last of his drink.

"I know you know. But it's good to tell the people you love that you love them."

"Life's short," Marshall agreed, handing over his empty cup.

"Yes," Shane said, thinking Marshall far too young to understand a statement like that.

That night, after they were convinced Marshall was indeed okay and all the kids had all been tucked in, Maggie cornered Shane in their bedroom while he was putting away laundry. She emerged from the bathroom wearing a short black nightgown she hadn't worn since their anniversary. It caught him by surprise.

"Hello, stranger," she purred, seductively walking towards him, her toenails painted fire engine red. Her hair was long and wild, strategically revealing bits of her, yet leaving most to the imagination. He looked at her, assessing the goddess he had married. Something stirred in him, but it was not the stirring she probably wanted, at the moment.

Maggie pushed him onto the edge of the bed, straddling him, then kissed him deeply. Her hand explored beneath his t-shirt. She smelled good. Sexy. Funny. *Familiar.* "What's wrong?" she asked, sliding off of him after he failed to properly respond. "You don't seem too interested."

"It's been a long day," he said, his eyelids heavy. "The restaurant. Marshall. The hospital..." he tried to stifle his yawn with his forearm.

"Yeah, you're right." She sighed, climbing under the blankets, but he could sense her disappointment.

He took his side, and wondered if this was what marriage was? Appreciation, even desire, without urgency. *Comfortable*, he thought, then dismissed it. Comfort implied boring, and his life was not boring.

"I'm glad things went okay with Marshall," she said, leaning close. Her hair smelled clean. "Jillian says he can stay with her tomorrow, if you want to keep him home."

Shane nodded. "That's a great idea. But only one day. He might get too far behind in school."

"The kid reads Ruth Anne's old college textbooks for fun. He'll be fine." Maggie kissed his cheek. "Maybe..." she said, nuzzling his neck, wrapping one leg over his thigh. "We could meet in your dreams tonight?" She walked her fingers up his chest.

"Maybe," he agreed. "Let me see what I can summon up. Then I'll call you in."

She nodded contently, then closed her eyes and fell asleep on his shoulder. *I love you*, he thought, smelling her hair again.

When he closed his own eyes, he opened them just as quickly. What waited for him behind those eyelids was darkness, flooding, fire. And Erin's eyes. He touched Maggie's thigh, still twisted over his leg, returning himself to home.

In the quiet house, Shane became aware of a knocking sound. A tap...tap...tap, like a small child knocking on a door. It was a constant sound, buried somewhere inside the walls. He was sure he'd never heard it before.

He strained his ears to listen. It was coming from below. *Way,* way down below. *An old pipe?*

He burrowed into his pillow, telling himself he would deal with it tomorrow. But this only made the sound clearer, thumping inside the batting of his pillow like an overtaxed heart.

THUMP. THUMP. THUMP.

He slid out of Maggie's arms and crept across the room to the door, knowing he wouldn't sleep until he discovered the source.

CHAPTER 8
RUTH ANNE

"Kiss. Kiss. Kiss. I love you, too, my snookums, sweetie, honey bee," Ruth Anne said into her cellphone. The response on the other end was an annoyed grunt.

"Can't you just call me by my name?" Sophie asked.

"But you said I wasn't romantic enough," Ruth Anne countered, scratching her head.

"I said that back when you were wooing me. But now, we're living together, planning our marriage, and you're having my baby. That's all the romance I need these days."

Ruth Anne chewed on her lip. She had never actually volunteered to carry their child, but that was a discussion for when Sophie returned from New Mexico, where she was caring for her sick *abuela*. "How's Nana Marianna?" Ruth Anne asked. Sophie's grandmother had been sick for some time, with an unknown illness. Undiagnosed, in part, because she refused to go to a doctor, claiming they were all hacks.

"She's hanging in there. She even made menudo this weekend, with my supervision. She's a bone of a thing, but everyone says she's perked up since I came home. Now, I'm scared to leave."

"Take as long as you need. I'm just writing my book and doing ghost tours," Ruth Anne said, wrapping a rubber tube around her elbow, tying it off, and jamming a syringe into her forearm.

Almost immediately, her building tremors began to cease. It was instantly invigorating--every sense coming alive--leaving her feeling both younger and stronger. But within minutes, the full effects of the serum would take hold and she was as likely to vomit as to hallucinate. Either way, Sophie would know that something was wrong if she stayed on the phone much longer.

"I better go." Ruth Anne feigned a yawn as the drug pumped through her veins. "Big day tomorrow. The *Haunted Dark Root* tours resume for the season."

"Did you get the windshield wipers replaced on the Jeep, like I asked you to?"

Ruth Anne scrunched her eyes. "Yep. Tomorrow morning. First thing"

Fortunately, Sophie laughed. "Have the breaks and the tires checked out while you're at it. It's the beginning of the rainy season, if I remember."

"You remember way too much. I love you. Now let me sleep, woman."

Sophie laughed, her voice like tinkling bells. "Goodnight. Dream of me."

"Only you," Ruth Anne promised.

After hanging up, Ruth Anne put away the rubber tube, the serum, and the syringe, hiding them inside an old spirit box case. It was someplace Sophie would never look.

Flexing her fingers, she felt free again. She loved Sophie--with a love she hadn't known she could feel again, after losing someone important years ago--but it was still strange being part of a 'couple.' She wasn't used to being reminded to eat healthy, check the brakes, or that she would be forty in a few years and had very little time left on the biological clock to manufacture a new human.

And then there was Ruth Anne's secret life--much easier to keep since Sophie left town.

She applied a cotton ball to her poke mark and secured it with a Band-Aid as a wave of nausea overtook her. Clenching the counter of her kitchenette, she waited for it to pass. Sweat beaded on her forehead and her legs quaked, but it was over quickly. No pink elephants or green leprechauns appeared this time, and she kept her dinner down. *Whew.* She didn't need to worry for another week.

Worry wasn't the right word, and Ruth Anne was a stickler for words. Of course she'd worry. She was almost out. There would be no more quick hits in between dosages to 'get her through'. When those agonizing, burning moments came, searing her forearm like a hot branding iron, she would just breathe through it. Maybe she'd have Merry work with her on meditation. And Jillian's topical salves did help some, though she seemed to be developing a tolerance.

It was cold in her rustic cabin, and she added a small log to the fireplace, knowing it would do little good. No matter how many logs she burned, she was always cold these days.

She looked at her dwindling woodpile. It wouldn't get her through the end of September, let alone the fall and winter. She'd have to get to lumberjacking soon if she were going to keep warm. She cringed, remembering when she chopped wood a few weeks ago. She had the ax raised high overhead when the fiery pain returned, and she nearly took off her hand when it fell.

"Maybe I'll just hire someone," she said to the empty cabin. "Or do it in the morning, while the serum is still fresh in my veins."

Of course, there was also the issue of the Hellhounds. Though she hadn't seen them in months, she smelled them--their trails of sulphur collecting in the eddies of wind. She was keener to their scent now, having been marked by one, but there wasn't much to be done except for the usual precautions: A salt circle around her property, and iron placed strategically about.

"Time to get back to work," she said to her sleeping cat, curled up before the fire. She rubbed her palms together. The Hellhounds weren't here now, and she had stuff to do.

Her cabin was simple, with a new queen bed and old everything else. A few chairs, a small table, a writing desk, a patchwork kitchen, and a fireplace. There were a few cozy pillows and blankets draped about, Sophie's doing, and a faux bearskin rug. She had a hulking, old-time radio, but no television, fearing it would be a distraction. She moved to the cabin specifically to avoid distractions, to focus on her books.

She went to her writing desk, looking at the stack of digital mock-ups Merry had dropped off. *The Haunted Dark Root Tour,* and she felt guilty. Ruth Anne hadn't been fully honest with Sophie. Tomorrow was the beginning of the tours, but she only had one tour scheduled, and it was with Merry. *Her Mayorship* wanted to ride along and ensure that plaques were properly placed, and all the historical signs legible. Ruth Anne preferred the grittier version of her tours--without signs or historical markers, replete with screaming kids and off-road mudding—but Merry was trying to class up the town. At least she hadn't gentrified her *Haunted Swamp Tours*. Yet. She pushed the proofs aside after a quick shuffle. Merry wouldn't make a mistake.

Turning on her computer, she gazed at the first page of her half-written paranormal romance novel, left untouched for nearly a month. She'd promised Sophie she'd use her alone time to finish the book. Her publisher had been calling and Ruth Anne assured them she was on track, but her mind was distracted with other things—the tours, Sophie and babies, and most of all, the constant pain.

Writing had lost its luster lately, for other reasons, too. When she was single, writing romance was all dewy and dreamy, with characters who wore sexy clothing and made passionate love in exotic locations. But now that she was in a relationship, Ruth Anne caught herself writing things like: *Corey left in a pair of sweat pants and flip flops, slamming the door behind him. Beth dropped to her knees, wondering if he was ever coming home. And why the hell didn't he take out the trash on the way out?*

Not exactly words her publisher appreciated.

"Not today," she told her manuscript, minimizing the window. "I'll do twice as many words tomorrow," she promised herself and her sleeping cat, wondering how deep her writing tab had become.

Instead, she needed to work on a puzzle that wouldn't stop gnawing at her: Marshall's seizure in *Dip Stix*. Ruth Anne suspected it was more than a medical, or mental issue. There was something to his bizarre words: lyrical, deliberate, even in their coarseness.

Ruth Anne tried playing the video she'd made of that morning, frowning when remembering that Maggie had erased it, along with everything else on the chip. She couldn't blame her, but boy, would she like to listen to those sounds again. She closed her eyes, trying to remember them—writing down every strange syllable she could recall.

She looked down at her notebook, tapping her pen against the page, as she paced the living room. It was a language, she was sure of it, evidenced by the cadence and the repetition of the sounds. An old language...maybe Akkadian...with Coptic influence?

Or maybe it was just gibberish.

"Why does it even matter?" she wondered, stopping at the window to look at a family of deer moving through the trees. "I'm sure it meant nothing." She caught herself tracing the word *nothing* into the steamed-up window.

No, it meant something. She had *seen* those words before, strange as they were. Had read them in a book, perhaps. And she had heard them before, too. But where?

She squinted her eyes, willing herself to draw out the memory. She saw words in a book—a fat, golden book. Old. Very, very old. She saw the words that Marshall spoke, dance briefly in her mind, before drifting frustratingly away. *Where...where...where...* She balled up her fists. *Damnit...where?*

A book...at the school...the school that was no longer there.

It came back to her, in confetti-sized pieces, but it was there!

She vaguely recalled other pages from that book. Chapters on binding spells and secret societies and fantastic creatures, with elaborate drawings, written in old-fashioned handwriting by pens dipped in inkwells. For a book lover like Ruth Anne, the golden book had been as enticing as real gold. When Sasha wasn't looking, Ruth Anne remembered sneaking peaks, speed-reading through passages on mirror magick, magickal entities, and ancient prophecies. She also remembered a chapter on Hellhounds.

This could not all be a coincidence. In fact, they were taught there were no coincidences.

She was being led to find the school. And the book. It held her antidote.

Looking outside again, she realized it was almost dawn. She had stayed awake the entire night again, yet it only felt like a few hours. That was another side effect of the medicine, or perhaps the Hellhound's mark—nocturnal tendencies and the need for less sleep.

She texted Jillian, who would be opening *Miss Sasha's Magick Shoppe*: *I'll be over soon.*

Ruth Anne entered *Miss Sasha's Magick Shoppe* through the back door, promptly at 7 AM. She had been milling around the alleyway, checking her watch every minute, fearing she'd appear desperate if she arrived any earlier.

"Hey, Jillian." Ruth Anne called a greeting into the back room where they conducted private Tarot readings, held merchandise available only to select customers, crafted their potions, and stored paper towels.

"Hello," Jillian said with sparkling eyes, as Ruth Anne came into the storefront. "You're just in time for coffee." She pointed to a steaming pot in the reading area, and a stack of cups. Jillian was a pretty woman, with perfect teeth and neat, graying hair. Impeccably dressed, as always, today in slacks and a festive blouse. She sat down on one of the chairs, crossing one leg over the other, and motioned for Ruth Anne to join her. "Come, sit."

"Okay." Ruth Anne removed her baseball cap, raking her hand through her mop of brown waves, loosening her glasses in the process. She sidestepped her way through a sea of supply boxes, nearly stumbling into a love-potion display. "Sorry," she apologized. "Just took my dose and I'm still feeling a bit woozy."

"You don't have to apologize to me," Jillian said, clasping Ruth Anne's hand as she sat down on the chair beside her. Jillian's hands were always warm. Motherly. Comforting. "That's one of the reasons I like opening the shop after I dose up--I get a few quiet hours to just...allow."

"Allow. Good word. Allow." *I allow the serum to filter through my blood and battle the nasty virus,* she thought, wriggling her fingers. It did feel better than fighting it, she admitted. "Looks great in here," Ruth Anne said, uncomfortable with the small talk. "Maggie's lucky to have your help."

"Well, she's got her hands full with her brood. And I'm happy to do it."

Ruth Anne drank down her coffee quickly, drinking it only because she thought it would look rude to refuse. Then, she threw away her paper cup and returned to the love potion display. She licked her lips, nerving herself to ask for what brought her to the shop, when Jillian appeared beside her and handed her a vial. Ruth Anne noted the deep purple liquid inside and immediately felt calmer. Her fingers twitched as she pocketed the tube, and her mind went to how good it would feel to use it right now. *No! Only for emergencies. Or in another week.*

"Did you keep enough for yourself?" Ruth Anne looked out the window. Cars were starting to appear, parking along the sidewalk. A line was gathering at *Java Juicer*. Maggie would be around as soon as the kids were in school; she needed to leave before then.

Jillian nodded, giving her an easy smile. "Ruth Anne, don't worry so much. I'll make another batch next week when the moon is full. I'll keep us both going until we can find a cure. Or until the elderberries run out. You've got a backup supply, right?"

Ruth Anne nodded. She was supposed to have a month's supply put away—in case of emergencies, but she had been nipping at it during those extreme moments, and now she was down to one vial, locked up in her safe so it was not easily accessible. "Yep. It's nice to have. Let's just hope we don't have to use it."

"We have to be honest with ourselves that it could happen," Jillian said, handing her a jar of the topical salve, too.

"Roger that," Ruth Anne said, wincing at the thought of running out of the serum. The special species of elderberries required for their serum were extremely rare, growing only in the Basque region. And this year's harvest had not been good. Add to that, the potion could only be brewed during a full moon. Her fingers twitched and she wrung her cap in her hands. "Maybe we could try growing our own bushes. There's enough magick here, I think. I could do some research. I'm sure it can be done."

"Perhaps. But..." Jillian sighed, blowing an errant curl away from her face. Sometimes, she reminded Ruth Anne of Elizabeth Taylor, with her poise and shimmering cat eyes. "We can't rely on the serum and salves forever. We're still being weakened by it, despite my best efforts." She turned her head and coughed into the crook of her arm, so hard she rocked backward.

"We will find a cure," Ruth Anne nodded, resolute, returning her cap back to her head. She reached into her jacket and removed the spell book she had borrowed from the shop nearly a year ago—Sasha's spell book, and a family heirloom. There was a chapter on Hellhounds which had helped them craft the serum and the salve—but there was nothing that mentioned a permanent cure. Nor had she found a cure in any of the other books she'd read—or anything she'd found on the internet. It seemed to be lost knowledge. But she had a new hope.

"There is another book that might have the antidote. A golden spell book. I think it might be in the old school Mama and Dora once ran. Do you remember anything about the school? Aunt Dora says Sasha hid it with a spell, back when we were kids."

"Old school?" Jillian's face paled. "I have no clear memory of it, but I feel as if I've been there, too. And when you mentioned the book, I got the shivers. You may be on to something." She showed Ruth Anne the goosebumps on her wrist. "But I will say this: If there was a school, Sasha must have hidden it for a good reason. And someone else, or something else, may be looking for it, too."

"You think finding the school might attract something *unwanted*? Even after all these years?"

"It's a possibility."

"Roger that." Ruth Anne nodded, having heard the same from Aunt Dora. "But if there's a chance it holds our cure, then it's worth the risk. At least we'll be alive to fight back."

With that, Ruth Anne gave Julianne a quick hug and left through the back door, lowering her head as she hustled to her Jeep.

Crap. She grimaced when she saw Erin, the pretty owner of Charmed, standing beside her vehicle. Her clothing was especially form-fitting today, and her heels especially high.

"Sorry, tours don't officially start until this weekend," Ruth Anne said, feeling anxious as she approached. She loved Sophie, but whenever she got near Erin, she got...nervous.

"I'm not here for a tour," Erin said, twisting Ruth Anne's cap into place. "I was just wondering what you were up to so early in the morning?" She smiled sweetly, nodding at *Miss Sasha's Magick Shoppe*.

"Just stopping by my family's shop," Ruth Anne said, trying to slide by Erin and get to the door.

"It was just curious that you left through the back door. How are you feeling?" She placed her hand on Ruth Anne's forehead. "Clammy. Not one-hundred percent." She extended her bottom lip. "Come by *Charmed*. I might have something for that, and other things that ail you."

"Thanks. I gotta go. These houses don't haunt themselves. Well, I suppose they do..." Ruth Anne squeezed past and made it safely into the driver's seat. *Does she know about my mark?*

"Stop by my shop sometime." Erin waved and crossed the street to her shop. "Sooner rather than later."

Ruth Anne patted the vial in her pocket, relishing in the sense of security it brought. She would not dip into it until the week's end, no matter how difficult it got.

"Hey, Sis," Merry called as Ruth Anne rolled up to *Merry's Mentionables.* Merry climbed in the passenger side, removing a map from her petal pink tote bag and spreading it onto her lap.

"Welcome to my *Haunted Dark Root Tour,*" Ruth Anne teased. "Have you signed the waiver stating you won't hold me responsible for heart attacks, possessions, or monsters under the bed?"

"A monster under the bed would be a vast improvement to my love life," Merry said.

As Ruth Anne drove, Merry kicked off her pumps and traded them for a pair of extra-white Keds, sealed in a large Ziplock inside her bag. "Ooh, that's better. Between you and me, this teaching thing is more exhausting than I thought it would be. I put out an employment ad in the Linsburg paper, but I'm not getting many bites. I may have to cast my reel further."

Ruth Anne licked her lips, leaning forward to see the path ahead as they left town and entered the woods on a dirt lane. "You know, I could fill in for you sometimes."

Merry gave her a sideways look. "Does that mean you're done with your novel? Because I have explicit instructions from Sophie to keep you on track."

"Sophie have you on her payroll too, huh?"

Ruth Anne felt Merry assessing her. "You're tired," her sister said, putting her hand on her shoulder. Ruth Anne felt Merry's rejuvenating magick, like crisp cool mountain water on a hot day. She sank into it, knowing its effects wouldn't last long. Merry was a gifted healer, but she didn't know what she was up against here. "We'll talk about you filling in for me after your book's done and you've had time to rest."

"I've just been missing Sophie. That's all."

"Ah, love," Merry said, buying it. "I remember that feeling of not being able to sleep because you missed someone." She smiled, and Ruth Anne wondered which of Merry's old suitors she was thinking of.

They bounced along nameless roads, stopping at old landmarks and buildings of Dark Root's past—an abandoned farm, a house where moonshiners once hid out, an abandoned old shack. Each stop now had a painted wood plaque, proclaiming what it was, when it was founded, and any relevant history or rumors of hauntings.

"So, did you like any of my ideas?" Merry asked as they pulled up to the old brick library, built in 1938 and closed in the '70s.

Ruth Anne scratched her cheek. "I kinda miss the old ways. I hate schedules and routes and waivers. The plaques look good, but doesn't it all feel a bit inauthentic?" She stopped directly outside the wrought iron gate that enclosed the crumbling dwelling.

"I think the new painted door looks great," Merry said, leaning out the window to take a photo and then consult her map. "Okay, next stop, the cemetery."

Merry didn't seem to hear what she was saying, and Ruth Anne had more important fights to fight, so she held her tongue as she drove in the direction of the cemetery. But as they neared the property, she made a sudden U-turn, surprising even herself. *Cemetery.* The word jogged something in Ruth Anne's memory. Merry grabbed the door handle, pushing her foot against an imaginary brake, as the Jeep's tires sprayed the nearby trees with mud.

"I think this is illegal," Merry said, grabbing for the map sliding off her lap.

"Can you take your mayor hat off, for just a minute?"

"Fine," Merry said, breathing deeply. "I can go with the flow. I'm just along for the ride. But Ruth Anne...are you driving to the Dune house?"

"Maybe."

"I already asked Peter Dune about adding his house to the tour, but he's not on board. He's a very private person and... Ruth Anne? You okay?" Merry snapped her fingers before her sister's eyes. "Did you hear a word I said?"

Ruth Anne swatted her hand away. "I just wanna check something out."

She did not actually stop at the Dune House, as initially intended, but sped past as Merry objected further, wedging through the trees, barreling in the direction where the school should be. At least, according to periscope calculations. But there was nothing there. Just trees and moss. Not even a gate.

"Are you still trying to find the school?" Merry asked "I don't understand why you all are so obsessed with it. We have a nice school—a new school—not some stale old— "

"Keep your eyes out for any anomalies," Ruth Anne interrupted, braking sharply to a stop.

"Maybe we should let the past stay in the past," Merry warned.

"Maybe there are valuable things we can learn from the past," Ruth Anne said, grabbing her backpack as she opened the door. "If the school had been cloaked by a spell, there should be some trace of it. Some evidence we can find."

"Why can't you leave things alone?" Merry climbed out of the Jeep and chased after her, mucking up her white Keds. "Dark Root's darker days are behind it. Let's move forward."

"Says the woman tagging and labeling the aforementioned 'darker days', all in the name of town charm." Ruth Anne pulled her electromagnetic frequency reader out of her pack, flipped it on, and waved it in the air before her. "I know you want everything neat and packaged and pretty, but sometimes life just isn't that way."

"You feel like our childhood was stolen from us, don't you?"

Merry said, looking about. "I understand. I have big holes in my memory bank, too. But I'm afraid of what I'll find in those gaps. They aren't all good memories, waiting patiently to be uncovered. Let's let them remain where they belong, Ruth Anne, bottled up and properly corked. We can never go back."

CHAPTER 9
MAGGIE

"Any word on Marshall?" Merry asked from behind the counter, the moment I stepped through the front door of her collectibles shop, *Merry's Mentionables (Now on Main!)*. The bell chimed to announce me but she didn't need the alert--she had a knack for knowing who was coming, and when.

"The good folks at Linsburg General think he's a-okay," I said, wiping my boots on the welcome mat. The shop was cozy, a mix of old-time nostalgia and modern country cuteness. It was pleasantly warm inside, and I went to the 'make your own hot cocoa' station near the window, pouring myself a Dixie cup full of mini-marshmallows. "I wished Shane would've let us work on Marshall, before bringing the hospital into it. They keep records on all that stuff. I prefer we handle these things privately, especially when it comes to the kids. What good is magick, if we aren't using it?"

"Shane is his father. He has to do what he thinks is best for Marshall." Merry shrugged, tossing me a butterscotch from the tray by the register as I meandered about, which I plucked it from the air with one hand." I didn't pick up that it was physical when I was touching him. I think it is a mental issue—and I can't cure that, though if it persists, we might try one of Eve's charms or Auntie's teas"

"Marshall isn't crazy," I said. The boy was odd, sure, and off in his own world much of the time, but that didn't mean he was 'coo-coo for Cocoa Puffs'.

"I'm not suggesting that. Perhaps I should've said he has a condition of the *spirit.* As in...not of this realm." She grabbed her ledger and crossed the plank wood floor, joining me at the circular *Choose Your Own Adventure* book stand, which I was spinning around. "What did the doctors say exactly?"

"Just that there's nothing wrong with him that they can detect. They attributed his slurred speech to low blood sugar. Or high blood sugar. I can't remember."

"That wasn't slurred speech, Maggie," Merry said, her cornflower blue eyes narrowing. "They weren't just random sounds, either. It almost sounded like a spell."

"Ooh-Ee-Ooh-Ahh-Ahh is a spell?" I asked, moving to a wall rack filled with Norman Rockwell reprints and old copies of The Saturday Evening Post--remnants of a more innocent era, though one that existed largely in the heart of the artist. My sister followed.

"It was either a spell or a message. But from who?" Merry removed the sharpened pencil tucked behind her ear and twirled it between her fingers, trying to put the pieces together. "He hasn't been...playing with a Ouija board or anything lately?" she asked, clenching her teeth. I knew where she was going.

"Marshal isn't possessed," I said. Ouija boards were often associated with dark spirits, as they were an open communication channel for anything wanting to jump into our dimension. And *darklings* were always eager to get to the head of that line. "I can't remember his exact words? Can you?"

"Nope. I can't recall either." Merry shook her head, swinging her long ponytail from one shoulder to the other. "Maybe someone shouldn't have recklessly released a very dangerous power surge, and then we'd have Ruth Anne's audio evidence to listen to?"

I ignored her with a scoff.

She put on her reading glasses. Merry didn't need them, not like Ruth Anne, but she radiated confidence whenever she wore them. Taller. Smarter. Her glasses worked a magick that even Eve's potions couldn't duplicate.

"With luck, whatever happened to him was a one-time freak incident." I said, cringing when I caught myself saying 'freak' with regards to one of my children. "A one-time incident," I corrected.

"Agreed."

As Merry locked up and turned off lights, I strolled around her shop, touching things I probably shouldn't touch, like a toy monkey with brass symbols who clanged himself right off a shelf when I pushed the button on his foot.

"Nothing!" I called to Merry, who was straightening up the back room.

I picked up the crashed monkey and moved away from the shelf. *Merry's Mentionables* was becoming known for its collection of old toys and dolls, most recovered from our attics; but I preferred her simpler offerings: Louie L'Amoure paperbacks, Mr. Peanut memorabilia, Duke Ellington records, a pair of old-fashioned ice skates with extra-long blades. There was even a 1940s newspaper announcing that America had entered the war. Being inside Merry's shop was like being in your grandparent's home during the holidays. It felt familiar and safe, yet you knew there had been struggles there, too. There was always the smell of something baking, courtesy of one of Eve's tinctures. Today, it was the scent of banana bread.

"Your store looks great," I said, as Merry joined me at the front door.

My sister looked around and sighed. "Thanks. Unfortunately, it leads to a lot of lookie-loos but not many actual buyers."

"Hence your other jobs," I said, now understanding. "Sorry I questioned you about all the hats you're wearing these days. I shouldn't judge your life until I've walked a mile in your Keds." I gave her a side squeeze. Merry made everything look so effortless that it was easy to forget she was only one woman, doing the best she could, just like the rest of us.

My sister slid on her corduroy jacket and tightened her ponytail. "As Mama used to say, 'Suck it up, Buttercup. Or maybe that was Ruth Anne."

"We should get a more modern saying. What about...Broom up and witch, or you'll never get rich?"

She raised an eyebrow.

"I'll work on it."

We left *Merry's Mentionables*, fighting the wind to close the front door. Hooking my arm, Merry pulled me across the street, not to the pie shop as I'd hoped, but to *The Imaginarium*. Herman was outside, cleaning his windows and shooing away a few curious squirrels. His long purple robe billowed up around his ankles, revealing sandals and otherwise bare feet. "Have you seen his new display?" Merry asked as we approached the store window.

"Nope. My dance card's been pretty full lately."

Herman always had the best window displays in town, and his latest was no exception. It was an autumn graveyard landscape, with ravens that flew, without strings or noise, behind the glass. The birds landed on various tombstones and squawked out 'Nevermore!' as they turned their red eyes to the audience. Zigs of blue lightning in the background made the scene playfully eerie. Though it was mesmerizing to watch, the display felt a little gloomy for early September.

Herman went inside without a word to us, shut the curtains, and put out the 'CLOSED' sign, before locking the door.

"It's good to see you, too Herman," I called into the locked door. "Friendly guy. I can see why Aunt Dora's so fond of him."

"He's an old grump sometimes," Merry agreed, "but his shop has energized this sleepy town."

"Psshhh." We walked along Main Street, passing the pie shop without stopping. Most of the stores were closed now, their windows dark. The Victorian streetlights began lighting up, casting yellow halos, illuminating the few cars parked along the curb. As we approached *Miss Sasha's Magick Shoppe*, my fingers began to tingle. Looking up and down the street, I knew this might be my only chance.

"Merry, I need to stop at my store real fast."

"Okie-dokey."

She didn't ask any questions and I didn't offer any explanation. But then again, no one knew my secret besides Shane.

Merry opened her rose-gold handbag and applied clear lip balm while I searched my purse for my keys. As my fingers dug along the bottom of my bag, I felt the sensation of being watched. I turned my head to see Erin, crossing the street from *Charmed*, and coming our way. *Great.*

"Whatcha doin', Maggie?" Erin said, giving Merry a quick hello hug. "I thought for sure you'd be home right now, helping that sweet husband of yours with the kids. Especially after what happened with Marshall."

"This is a modern world, Erin, not the 50's. You own a shop, you should know that."

"Yes, but I'm a single woman. I can be as fancy-free and footloose as I choose. But if I had your family, you bet your bottom dollar I'd be at home."

"Well, it's too bad you'll never have my family then, isn't it?" I said, smiling back just as sweetly. *Or maybe any family*, I thought, then wiped it away. Dark thoughts weren't helping my enlightenment, even if they felt justified.

"I saw Ruth Anne today. She looked tired, poor thing." Erin looked at me with those blue-lagoon eyes of hers. "There seems to be a lot of that going around."

"I'm feeling wide awake right now," I said, turning to face her.

"Anyway, I won't keep you." There was a perceptive smile in her eyes. "I just had the sense you might have lost something, and I came to see if I could help."

"Not unless you've found my temper," I said, smiling wider as I stood up taller.

"Oh, Maggie! You're too funny. That wit of yours must have enchanted Shane, once upon a time." Her twinkling eyes implied she felt superior; but she'd need more than an hourglass figure and pheromones to go up against me.

"You know what, Merry?" I said, way too loudly. "I don't need to check the store, after all. I think I'll just go home and rock my husband's world instead."

"Good for you, Maggie." Erin winked, as she turned away. "If I've learned anything, it's that we shouldn't take the ones we love for granted."

The nearest lamppost sputtered as my eyes burrowed into the back of her skull.

"I don't know why you let her get to you," Merry said, ushering me away before I caused a power surge up and down Main.

"Possibly because she flirts with my husband every chance she gets, and implies I'm not good enough for him, or my kiddos." My steps quickened and Merry jogged to catch up. "I keep telling myself that she's here to test my enlightenment."

"And have you passed?"

The headlights of the nearest parked car flickered on and off, answering her question.

We entered the woods through an enchanted hedgerow, separating our expansive property from the rest of Dark Root. The wind picked up again, rolling the leaves along either side of the dirt trail, and we talked of how we'd miss the fall colors when winter came.

We soon reached the fork in the path—one leading to Harvest Home, where Merry stayed with Aunt Dora, and the other to Sister House, where I lived. "See you tomorrow," I said. "I think Marshall will be back in school."

"Is he still working with Jillian?"

"Not right now. She's been busy helping Luna with her tree, and she's opening the store in the mornings so that I can get the kids to school." Jillian was my biological mother, whom I met well after I was grown. Over the summer, she had been helping Marshall with his 'visions,' but that had tapered off as she helped out more in the store.

Merry hugged me. She smelled like fresh linen and old books. "See you and the kids tomorrow."

I loved the Dark Root forests in the autumn, especially in the hours of twilight and dawn, when the magick felt crisper and the colors more vibrant. The rich smell of moss and earth filled the air, and the sound of small scampering creatures and chirping birds echoed around me. I had wandered these woods often, with an affinity that was partly lineage and partly nurtured by years of living among the trees. But this evening, once Merry and I parted, something felt different.

A crackling noise popped inside my ears, like candy rocks on my tongue, leaving me slightly disorientated. The pathway home blurred. Everything was in its place... but not quite. As if the world had skipped a beat, like a record with a scratch, and I was just catching up.

The noxious smell of sulphur now mixed with the smells of soil and moss. I stopped walking, trying to lock down where it originated from. I was familiar with the scent—it was the smell of Hellhounds and cauldrons. There was also another smell, far off, and I had to stand very still to place it. *Smoke.*

The disorientation and aromas passed as quickly as they'd come. I continued towards home, quickening my footsteps, looking over my shoulder at each little noise, aware that my heart was racing faster than my footsteps.

My pounding heart slowed only when the woods opened to the large clearing surrounding Sister House. Our ancestral home, with its wrap-around porch and sturdy columns, was always a warm and welcome sight.

I ran, clunking across the open field into the grass yard, in my furry boots, my beaded bag thwacking the side of my leg with every other step.

I was anxious, but I couldn't say why. Only that something was changing. I felt it in the woods. *Smelled it*, in the woods. A harkening or a reckoning? Perhaps both.

The Victorian home where Sasha raised us once felt palatial and eternal, but youth had a way of making us feel both immortal and small. I had wandered its many rooms as a child, seemingly as far apart from one another as the Earth to the moon. Sister House, like my life then, unfolded out indefinitely before me, offering tantalizing mysteries behind every closed door. These days, with three children of my own, a husband, various pets, and more toys on the floor than *The Imaginarium* had on its shelves, the house felt crowded. And the only mysteries left to solve were 'what's for dinner?' and 'where did Montana leave his shoes?'

I was met with a whirl of activity as I stepped inside the house, or rather, stepped over a pile of toy cars parked in front of the door. Montana was chasing Luna around the coffee table, breaking crayons on the floor with every step. The TV blared as Marshall strained to hear old Bugs Bunny cartons above the clatter, while eating cereal with a wooden spoon from Shane's recliner. A heaping pile of unfolded laundry was waiting for me on my chair.

"Hey guys." I dropped my purse and coat beside a laundry basket, then made the rounds, kissing everyone's cheeks. Montana immediately wiped his away. I looked around for Shane, on dinner duty tonight, but he was nowhere to be seen. Or even heard.

"You feeling okay, champ?" I asked Marshall, checking his forehead with my hand for signs of fever. He nodded yes, without blinking or missing a bite.

"He won't let us turn the channel," Montana said, crossing his arms and extending his lower lip. “Daddy says we have to let him ‘cuz he’s sick.”

“I’m not sick,” Marshall said flatly. “Just resting.”

“It’s a rule in this house that if you go to the hospital, you get to lord over the TV,” I agreed. Marshall cast a smile my way before returning to the cartoon. “Now, where is this dad you speak of?”

Luna pointed to the storage closet, which was usually locked, often dead-bolted, but now wide open. I didn’t like this. At all. That was my office and workshop down there, or would be, if I ever had the time and privacy to use it.

My mind ran through the list of things I might have forgotten to hide away—scales, powders, bones--wondering what Shane would say of them. The workshop once belonged to Sasha, and before her, Juliana. Shane had mentioned several times that perhaps I had bonded too much with my grandmother’s ghost, and that it might be wise to take a reprieve. He was careful never to tell me explicitly not to, knowing that would incite my rebellious nature, but when he asked with that kind, yet concerned, look in his eyes, I felt obliged to comply. Not because I agreed with him, but because I loved him. And, most honestly, I didn’t like him looking at me like *I had a problem.*

“What’s he doing down there?” I asked, and they all shrugged. “Luna, I’m going to check on your father. You’re in charge, okay? Mommy will be back soon.”

“Heyyy!” groaned both boys, while Luna gave a firm nod and a smug smile. “But no magick!” I said, heading for the open closet door. “Just tell me what they did wrong and I’ll deal with it when I come back.”

Montana stuck his tongue out at Luna, who lifted a finger, letting him know she was not to be intimidated.

I poked my head inside the closet, which was long and narrow and large enough to qualify as a room. I flipped the light switch but it remained dark, the bulb dead. “Shane?” I called as I stepped inside, half closing the door behind me.

This closet had once housed hundreds of magickal artifacts, collected by Sasha and Aunt Dora over many years, from around the world. We had organized the room a few years back and found new homes for some of the items, but many still remained, in boxes stacked up along the walls. The room smelled like a sawblade, left out too long in the rain. I found the aroma pleasant, but most people couldn't take it for long, especially in such a concentrated amount. Shane was one such person, which made it all the more intriguing as to what he was doing.

"Babe?"

Attuned as I was, I heard the artifact boxes hum--ever so slightly, and even glow – ever so lightly, in response to my own magick. One of the few defining characteristics of all witches that I've met, no matter what they called themselves or how they practiced, is that magick items had a way of finding them, just as a familiar did. There was a co-dependency between a special artifact and the witch. Some could wield such an item, but only an adept could master it. And more than anything, they longed to be mastered, just as was intended during their creation.

I picked my way towards the back, to the hatch normally hidden beneath a rug, leading to the workshop below. "Baby?" I called down, grabbing the ledge and lowering myself into the dim light, landing on a long desk and scattering a few papers.

There was a small gas lamp lit in the far corner of the room, evidence Shane was here recently. At least, I hoped it was Shane.

I smiled as I slid from the desk, remembering how I loved this room and its connection to my grandmother, Juliana. I walked about, taking in the familiar maps, diagrams, books, scales, small dead animals pickled in jars, and bottles containing unlabeled liquids that filled the workshop. Juliana studied not only witchcraft, but medicine, astronomy, divination, and alchemy--a subject I'd begun to explore myself, before my self-imposed workshop embargo, though my mind had difficulty making sense of it.

Juliana was deep into alchemy—the quest to transform one form of matter into another--proven by the strange symbols painted on the walls and even floor, of suns with weird faces and upside-down pyramids, both beautiful and disturbing. I skirted the outside of a pentagram drawn on the floor a century ago. That particular symbol was protective, but could also be a portal, and I didn't want to take my chances. Someday, I'd dispel it, just to be safe, but that was at the far end of my to-do list.

It was cold down in this basement and the lamp provided scant light. I rubbed my hands together, producing a warm, blue-white flame between my palms. It served as both light and heat. This spell took a lot of concentration and energy to maintain, but it was definitely handy to have.

Shane wasn't here. He probably checked on some pipes or something, then left to get a tool and was planning to return. That explained the open hatch and lit lamp.

I should get back upstairs. Who knew what the kids were into right now? Well, Montana anyway. But being here made me so...*happy?* Was that the right word? My own subterranean world, where there were still corners to explore.

I tapped a set of brass scales, then ran my finger along the page of the alchemy book I'd started reading, stopping at a picture of a lion eating a snake that was eating itself. *Calcination,* the title read. Page eleven. That was as far as I'd gotten.

A cold, bony hand touched the back of my neck. I screamed as I spun to face my attacker, readying my palm flame. A full skeleton rattled before me.

"Maaaagie."

I heard Shane's laugh as he moved the skeleton on a frame to the side, revealing himself, then returned it to its rightful place near the medical charts.

"I don't like you," I said, dowsing my flame. "And you shouldn't disturb the dead."

"Maybe it's the dead who are disturbing me?" he said, kissing my cheek to show that he was sorry.

“You’re in a good mood,” I observed, seeing the sparkle in his eyes . Then, more cynically, “What are you doing down here?”

“Man stuff.” I noticed he was wearing a tool belt and a headlight band around his head. Somehow, it looked sexy.

“What kind of man stuff?” I asked, looping my fingers through his tool belt and drawing him near.

He gently lifted my chin and kissed me. I melted immediately, kissing him back, forgiving him for his dumb prank, and even for invading my space. It had been days since we’d kissed with that passion, but it felt much longer. Whenever there was a distance between us, physical or otherwise, I felt it, even if I didn’t say anything.

“Your dreams aren’t the only way we can spice up our sex life,” I whispered, nibbling on his ear. The idea of him taking me here—or anywhere that wasn’t our bedroom--was oddly arousing, even with a skeleton watching. I kissed him deeper, pulling him down on top of me on the edge of the desk, hiking my skirt up to my thighs. “We can play handy-man and lonely wife.”

But there was definite hesitation on his part.

“If you’re worried about the kids, there’s still plenty of cartoons left,” I said.

“Maggie, I’d love to but...” He stood, shaking his head as if shaking away a spell. He removed phone out of his jeans pocket. “I’ll text Jillian to come watch the kids. I have to show you something.”

“Now?”

“Now. Come with me.”

CHAPTER 10
MAGGIE

Shane gently pulled my arm, guiding me across the room, to a full-height eye chart hanging on the brick wall. "You ready?" he asked with gleaming eyes.

"While I admire your spark," I said, "is there something about this side of the room that turns you on more than the desk?" I looked about. I was all for bringing more adventure into our lives, but there was no place to even brace against, except the slick eye chart and a shelf filled with jarred rats, swimming in blue goo. Not exactly sexy. Or safe.

Instead of answering, he lifted the corner of the eye chart. I heard myself gasp as he pulled it back, revealing a narrow brick corridor, wide enough to walk through. I crouched down, finding rat droppings, then glanced back over at the embalmed rats. Probably not the same culprits. Dusty spiderwebs encroached down from the ceiling and corners. I was frightened and giddy as if we'd discovered Dr. Jekyll's secret lab.

Shane peered over my shoulder and I could *hear* him grinning. He cast his headlight down the narrow passage, that appeared to end at a distant brick wall. "Shall we?" he asked.

"You found a secret passage?! I've never loved you more." I turned and kissing him hard on the lips. "What is this place?"

"I don't know exactly." Shane scratched the back of his neck. "I heard noises down here. Thought it might be bad pipes or rats, and I traced the sound here."

"Well, you guessed right on the rats." I crisscrossed my arms protectively over my chest, standing on my tiptoes as I imagined an army of rats, readying to take over as new owners of the house.

"Follow me," he said, stepping in front. "I don't think there's any critters running about right now."

Now?

We sidestepped to avoid the webs, our footsteps echoing on the chipped cement floor. The bricks were perfectly laid—this was no afterthought, but built deliberately. It felt very 'secret circle' inside the tunnel, as if I were a disciple in a mystery school, about to get initiated. I assumed we'd continue all the way to the end, but Shane stopped at about halfway.

"I didn't see it at first. Took several passes. But look..." Stepping as far back as he could, his light was able to pick up a faint chalk circle on the sidewall. Shane knocked on the circle and it sounded hollow beyond. "I think this opens up to something else," he said, pushing on several bricks, one at a time. "But I can't figure out how. Couldn't find any latches or levers or buttons or anything like that. I think this is where that noise was coming from."

"Maybe there's an old furnace or oil tank locked away on the other side?" It was a bad guess, but it was better than the darker images conjuring up in my mind. There were rumors that Juliana was not only a witch, but also a murderess, and that her victim's bodies were never found. They were rumors I had paid little heed to, until this moment. If one were needing to hide a body—really hide a body—then carving out a secret tunnel inside a secret basement room, beneath a storage closet, would probably make sense. *Did the spirit of one of her victims bring Shane down here?*

It was hard to have perspective in such a tight space, but I did notice an anomaly in the brick pattern near the center of the circle. They weren't staggered like the others. "There's a vertical line through the middle of it," I said, tracing my fingers through the mortar joint.

"Yeah, you are right." Shane tilted his head. "Mean anything to you?"

"That the mason got lazy?" I joked. But as I broadened out my view, I realized it did mean something. "It forms a different symbol, along with the chalk circle." I traced my finger along the shape. "I've seen it in Juliana's alchemy book. Wait here."

I scurried back to the workshop and opened the alchemy book I'd been studying to one of the first pages. *I'm right!* I thought, exhilarated by the way events were lining up. I searched for, and quickly found, a glass bottle of sea salt, and returned to Shane. "A circle with a center line dissecting it is the symbol for one of the three alchemical elements: Salt." I held it out to my side, like a prize on a game show.

"Wow! That's impressive you knew that," Shane said.

"I'm smart," I said.

"Damn right you are. Now what do we do with the salt?"

I took a pinch of the sea salt, then ran it along the chalk circle. Next, I rubbed some into the straight length of mortar. The wall rumbled before us. *Oh crap, what did I do?* The brick wall split neatly in two, dust falling on the floor, and slid open to reveal a dark space beyond.

"That's my Maggie Magick." Shane kissed my cheek before we stepped inside, hand in hand. The crystal bracelet purred against my wrist--a gentle warning. It was so dark that even Shane's headlamp hardly cut through it. The air was colder than it should be.

"Feels like old times," I said, as we began feeling our way around the curving wall. From what I could tell, the room was a circle. There were no rat droppings or webs, and the air smelled both sweet and stale. "How did we not know this was here?"

"Never thought to look, I guess. Makes you wonder what else is hidden in this town, and who did the hiding?"

I squeezed his hand. "Shhh...We're not alone," I whispered. In the middle of the room, I detected faint blue glowing lights that came and went like the notes of a song. And I felt the presence of strength. So much strength. Something was definitely in the room with us, something much stronger than a single lingering spirit.

"Turn off your lamp," I whispered again, and he quickly complied. "Do you see the lights?" I asked as they brightened in the deepening darkness.

"I don't see anything," he said.

"In the middle of the room," I began moving towards them, my hand stretched out before me.

"I should lead," Shane said.

"No offense, but this job requires a wand, not a tool belt. Not that I have a wand."

We slowly made our way, caution in every step, my awareness of the 'something' growing by the moment. It was vile, whatever it was. Even darker than this underground cavern Juliana likely built specifically for it.

The amount of magick concentrated in the center of the room was dizzying. We might have been walking into a vortex, for all I knew. But come what may, for I had lost sense of reason and time. It seemed Shane had too, because we were not turning away until we found the source. We would feel neither safe nor sated, until we knew what shared the house with us.

Then we saw the mirror appear out of the darkness, standing unexpectedly before us like an old hermit on a mountain summit, both wizened and worrisome. A tall, ornate mirror with a dull brass frame and obsidian glass. The type once used by alchemists and magicians for channeling supernatural entities, and by witches and wise women, for fortunes and prophecy.

It was within the obsidian glass that the blue symbols glowed, randomly pulsating, like unmelodic beats of a drum. I reached out to touch one, even as my mind scolded my hand for its foolishness, and was immediately zapped by a charge from the frame. My bracelet flashed simultaneously, illuminating the room in a brief ring of light, before returning us to darkness.

"Shane, turn on your light again."

"On it." His headlamp on, the symbols disappeared. When he turned it off again, they did not return. "Why did your bracelet go off?" he asked.

"You still didn't see any lights?" I asked, hoping.

"No. Let's get out of here--this room is making me feel ill." I felt it too. My stomach ached, and my head throbbed. Our joined hands were sticky. "I never should have brought you down here. We should keep away for now."

"We were meant to find it, Shane. Don't you want to know why?"

"No. That mirror...I was fine with some minor dungeon exploration, a few bats, even a ghost or two...but I don't like that thing at all." He stepped back towards the opening to the tunnel. "It's evil, Maggie."

"Objects can't be evil. They can only be imbued with evil."

I followed him out, relieved that my head was clearing, yet disappointed that we were no longer sharing this sense of adventure.

"Well, someone or something imbued the hell out of it. I'm boarding this wall up, just like we did to the wall in the upstairs library, and we'll never speak of it again." When we stepped out, the wall shut behind us. Shane took my hand and pulled me back through the passage, into the workshop. He looked at me directly. "I know I've asked you to back off on your magick use lately, but I give you full permission to put up whatever spells or domes or charms you want to, to keep that thing, and whatever it wants, firmly locked up."

"Permission? You can't give it to me and I don't need it," I reminded him.

"Fine. Then I'm asking you..." he said, as he secured the eye chart back into place. “Maggie, let’s please have a Council meeting and figure out what to do with that room. It’s either that or move.”

I took a deep breath. It was time for me to confess. “Shane, I’ve been seeing Juliana again. I think she’s trying to get us to help her.”

“What? You’ve been seeing her again and you didn’t tell me?”

“Don’t act like I’m the only one with secrets,” I said. “You’re not exactly an open book, either. When, exactly, did you find that tunnel?”

“Look...” he blinked, trying another approach. “I know you have an affinity for the dead woman, but have you considered she might be using you?”

“Using me for what?”

“To uncover that mirror. Who knows what magick she worked with it when she was alive? Do we really want to bring that into this reality? You promised me we’d leave Juliana in the past. For your mental health, as well as mine.”

“I promised, but she didn’t.”

In some ways, Shane was right. I had become a bit obsessed with Juliana after reading her journals. I’d dreamed of her, found myself speaking in her words at times, wondering about those missing years between her adolescence and full adulthood. But in trying to discover more about her, I had been neglecting my own life.

We left the storage closet and locked it, neither speaking another word of it that night. Thankfully, Jillian had fed the kids and took them upstairs for baths. Shane and I washed a tower of dirty dishes, momentarily forgetting the mirror in lieu of our domestic duties. Or perhaps, in my case, purposely avoiding it for now.

“How’s Marshall?” I asked, scraping crusted macaroni and cheese off a plate and into the trash.

“Physically, he seems fine. But he said he’s been having visions again." Shane shook the water from his hands, drying them on a towel draped over the oven handle.

"I'll ask Jillian to work with him again. She's just been so busy with the shop and Luna. And—" I lowered my voice, craning my neck to look into the living room. "I think Jillian might be sick. Her eyes are red at times, and she has this really bad cough. It worries me."

It was a bear's cough, kept mostly under control with a homemade tonic. But in between doses, she coughed so violently it rattled *my* bones. She never complained, nor even spoke of it.

"I've heard it, too. In the early mornings, when I'm warming up the pickup for work and she's out walking. I wondered if she were smoking again."

"She hasn't smoked since the '80s," I said. "At least, I don't think so."

"The world is getting weird, Maggie, and Jillian is very sensitive to everything around her. Maybe she took it up again, for nerves." He shrugged as we headed to the living room for our nightly toy round-up.

My mother wasn't a smoker. Was she? But at least that would be a reason for the coughing. If she just started, there was a chance we could still get her to stop.

"What do you mean about the world getting weird?" I asked, scooping up a herd of brightly colored horses from the couch. Shane's words were troubling. He was normally an optimist. He didn't see the world as weird, he saw it as unfolding. For him, it was always closer to dawn than dusk.

My husband clenched his jaw, sliding it side to side. "I can't explain what's wrong," he said, tapping his fingers together, "only that it *feels* like time is running out. But where it runs to, I can't say."

"You're just overdrawn at the moment, with work, and kids and... me. And I'm sure Marshall's just nervous about the new school year, like the doctor said. He'll settle down, you'll see."

"I'm having dreams too, Maggie." He threw a pink sock into a laundry basket. "They're disturbing."

"Dreams? What kind of dreams?" I didn't like where this was going. Not only was he a dream walker, a master of dreams, but Shane was also my rock. I was the one who got freaked out about things and he was usually talking me off the ledge. "Dreams that you can't control?"

"I wish I could control them," he said, his eyes far off as he returned pillows to their places on the sofa.

"We just need to get you some better dreams then," I purred, slinking over to him, breathing on the back of his neck. "Maybe I can help you relieve some of your stress?"

"I'd like that," he said, turning to kiss me.

"Shane, wait." I said, pulling away, remembering. There was something still nagging at me that couldn't wait until morning. "Did Marshall tell you what he saw in his visions?"

"Something about a teacher."

"You mean Merry? Did he mention a school?"

"Maybe. Why?"

I stepped back, trying to pull the threads together. "Brace yourself. Apparently, there used to be another school in Dark Root, and Sasha hid it with a spell. Then she zapped all of us with a forget spell, so we wouldn't remember it."

"That was a real place? I assumed he was talking about the school he went to when he lived with his mom. But come to think of it... I might have seen it in my dreams, too." He rubbed his eyes. "A creepy white building that looks like an abandoned asylum?"

"Yes. You must've gone there too, then, when you came to Dark Root. Sasha shut it down, fearing it would call something in. But who? And why was it so important that she blocked it from our memories?" I paced between two our two recliners. "I suspect this mirror in our basement, Marshall's vision, and the memories of the school all returning to us right now, just when our own kids are starting school, is no coincidence. Those symbols in the mirror I saw—what if they're the words to the spell Sasha used? If so, we could counter it and maybe bring the school back? Surely, that has to be what Juliana is trying to tell me."

"Why would she care about it? Juliana was long dead by the time you were in school," Shane said.

"True, but Sasha could see the future. She'd know I could communicate with Juliana..."

"You can talk to ghosts. Sasha could talk to you directly, if she needed you to know something, right?"

"You know that's not the way it always works," I said. "And it's certainly not the way that Sasha works." I knew—with everything in me—that this was all related. Somehow. "Maybe the school was meant to be found now, so that our children could go? We could pick up where Sasha and Dora left off. Train them away from the *normies*, where they'll be loved and accepted and—"

"The *normies*? Our kids *are* normal, Maggie."

I stopped pacing to look at him. "We both know that's not true. I'm not saying our kids aren't wonderful, but they're not normal. Neither are we. That's why we live in Dark Root, where we can be abnormal as hell—*I owe the curse jar a buck*—and still live a functional life, hidden from the Darkness that would destroy us. With all these outsiders moving in, people are going to figure out our kids are freaks."

I felt Shane's anger, even before his grey eyes turned black. "I didn't mean..."

He leveled a shaky finger at me. "Our kids are not freaks!"

"I know. I'm sorry for saying it that way. But people are talking, and it's only going to get worse."

Shane clenched his jaw as the truth registered. "We need to devote more time to helping them fine-tune their gifts, and teaching them when it is appropriate to use them. Where the hell is Luna getting all those marbles, anyway?"

I shrugged, knowing his anger came from fear. We had shielded

Dark Root from the outside world, but how did we protect it from within?

"This school is the answer. That's why we're all remembering it at once. We'll train them in a suitable environment, without worry."

Shane looked drained, the fight in him gone for the night. "Our kids are not freaks. I'm going to bed."

"Without me?"

"Your choice."

"And people say romance is dead. I think I'll go for a walk." I grabbed my coat and opened the front door. If he wanted to be grumpy and alone, so be it. My fingers tingled as I slipped on my mittens.

"I know you'll do whatever the hell you want, but please stay away from your shop when you're out walking. Nothing good can come of it." Then he disappeared up the stairs.

Ugh! I grunted. *How did he know that I was going to the shop?*

Because he knew me. We both knew each other too well. It was comforting, but also confining.

But as he also acknowledged--I was going to do whatever the hell I wanted.

I did not go to the shop, though it was heavily on my mind. Shane might ask me to stay away, but he would never check up on me. I would have the place to myself, and with it, the opportunity to unlock the hidden cubby in the back room. Ironically, I was relieved when I remembered I couldn't gain access to it without the ankh key I'd stashed away, in Juliana's desk back at the house.

I was going to the Dune House, I decided, almost as an afterthought. Why, I didn't know, only that I felt certain it was all tied into this. Perhaps I could break in again, and see if the school would return. Why was it visible from that location, anyway? And who constructed the shaft that showed the way, or at least a view of it?

Evening had become night as I traveled the same path through the dark forest. It was a damp and winding, skirting drainages and denser brush, and the air was thick like gravy. The foliage did not ferry me, as it had for Merry, leaving warning scratches on my face and hands, which I ignored.

The garish black-purple house appeared, more looming and ominous this time, now that I was alone. The lights were off in the windows and no smoke rose from any of the three chimneys. I took this to mean that no one was home. Merry said Peter Dune was spending the weekend in Linsburg. Perhaps he'd gone early? I hoped. I slowly circled the house, twice, when I was overcome by a forgotten memory:

"Ollie Ollie, all come free!" Merry called, trying to find us. We had been forbidden from coming to The Dune House, by Miss Sasha herself, which made our midnight game of hide-and-seek all the more delicious. We had even enticed rule-following Merry to join us, with the promise that she might see glowing fairy rings along the way. "Here I come!"

Eve was terrible at this game, squealing the moment Merry ran towards the small orchard where she huddled between the trees. From my spot by the small staircase leading to the outside basement entrance, I saw Merry charging towards Ruth Anne. My eldest sister ducked behind a wheelbarrow filled with stones but was caught anyway.

"Where's Maggie?" Merry asked, and they shrugged.

I felt a deep sense of satisfaction at having hidden so well, tucked down into the stairwell. My three sisters joined hands and swept across the backyard, quietly calling for me. I considered coming out of hiding and joining them. It would be fun to run holding hands, feeling that current of energy pass between us, as we collectively became one. But I had so little individual freedom—we shared everything, from books to bedrooms to Mother. So I savored the moment alone, knowing I'd never get it back.

How long am I willing to wait here? I asked myself, as their cries for me grew louder. I had already technically won the game, and was thus awarded gloating privileges. Their shadows passed several times, apparently not seeing the stairwell. On their third pass, I drew close to the cellar door, padlocked from the outside. There was a strange noise inside, like an animal running loose. Odd, since Old Lady Dune was supposed to be off visiting family.

I bent low, listening intently to a muted thunder sound. And then a high-pitched bark. A deep growl. Was a dog trapped inside?

I beat on the door. "Here, puppy!" I called, no longer caring if I was discovered. My sisters quickly found me and I explained what happened, but none of us heard any further noises. Merry said I must have imagined it, because I ate too much sugar.

I wondered about the dog for several days after. It had been a dog; I was certain of it. Had I not feared getting in trouble, I would have told Sasha. And had I not feared what was behind the door even more, I would have gone back alone.

Returning myself to the present, I hurried past that cellar stairwell, not slowing until I reached the safety of the porch. This recovered memory would have to wait until later to fully traumatize me.

I easily disarmed the front door lock, then slipped inside, casting a light between my palms. The house was cold, unfriendly, and sad. And eerily quiet. Yet, it also felt alive; or at least aware of my presence. I imagined the eyes of the Dune bird-eyed ancestors following me from their portraits as I ascended to the second floor. The feeling of unease stayed with me until I reached the library.

I opened the door, startled by the form standing in the center of the room. It turned to me, a smile stretched across his face. Holding up the flame, I recognized him as Peter Dune.

"Hello, Maggie. I thought I might be seeing you tonight," he said.

"How?" I closed my hands to snuff out the light, hoping he hadn't gotten a good view of the magick flame.

"Intuition. Just a feeling." He turned on a lamp, sitting on the small table by the opposite door. The room remained dim, though my eyes adjusted quickly.

"You know who I am?" I asked, keeping to the doorway.

"Of course. You and I were friendly, back in school. I admired your spunk and curiosity, wishing I had more of the former and less of the latter. Curiosity is a good trait, but it always got me into trouble."

"I can relate," I said, wondering what trouble of my own I had just stepped into. My bracelet tickled my wrist, alerting me to magick in the room, but that much I already knew. "So...school, huh? I don't have many memories of back then. A few here and there, and none of my classmates. What do you remember?"

I cautiously entered the library. The room appeared much larger than it really was. I should have been fearful of this strange man that I didn't know, nor trust. But as I felt the energy in my palms, still fresh from the flame, I buzzed with the courage of a witch, fully tapped into her powers.

Peter was wearing a sweater vest over a collared shirt, slim slacks, and polished shoes, his hair glued into place with pomade. Not exactly an imposing figure. But I sensed his inner power, carefully hidden from most beneath his meticulous clothing. "I remember you liked cheese sandwiches. That you wore Ruth Anne's hand-me-down jeans. Had to pee a lot. And I remember that you were the most promising student Miss Sasha ever had."

"You knew my mother?"

"I knew you all. But we'll reminisce some other time. Coffee perhaps?" He smiled lazily as he went to turn on another lamp, illuminating the wall of books behind it. "Let's discuss what brings you here tonight."

"Your intuition didn't tell you that?" We were standing within a foot of each other now. Without the tall hat he wore the first time I saw him, he looked rather short.

Peter didn't answer, only tilted his head, looking more like bird-like than ever.

"I wanted to see the library before the place sold," I said.

Peter Dune smiled, stretching his arms wide like a circus ringmaster. "A wonder, isn't it? It was built by my grandfather. I'm not sure why the library wasn't looted or the books sold over the years, but I'm grateful this room was left relatively untouched. I can see why you were *called* here. Go ahead, look around. I don't mind at all."

"Uh, thank you," I said, wary at how accommodating he was. I inspected the book case, hoping to find the spot where I'd seen *The School of Magick.* The circular walls made it difficult to orient myself. Plus, there were no orbs guiding me this time. After a few moments, I thought I found the approximate location, though it was hard to tell in the dark.

"There's no rhyme or reason to their order," Peter said. "They were just stuffed in as they were collected. I'll be reorganizing them, alphabetically." He knocked on a stack of books on the nearest lamp table. "I've already started reading through a few of them."

"Yeah? Find anything interesting so far?" I asked as I climbed the sliding ladder, pretending to be interested in a book entitled '*More Magic Mushrooms'*.

"Everything is interesting." He lifted the top book from his stack and physically smelled it, his eyes rolling back into his head, as if sniffing a fine cigar. "I am fascinated by words, aren't you?" he continued. "They are nothing, and yet they mean everything. Changing one little sound can completely alter the entire meaning. That is real magick, if you ask me."

"So true," I agreed, shifting slightly to the right, closer to the book I'd come for. If he knew what I was doing, he made no show of it, caught up in his discourse.

"Books are the greatest gift we've been given, Maggie. With just a few little marks, they give us the entire world. Words themselves are spells, you know? Abracadabra—some believe it to mean *I create what I speak*; and though it doesn't literally translate that way, because enough people believe it, that is exactly what it means!"

"That's actually a really smart observation," I said, finally resting my hand on *The School of Magick.*

"It won't be there," he said, returning the book in his hand to the stack.

"What won't be there?" I asked, freezing in place.

"You're looking for the shaft that points to the school, right? It's not there anymore. There are 365 books on each of the shelves circling this room, and every day the light shaft changes a degree. Go ahead, pull it out."

Knowing I'd been caught, I lifted out *The School of Magick*, revealing nothing but oak paneling behind it. I went to the next book to the right, *Discussions with a Woodsman*. The kaleidoscope shaft was there but showed only a copse of trees in the far distance. Unreasonably disappointed, I came down off the ladder and approached Peter.

"When you were here last, it was the one day all year you could see it," Peter said, holding up one thin finger. "What a coincidence. But as Miss Sasha used to say, *'there are no coincidences.'* One of her few lessons that actually stuck with me."

"I'm sorry to bother you," I said, not offering him an excuse, as he seemed to know too much already.

"Care to borrow a book on alchemy?" he asked, the corners of his mouth tilting up into a smile. "The quest for eternal life can be addicting. Then again, maybe you don't need any new addictions?"

What game is he playing? I glowered at him but said nothing, marching straight by him, without a goodbye.

Leaving the room, I heard the distinct rustle of stiff skirts in the hallway, and detected the scent of floral perfume. I looked back at Peter, to inquire if his sister Isabella was here in the house with him, but he was already closing the doors behind me.

CHAPTER 11
MAGGIE

I wandered through *Miss Sasha's Magick Shoppe* storefront, inspecting our inventory. We were low on smudge kits, as well as lavender and patchouli incense sticks. The glass cabinets flanking the register were still brimming with crystals and pendants, and there were enough mood rings to last through early October.

"I'm going to check the tea supply," I said to Jillian, carefully draping an autumn garland around the display window.

"We should have plenty of tea," she said, smiling my way. Though Jillian was naturally slim, I could see the hollows of her cheeks today. Her upper ribs were visible beneath her fitted maize turtle neck.

"I'll double-check, just in case." I went into the back room, looking through the boxes of teas. *Caffeinated, sleeping, healing...* "Yep!" I called. "All full."

I stooped to open a small cardboard box filled with ceramic fairies, and another filled with coffee filters. But my mind was not on fairy wings nor dark roast coffee. Standing, I lingered near the archway, busying myself with more boxes while casting glances up at the portrait of Juliana Benbridge. She looked down on me in return, whether in judgement or encouragement, I could not say.

I lifted the ankh key out of my jacket pocket, that I retrieved from Juliana's workshop just before leaving the house. I stared at the looped cross in my hand for nearly a minute. *No!* I dug my nails into my palms to distract myself. That cubby had been locked for over six months now. It could stay locked one day more.

I had promised both Shane and myself, that I would remove the relic from the trunk, only if necessary.

But what constituted necessity?

Before I did something I'd regret, I quickly lifted an old sweater hanging on a wall hook and hung the ankh on the peg beneath it. I congratulated myself for once again resisting the temptation, wiping the bead of perspiration off my forehead. It was a fool's win. Keeping the ankh here would only make it easier to unlock the cubby in the future. But, it was a win for today.

"You look tired," Jillian said when I returned to the front. She was standing back to view her garland display, adding a few fake pumpkins to the mix. "You should try my sunrise tea. Will pep you right up."

"I don't need any sunrise tea," I said, immediately regretting my rude response. Jillian shouldn't be the target of my withdrawals. Nor my personal problems. "Sorry. Shane and I had a *disagreement* last night, and I guess it's still weighing on me."

"Oh, bummer. I'd hoped you two would use the time to reconnect."

"We did for a moment, but then, like usual, we screwed it up again. Why can't he just agree with me on everything? It would make life so much easier."

"And you'd be bored out of your mind. Give yourselves some credit for how well you're doing. Marshall hasn't been in your lives that long, and you're still adjusting to the new family situation."

"I know. I just want everything to fall into place, to have those *Saturday Evening Post* moments, like in Merry's store."

"Honey, that was just art." She squeezed my shoulders before hanging a leafy wreath on the glass door. "Relationships are supposed to be challenging. It's how we grow."

I arranged the pillows on the love seat of the reading section, and then turned on the arrangement of orange salt lamps. This was my favorite part of the store, though today there were noticeably few magazines in the case.

"You know, I can help out more with inventory," I offered.

"Maggie, you have your hands full and this makes me feel useful." She stepped back to view the wreath, wrinkled her brow, and then fluffed up one of its boughs. Next, she moved on to straighten the books, returning me of my strange evening visit with the strange Peter Dune in his equally strange library. I watched as Jillian placed a reincarnation books next to a section on soul mates. In the adults-only section, she added one titled: 'Sacred Sexuality'.

"Did Marshall go to school today?" she asked.

"Yeah. Poor thing was petrified. I reminded him that tomorrow was Friday and he had an entire weekend at home to look forward to."

"Did it help?"

"Doubtful, but he went without a fuss." Marshall never wanted to make trouble for anyone, so his anxieties came out in other ways. "Between us, he wet the bed last night. I caught him trying to stuff his quilt in the dryer this morning."

Outside the shop, customers were lining up for our *Autumn Equinox Extravaganza*—25% off all fall décor and scents. "Fifteen minutes until detonation," I said, as Jillian ran a lint remover over the front of her pant legs. "Hope we're stocked up on pumpkin candles."

"Uh, oh." She looked at me, lips pursed, eyes round.

I groaned, remembering their prominent spot in the flier that went out. "Get ready to write a lot of rain checks."

Jillian smiled, lifting a drop cloth from a table corner, revealing dozens of orange candles in every size, shape, and design displayed among a few real pumpkins. "Crisis averted, super team."

"Funny, Jillian." I laughed, swatting her with a hand towel, her prank a welcome reprieve from the seriousness of everything else going on. I "Jillian," I began, nonchalantly picking through a basket of fun-sized candy bars, sitting beside a jar half-filled with dollar bills. The sticky note on the jar read: 'Curse Words'. "We were wondering if you could start working with Marshall again?"

She seemed surprised. "You think his episode was a vision?"

"His medical tests came out fine. I'm worried he's going to have a hard time in school if we don't get this under control."

"Oh, Maggie, he's just young and fears his own abilities. And Dark Root amplifies them. Remember, he hasn't been here that long. I'll be happy to work with him some more. He just needs to learn boundaries and control."

"That goes for all my kids," I said. "Montana nearly caused a power outage throwing a tantrum this morning, because he couldn't wear his race car pajama pants to school." I popped a fun-sized Milky Way into my mouth and immediately reached for another. "It's hard to raise kids with these *talents.* I'm not sure how my mother handled—"

I sealed my lips before I put my entire foot in my mouth. Sasha had adopted me, but Jillian was my birth mother, and it made the language tricky at times. I never wanted to hurt Jillian, nor dishonor Sasha.

"Anyway," I continued, red-faced. "I still don't have complete control, myself. This morning I tried locking the house up with magick and I set off the smoke alarm."

Jillian's cat eyes flashed as she laughed. "Yes, I heard. Don't be too hard on yourself. My visions are erratic right now, too, and... disturbing." She bit her lip, taking a beat before speaking again. "Maggie, I think I saw your father."

My father? My hand went to my heart. "In your visions?"

"No. I saw him walking by my window around sunrise. Smoking a cigarette."

"And you're just now telling me?"

She sighed. "It's a hard subject to bring up, and honestly, it was probably a trick of the mind." She waved her hand dismissively.

I nodded, wanting that to be correct. Nothing good could come of my father's sudden reappearance in Dark root. If he actually returned, I'd need all my strength to deal with it.

"Jillian, do you remember a school that Sasha and Aunt Dora used to run?" I asked.

Jillian's eyes turned glassy, but only briefly. "Not really..." She spoke with hesitation. "But Ruth Anne mentioned she's looking for a *missing* school, too."

"And it didn't jog any memories for you?"

"Um..."

"Are you open?" A sing-songy voice accompanied a sharp rap on the window. We turned to see a woman tapping on her watch.

Oops! The store clock read two minutes past nine.

"We'll talk later," Jillian promised, hurrying to open the door.

"Welcome to *Miss Sasha's Magick Shoppe*," I greeted the customers. "Here, you'll find a pumpkin candle to fit every lifestyle and price point." I pointed to Jillian's orange display. "We've got Pumpkin spice, pumpkin-vanilla, pumpkin-chocolate, and even pumpkin-pumpkin. It's your one-stop, pumpkin-candle shop, where the prices are craaazy." I waved my hands frenetically, as the line filed in.

"Oh, dear, you're just so funny. Must be the red hair," said an older lady, pinching my cheek before shuffling towards the knick-knacks.

As our shop filled, I watched Jillian, thinking about the look in her eyes when I asked about the school. *Did she remember it?*

She seemed a thousand miles away, even as she gabbed with customers and bagged up gifts. *Where is she?* Another time? Or another place? I couldn't tell, but I knew she wasn't here.

~

"I don't know how you stand it, Maggie. If it were me, I'd have drugged her with an Ugly Potion so concentrated that it would take three lifetimes to wear off."

Eve stood before the window of my shop, watching the scene unfold across the street. Erin and Shane were talking in front of *Dip Stix*. More accurately, he was talking while she appeared to be grooming him--smoothing his hair, adjusting his collar, tightening his apron. She stood back to inspect her work, nodding her approval. "If she ever touches Paul that way..." Eve's eyes flashed, her stare practically burning a hole through the windowpane.

"I'm not going to let her get to me," I said, casually, though inside me there was a flame. But I wouldn't give Erin that kind of leverage over me, as she was obviously putting on the show for my benefit. "She did work for him at one point," I rationalized, "and they are friends."

"I worked for him, too, and I give you full permission to smack me if I ever feel your husband up like that. And I'd expect the same of you. Aren't you furious at Shane? I mean, he's just letting her!"

"Men can be dumb when it comes to women."

"They pretend to be dumb, so they don't get in trouble."

"I'll just take it out on him later, in a passive-aggressive manner, and that will be that. I've been working hard on my temper. She can't be the one who breaks me."

"At least yell at him. Or deny him sex. Something. I mean, he still hasn't moved away. Her conversation can't be that interesting." Eve wriggled her finger, and Erin's skirt flipped up, revealing her shapely legs. She pretended to blush as she smoothed it back down.

"Oh, that was helpful," I said. "Why not just strip her naked, while you're at it"

"Maggie, you know my magick doesn't work that way. Like me, it's subtle."

I inwardly laughed. Nothing about Eve was subtle.

I left the window and pretended to dust the counter while keeping an eye on Shane and Erin. He had been acting odd, distant, impulsive, disinterested. All at once sometimes. Did Erin have anything to do with it?

"You seem worried," Eve said, appraising me over her shoulder.

"I'm not worried!" I snapped, tightening my grip on the feather duster.

"I'd be worried."

The confession surprised me. If I were as beautiful and fashionable and alluring as Eve, I'd never worry about keeping any man's attention. Even today, when she was just hanging out with me, she wore skinny jeans, a cropped leather jacket, shiny heels, and three delicate gold chains. Every inch of her attire showcased her figure. Her hair and makeup were perfect, as always.

I, however, looked like it was laundry day. Faded skirt, stretched-out sweater, and sneakers with mismatched socks that I hoped no one would notice. My hair was bunched up on top of my head, and my make-up routine consisted of a drop of Visine in my eyes, and a swab of Vaseline on my lips.

"Oh, Shane, you're so sweet and funny," Eve pantomimed from the window, as Erin touched Shane's arm. "What big muscles you have! I bet you grew up on a ranch."

I rejoined Eve at the window. Whatever Erin said next, Shane looked down at his feet and I could tell he was blushing.

"You can't trust men around boobs like that," Eve said.

Eve had impressive *boobs* of her own, purchased on a credit card she hadn't quite paid off. "Noted," I said.

Shane looked at his watch and Erin gave him a quick hug.

The lights in our shop flickered, and my sister shot me a knowing smile.

Shane walked across the street and came inside, shaking a leaf from his hair. "Hey, Honey. Sorry about that. I got held up."

"You're only thirty minutes late," I said, cooly.

"Where's the kids?" he asked, looking around the empty shop.

"I sent them home with Jillian twenty-seven minutes ago, when Erin cornered you across the street. I had a feeling you'd be *held-up.*"

"Didn't mean to be that long. We were talking about our employee situations. Hard to find good help these days." He looked at Eve. "I lost the best employee I ever had when you quit, and the new kids don't seem to understand hard work."

"Betrothal is a full-time job," Eve explained, looking at her nails.

"Speaking of betrothal, have you gone dress shopping yet?" I asked Eve.

She rolled her eyes. "Where? The *Dark Root Apparel Company*? The Linsburg Mall? Yum." She looped her finger in the air, unenthusiastically. Having lived in New York City, Eve had more refined tastes than the rest of us. She often referred to local fashion as 'bumpkin wear.' "Merry wants to *make* me a dress," she said, sounding both depressed and distressed at once.

"Oh?" Merry was a good seamstress, if you liked the *'Little House on the Prairie'* look. Which Merry did, but Eve definitely did not.

"I can see you ladies have a lot to talk about. I'm gonna run home and relieve Jillian," Shane said, kissing me on my forehead. "You coming straight home? I'm making lasagna. Your favorite."

"Nah," I said. Lasagna was his making-amends food. But I wasn't quite ready, nor hungry enough, to take the bait. "We're meeting at the pie shop. I won't be too late."

"Gotcha," Shane said, appearing confused as he left the store.

"Way to lay down the law, Maggie. You really gave it to him. That will teach him."

"I know what I'm doing."

We watched him make his way down the street to his pickup. Erin was still standing on the sidewalk and waved as he drove away. He waved back. The front door flew open in a burst of energy, slamming against the brick entry. I quickly closed it again.

"Yep. Looks like you have everything under control," Eve said, grabbing her red purse. “Mark my words--that girl wants something. And whether it’s your man or something else, she’s going to get it if you don’t do something a whole lot firmer than opening a door.”

CHAPTER 12
MERRY

"Heya, Merry!" Shane waved to her from his pick-up as she bounded up the sidewalk, her ponytail swinging behind her. She had put away her teacher's badge for the day and was now wearing her Mayor tag over a fitted blazer, carrying a binder as thick as a briefcase beneath her left arm. "Can we talk?" he asked, pulling up to the curb alongside her.

"Hi, Shane!" She smiled, approaching the window as she looked at her watch. "Sure, but I only have a minute before I meet the girls." She twirled her ponytail around her hand like spaghetti around a fork, sensing what was on his mind.

"I'll make it quick. Marshall didn't want to go to school today. He was up all night, worrying what the other kids would say after his..." he rolled his hand.

"Incident?"

"Yes. So, how did he do today in class?"

She nodded absently. "Fine. Fine."

"Really?"

"He kept mostly to himself, but he turned in all of his assignments and ate his entire lunch. So... yay?" She lifted one hand, mimicking a pom-pom.

Shane thought on this a moment. "Luna and Montana didn't want to go either. Any idea why?"

"Well... a few of the newer students have been whispering."

"About my kids?"

"Yes, but don't worry about it. I talked to their parents and next Monday we are having *Good Citizens Day.* I think a day focused on the community will do everyone some good." She opened her binder and handed Shane a freshly-minted newsletter, detailing the itinerary for the day. That morning, she would lead the children on a tour through town. Local store owners were encouraged to teach the kids something related to their professions, beginning with a different letter of the alphabet, and then talk about the importance of community.

"So, you think if I gave a lecture on biscuits it would turn things around?" he chuckled, setting it on his dashboard.

"We already have B... can you do anything with letter D?" She got out her pen and began writing notes on the back of a flier. "Here's an idea--after the lecture, you could give away freshly baked donuts! Or something else starting with the letter D. Donut *holes* maybe?"

"Sure" he scratched the back of his neck. "Do you really think Good Guys day is going to help?"

"Good citizens day," she gently corrected, "as in, we are all a part of this little ecosystem. And this is just a starting point," she said, confidently. "And every change begins with a starting point."

Shane drummed his fingers on the outside of his door, letting out a long sigh. "Maggie's convinced we should find some old school that Sasha closed when we were kids. And that we let them learn there, away from the others."

Merry pursed her lips. "Yes. She's expressed that opinion to me, as well. How do you feel about it?"

"I know what it's like to be an outsider. In Montana, kids like me weren't exactly welcomed. I don't want to put my kids through that same experience, but unless they start fitting in a little better, we may have to pull them out. That's assuming there is some mystery school, and it's not all in our collective imaginations." He skipped his hand outside the window as if it were riding a wave. "I guess we could home school them, if it came down to it."

"Oh, please don't!" She begged, her heart sinking. The new school was the first really big project she had taken on. She couldn't have families, especially her own, deserting before it ever got off the ground. "We've worked really hard getting this schoolhouse updated. I've put my heart and soul into it. Just give them one more week, okay? I promise I'll do my best to assimilate them."

"Assimilate who? My kids, or the other kids?"

Merry smiled and patted his arm. She didn't know the answer to that. She only knew she had to make this work. Somehow.

"Thanks everyone for coming." Merry smiled at each of her sisters and Aunt Dora, before ceremoniously poking her fork into her pie crust, thus opening the meeting. "Oh, this is good," she said after the first bite practically melted on her tongue. She was pretty strict on her diet most of the time, but she let herself slide on meeting days. She took another large bite, letting it roll around her mouth, then pushed the plate away.

"I don't know why I have to be at your school meeting Merry," Eve said, picking at her cherry pie but not taking a bite.

"Really, Eve?"

"Oh, yeah, Nova. Sometimes I forget that I'm a parent."

"Well, that's ap-parent," said Ruth Anne, doing a Groucho Marx cigar impression with her spoon.

"It's impossible to forget you're a parent when your house is always a disaster," Maggie said. "It's either kids or ghosts. Might be easier if it were ghosts."

Merry coughed, returning everyone to the subject at hand. She opened her binder and handed out her *Good Citizens* fliers. “I know a few of you have expressed concerns over having our children go to school with kids that might not share their gifts. Though it won’t fix everything, I think this might begin to solve our problems.”

Maggie looked it over, front and back. “A workshop on citizenry?”

“One fully immersive day,” Merry nodded brightly. “This is a good opportunity to show the kids how important community is, and that we’re all connected in our little town.”

“I don’t know...” Maggie pushed the flyer away. “A *Good Citizens* workshop is not going to stop Marshall’s visions, or Montana and Luna from using their magick when they feel justified.”

“I know.” Merry sighed, bridging her hands before her. “But maybe we work more on that aspect of their development ourselves. Privately. If we all pull together, we can make this work. I know it.”

“Since Nova has no magick, I still fail to see how this concerns me,” said Eve, sliding back into the booth bench and opening her phone game.

“It concerns us all. We’re a community, Eve. Besides, this is also a family thing.”

“Montana said a kid called them freaks at school,” Maggie said. “Luckily, he thought it was a compliment, or that kid might’ve experienced a fire-starter moment.”

“And our *Citizens Day* will highlight that there are no freaks in this community, only friends.”

Maggie rolled her eyes.

“Do you two want to weigh in?” Merry asked, turning to Dora and Ruth Anne, both chin deep in sweet potato pie.

Ruth Anne sat up, wiping her face with her napkin, appearing way more interested in the topic than Merry would have guessed. “I think we need to find the old school and possibly open it back up. I’m not sure we need to send the kids there immediately, but it’s an option worth exploring. There are way too many signs pointing that way.”

"And you, Aunt Dora?" Merry asked, stiffly. She had not expected that from Ruth Anne.

"I don' think we should shut away children cuz they're different. But I do think we need ta protect 'em, too."

"So...you're neutral?"

"Cautious."

"Exactly." Merry directed her attention to the entire table. "We still don't know exactly why Sasha closed the school. Was it supposed to be temporary, or forever? I'm not comfortable with finding that old place until we know more, if it even still physically exists. Aunt Dora, have you gotten anything else from the tapestry and memory globe."

"Aye." Aunt Dora sipped her cocoa as the waitress took her empty pie plate. "Been readin' the tapestry. Hard on the ol' eyes, though." It got quiet around the table, as Aunt Dora twirled her thumbs together, weighing her words. "Somethin' was unleashed that night. Somethin' big enough that Sasha used a spell from *the old book* to cover it up. That book oozed ancient magick--not something ta be trifled with."

"Did the book have a gold cover?" Ruth Anne asked, leaning in, her hands pressed into the table on either side of her plate.

"Can' remember."

"We need to find that book then," Maggie said. "It might have the counter spell. Or maybe we can reverse the original."

"Did ya not hear me?" Dora banged her fist on the table. Every plate moved and every eye widened. "Findin' it might bring the shadows back."

"Okay, let's all calm down." Merry took an audible breath, letting it out. "We'll put the pros and cons of finding the old school on our agenda for next month. Agreed? But for now, let's concentrate on the school we have, and how we can make it better. The children are our future, you know?"

"I'm reminded every time I read your bumper sticker," Maggie said. "I'm not trying to dismantle your school, Merry. I'll withhold any further opinions until after your *Good Citizens* experiment. And, I'll set aside more time to work with my kids on their talents. Maybe we can all do this together? Hold informal classes or something?"

"Maybe," Merry agreed. It was a good idea, but it was sliding uncomfortably close to 'new school' territory. "I'll put that on the list of after school options."

"What if we convert Jillian's old painting studio?" Maggie continued, the idea firmly taking root inside her head. She turned to the others for support. "Or fix up one of the old barns?"

"Not the old barns. Something newer," Eve suggested.

"No!" Ruth Anne nearly growled."We need to find that school. It's there, and it wants to be found."

"But the shadows!" Dora contested.

As they continued their debate, Merry tried not to feel deflated. Who knew this would have turned into such a heated dispute? Why could no one else share her vision?

She looked out the café window at the town she loved. The town she'd grown up in, and was now raising her own daughter in. Two very different worlds, she admitted.

Maybe progress isn't the answer for Dark Root? Then again, does going backward ever solve anything, either?

CHAPTER 13
JILLIAN

The sky that afternoon was neon orange, as if *The Great Pumpkin* itself had risen on the horizon, for all of Dark Root to witness.

Jillian smiled from the tree stump where she sat with her analogy, remembering when she watched that Charlie Brown special with her father, decades ago when it first aired. The two were curled up on the plaid family couch one raining October night, sharing a batch of Jiffy Pop popcorn--only slightly burnt on the bottom—and sipping on orange Tang. During the commercials, Jillian would ramble on about school, grades, and boys. And her father told tales of his time in the Marines, and how he met her mother, who was working at an airport gift shop. "She was pretty," he said, whistling. "That's where you get your looks. But you and your brother get your smarts from me," he added, tapping his head.

Closing her eyes, Jillian was back again in her childhood home. She could smell the lemony pine of freshly-scrubbed floors, the still-warm meatloaf on the counter, and the buttery/burnt smell of the Jiffy Pop. She could even smell the Camel cigarettes on her father's breath, and see his eyes sparkle when he asked if she still believed in Santa Claus. She could hear the rattle in his throat when he laughed at her terrible 6th-grade jokes.

The memory tore at her heart, both with its clarity and the realization that she could never return to that moment—no matter how good a witch she was. That house was long gone, and so were both her parents. And her brother, killed in the war. Jillian had never gotten to say goodbye to any of them.

"I still miss you, Daddy," she said, feeling a warm tear slide down her cheek, cooled by the breeze sweeping through the meadow. What she wouldn't give to go back, just for a day, to smell her father's aftershave, or to watch him read the newspaper before work. To hug him goodbye when he dropped her off at school.

So what if her mother hadn't accepted her gifts? In retrospect, it seemed foolish to have ended their relationship over something so silly as *belief.* But it had seemed so important to Jillian then--that her mother accept who she was--when she pulled her heavy suitcase out the door and into her boyfriend's waiting car. Her father had watched sadly from the doorway but did not try to stop her.

That was the last time she'd seen either of them in person—a moment permanently etched with a rusted nail into her heart. There were only letters and phone calls afterward, less and less frequent as the years passed, especially when her mother discovered she'd run off to join Sasha in some sort of 'cult.' That was not what good Catholic women did. It took time and maturity for Jillian to realize she had also been punishing her parents, for encouraging her brother enlist.

It didn't seem fair to Jillian that those moments happened when you were young, when you were too new on the planet to recognize the importance of them.

"You 'kay?" Luna asked, patting her grandmother on the knee and leaning against her. A sympathy tear slid down Luna's cheek as she sensed Jillian's sorrow. When it touched her arm, Jillian felt better, like the first ray of sunshine of a new morning.

"I was just remembering someone I missed," Jillian said, squeezing Luna's small hand. "I'm better now,"

"Who?" Luna asked, lifting her hand to allow a butterfly to land, letting it dance along her fingertip before sailing off with the gentle breeze.

"My dad. Your great-grandpa. You would have liked him. My mom, too. She was a lot like Aunt Dora, but not as grumpy." Luna snorted with laughter, covering her mouth with both hands. "Let's keep that to ourselves. Dora might not find it as funny as you do."

Luna held up a single finger—her version of a thumbs up. Luna had her own version of everything.

"Shall we go?" Jillian stood up from the broad tree stump, dusted off her slacks, gathered her basket, and then took Luna's hand. "Let's go this way today," she said, pointing west. She liked to change up paths so that Luna would always be able to find her way to the tree, no matter where she was.

They left the quiet meadow and hiked alongside a slow creek, now a wisp of its springtime glory. They stopped for a few moments to let Luna gather pink river stones, and then cut through a small grove, finally arriving at the tree.

Their tree.

All of humanity's tree, though very few outside of the family knew of its existence.

A *Tree of Life*.

It was a majestic sight, with a wide canopy of golden upturned boughs that reached for the sunshine. It was one of only a handful left in the world—and perhaps the only one still glowing with the light that came from within. But it was also blighted, affected by the negative energies of the world, and Jillian was very aware of the burden they were entrusted with, to ensure its survival. It was said that when the final *Tree* lost its light, the world would die. Their parent tree, the source of their seed, existed yet in the *Netherworld*.

Jillian stood reverently before their *Tree*, taking a moment of silence before inspecting it. She had kept watch over it for years, as

Sasha had before her, and Juliana before that. Now Jillian was training Luna to be its next guardian.

"I think it's looking better," Jillian said, nodding as she appraised the color of its bark and the suppleness of its limbs. "You have the magick touch."

Luna held up her pinky finger. It had the soft pink glow of magick. But the look in her granddaughter's eyes said she knew it wasn't *that* much better. "Well, it's not getting worse," Jillian said encouragingly, and Luna agreed.

Before Luna came to help with the tree, it had been on a steady decline. Jillian tried repairing with spells, reagents, and faith. Band-aids and crutches. But it was Luna, she believed, who would be the one to save it. The child had been conceived in the *Netherworld*, after all, where the original *Tree of Life* resided.

"Have you thought of a name for it yet?" Jillian asked. Each guardian chose a new name for the *Tree* they protected, to strengthen the bond between them.

"Per-sel-ly..." Luna lifted a finger with each syllable. "Like?"

"Excellent choice. Hello, Perselly," Jillian said to the tree. The boughs moved a little, and they took it to mean the *Tree* approved. They ducked under the many arcing branches, patting Perselly's solid trunk. "I think you're holding up better than I am," she said, inspecting its base. "Maybe Luna should be my guardian, too."

"I fix you?" Luna asked, surveying her.

Though Dark Root was abundant with magick these days, Jillian remembered older days, when magick was rare and hoarded. What if there was a drought again? "Don't waste your gifts on grandma," Jillian said, squeezing her hand. "Keep your magick for Perselly."

It was always hard to leave the *Tree*. Jillian had been bonded to it for so long. But like her own life force, she felt that connection fading, as a new generation stepped up to take her place.

"I'll meet you at our spot," Jillian said, blowing Luna a kiss and leaving the safety of the boughs.

Luna pressed herself against the trunk, her silvery hair turning the same golden hue as the branches above her head. The leaves jiggled as Luna spoke to it. Jillian smiled, proud that she had made this match. It was one good thing she'd done in this world, anyway.

While Luna and Perselly bonded, Jillian wandered towards the small clearing where she always waited for her granddaughter. There, Jillian would set up a picnic, and when Luna returned, they'd eat jelly sandwiches together. Jillian would make up stories about the pictures in the clouds, and they would laugh and laugh before returning home.

As she unpacked the basket of sandwiches, ripe pears, and goldfish crackers, Jillian felt a tickling in the back of her throat, and was seized by a violent coughing fit. She clutched her chest, trying to breathe through it. These fits were getting worse, and harder to cover up. While she gasped for breath, she checked to ensure Luna was not heading her way yet. Finally able to breathe again, she sat down on the blanket and pressed her hands to her chest to feel her lungs. They rattled like her fathers did, though she hadn't smoked in decades. "What's happening to me?" she asked herself, aloud.

You're dying Jillian.

"Armand?" Jillian looked for the familiar voice, ringing all around her. Had it been her imagination?

It's not your imagination.

"Where are you?" she demanded. She could feel him, too. Her first thought was that she *had* died; had coughed herself to death and was being greeted in the afterlife. Her next thought was that she hoped she and Armand were destined for separate afterlives, in different places.

"You're dying, not dead," he said, and she sensed his presence sitting on the blanket across from her. Soon, a fuzzy outline appeared of the man, older than she remembered, but younger than his true years. He was wearing his trademark cowboy hat and fringed jacket. *"I can't stay long."* His form shimmered. *"Materializing takes too much energy."*

"What do you want?" she asked. As far as she knew, he was stuck between life and death, wandering the tunnels of time and dimension. Why was he manifesting to her now?

As in life, he lit a cigarette, using a flame from the tip of his hazy finger, then taking a long draw. The smoke circles he exhaled were very real, and she could smell them, drifting towards her in ever-expanding rings. "*You need to take care of yourself Jillian...until I can take care of you.*"

"Take care of me? You tried to kill my grandson!"

"Correction--I tried to trade *your grandson. Our grandson. He was never in any physical danger. And I didn't do it, in the end."* He spread his hands. "*But that doesn't matter anymore. The Final Trial has come, Jillian, and soon we'll all be set free.*

"What do you mean?"

Armand began to fade. Jillian reached forward, unable to touch him. "Don't go," she said, surprising herself. Armand had never been a nice man, and she suspected his spirit hadn't gotten any nicer. But he had been the love of her life, despite herself. Her only love. She'd seen flickers of light in him, in their intimate moments alone, that no one else ever saw. And her love for the man felt as real in this moment as it did 30 years ago.

"Gran-ma?"

Jillian looked up slowly to see her granddaughter standing beside her. Armand was now gone. *Did she see him?*

"You 'kay?" Luna asked, patting her shoulder.

"Yes, yes darling." Jillian opened her arms wide, feeling foolish. Armand had been a hallucination. A byproduct of her illness or her medications. That was all. "Sit down and we'll share a pear, Little Looney Bird. Then, I'll tell you a story from the clouds."

Nothing more than a very vivid memory, just like the one of my father.

That's what happens when you were dying, she decided--you saw ghosts, and most of them came from your imagination.

"No." Luna stepped back, waving her hand before her nose.

"What's wrong, honey?"

Luna squatted to retrieve a smoking cigarette butt from the grass and handed it to Jillian. "Yucky."

CHAPTER 14

MARSHALL

Marshall sat on the corner of his bed, in the large room he shared with Montana, rubbing his temples with both hands. Aunt Ruth Anne had teased him about having 'alien fingers', long and spindly, but they weren't long enough to dig out the visions that played in his head. Some were his own memories, but more often they belonged to other people, and scant few of them were good. The visions came on suddenly, not only filling his mind but taking control of his body, as if some unseen hands were pulling the strings and he was the unwilling puppet.

Marshall had always had these experiences, but their quantity and intensity increased since moving to Dark Root. Jillian told him it was because Dark Root was saturated with *aether*—an invisible element, that when woven with other elements, created magick. She said that only a few could wield it, and he was one of the *lucky ones*. This ability gave him a direct connection to other timelines--whether he wanted it or not.

Maybe working with Jillian again would help. She was a *psychic* too--the word she used--and had learned to live with her visions.

With time and training, perhaps he could, also? And maybe even learn to control the episodes.

Episodes.

That's what the others were calling them. Even Luna said *'e-pi-zode'* when he returned from the hospital, before giving him her teddy bear and a pat on the hand.

Maybe they were right. The last event wasn't so much a memory, as a possession. He was viewing the world through someone else's eyes, speaking through someone else's voice. It was horrible, having those weird words pour out of him, unable to stop. At the very edge of his memory, he could almost recall them--words familiar enough that he could almost remember their taste. He certainly smelled them; and they smelled like ash.

That episode made him wet his bed. Mommy Maggie caught him in his wet pajamas, with his wet bedding. She looked at him kindly, but with such pity. He was next in line to be the man of the house, if, god forbid, something happened to Daddy. Then she hugged him as if he were still Montana's age. He never wanted to relive that scene.

Marshall shimmied his wrist out of the hospital bracelet he'd been wearing for the last three days, and set it around the knob of his bed frame. He'd kept it on, hoping the kids would be nicer to him when they saw it, but it was not a very effective charm. The girls laughed behind their hands, and the boys floated paper airplanes at his desk when Merry wasn't looking, with the word *'FREAK'* written across the wings.

"I bet he's weird because he lives with a witch," Susie openly said, as they lined up for lunch.

"My mom is not a witch!" Montana, defended, stepping out of line with his finger drawn in place of a wand. "And witches are cool, anyway. Your mom's stupid." It had shut Susie up for the moment, but further fueled the whispered rumors. On Friday morning, Luna received a paper airplane too, though Marshall stole it from beneath her desk before she noticed.

Marshall eyed Montana from across the bedroom. His younger

brother was sitting on his race-track carpet, beside his race car bed, talking to an assembled array of Matchbox cars. His deep auburn waves corked out in all directions, and his clothes were on crooked.

"Okay, you ready?" Montana asked his cars, kissing them before placing them in a line on the carpet track. "I pick green and yellow!" He said, tapping the corresponding colors. "Ready... set... GO!"

Only the yellow and green cars complied, reluctantly leaving their parking spots and sputtering towards a bridge, losing power just before crossing the lake. "Gah!" Montana grunted as he scooped them up, tossing them into the wastebasket like a bad report card. Marshall would wait until Montana was sleeping and then rescue them from their dumpster fate, storing them away in a box where he kept Montana's other discarded toys, until he was old enough to better understand the value of things.

At least Montana's abilities were useful, Marshall thought. And fun, too. Sometimes Marshall wished he could move things with his mind like Montana did, with just willpower and words. Or conjure things from one room to the next with a snap of his fingers--which Montana was forbidden from doing, but did anyway. Marshall didn't let himself think about it too long, fearing it would take him to dark places. He loved his brother and knew he shouldn't envy him, but sometimes it was hard to be happy with what you had when someone very close to you had so much more.

"Beep!" Luna suddenly appeared in their doorway, her hands and feet braced against the frame like a star in the sky. Her silver hair shone like moonlight, matching the diamond twinkle in her eyes. She ran into their bedroom, barefoot, pajama'd and ponytailed, snorting gleefully as she zipped about the room. She ran a lap around the car track, leapt over Marshall's plastic dinosaurs, rolled across the toy box, bounced on both beds, then darted back into the hall.

"She's so weird," Montana said, closing the door after she left.

"Yeah," Marshall agreed. *But so are we.*

Having lived elsewhere, Marshall understood that not every family was like this one, and that not every school was a one-room building with a small divider. And not every kid could make cars move with their mind. But Montana didn't know all this. Linsburg was the furthest he had ever been away from home.

"You know what's funny?" Marshall asked, rolling striped tube socks onto his feet. "Your name is Montana, but I'm from Montana."

It was funny, but also confusing. Part of him didn't like that Montana got the name of *his* birthplace, and *his* father's birthplace, even though Shane wasn't Montana's real dad. Montana laid claim to everything, like a prince who knows that one day he'll be king.

"That is funny," Montana agreed, taking a red car from his pocket and flying it around the room like an airplane. He navigated it past the Sesame Street posters, the bookshelf, the ball hamper, ruffling the plaid curtains as he whooshed by. "Maybe I'll tell everyone I'm from Montana, too. Then we can really be brothers."

"But you might go to Hell if you lie," Marshall said quickly.

"What's *Hell*?" Montana stopped flying, staring at him with his emerald eyes.

"I don't know. But my grandma used to talk about it before she died. She said if you weren't good, you'd go there. It's a scary place and there's fire everywhere."

"I like fire." Montana shrugged, returning to his flight.

Once his socks were straight and his sneakers tied, Marshall inspected himself in the full-length mirror. His jeans were long enough, his hair parted neatly down the middle, his face scrubbed clean. There was just one unruly hair sticking up from the back, and it wouldn't lie down no matter how much he combed it. Grabbing scissors from their craft table, he cut it down to the quick, leaving only the root behind. Perfect.

"Why are you getting so fancy?" Montana asked, eyeing him suspiciously. He came over and sniffed Marshall's neck. "And why do you smell like Daddy?"

Marshall blushed at having been caught wearing Shane's after-shave. "I'm going to Grandma Jillian's. She's going to help me with the bad thoughts I'm having," he said, trying to explain it to Montana in a way that a six-year-old could grasp.

"You should do what I do," Montana said. "Just think of something else when you get the bad thoughts. Then you'll forget about them."

"You get bad thoughts, too?" Marshall asked.

"All the time." He blinked several times. "I just think of something like a TV show or a superhero and they go away." Montana flew about the room again, this time his arms before him like Superman. After three quick laps, he flopped onto Marshall's bed, grinning and breathless.

"I can't think of other things when they happen," Marshal explained. "It's like a movie in my head, and there's no remote control. What are your bad thoughts like?"

Montana scrunched his nose to his eyes, collapsing his spray of freckles into the folds of his upper cheeks. "Mostly just voices, sometimes pictures, too. But not movies. Mine are just boring voices telling me to do things."

Marshall looked over his shoulder at Montana, to see if he was joking. "What do they want you to do?"

"Find things. It's mostly Grandpa and sometimes my real dad, but sometimes other people, too." Montana shrugged, running his car along Marshall's pillow.

As far as Marshall knew, Montana's real father and grandfather were dead. Weren't they?

"My dad says that he misses me." Montana reached for the hospital bracelet on the bed knob, absently spinning it. "My grandpa says that it's almost time to get my special present."

"A present?" Marshall turned from the mirror, curious and suspicious since Montana didn't always tell the truth. "What kind of present?"

"I don't know." Montana shrugged. "It's a surprise."

"You're not supposed to take presents from strangers," Marshall reminded him.

"He's not a stranger! He's my grandpa!"

"But you never met him."

"Yes I did! He said we met when I was a baby. And Mommy took me away from him. And then—" Montana clamped his hand over his mouth, aware that he was saying too much.

Montana didn't seem to be lying. If Mommy Maggie and Grandma Jillian talked to ghosts, maybe Montana could, too? Another gift that would probably be far more useful than his own visions. "I think you should tell the grownups." Marshall went to the window, checking to ensure it was locked. *Do locks work on ghosts?*

"No way."

"Why not?"

"Grandpa said not to."

"But what about-"

Montana stood up from the bed and stomped his foot, pointing his finger up at Marshall. "I said no!"

"I better go." Marshall turned towards the door, glad to be out from under his little brother's basilisk gaze.

Marshall had always feared the long upstairs hallway, ever since moving to Sister House. It was straight when he looked down it head-on, but seemed to slant this way or that when he went along. And though it was only thirty-one footsteps exactly, it seemed like miles from his bedroom to Shane and Mommy Maggie's, where it always felt safe.

The first challenge was getting by Luna's bedroom. It was a cheerful room in the daytime, with soft yellow walls, billowy curtains and stuffed toy bunnies on the bed. But when Marshall passed by her closed door at night, there appeared to be a storm going off inside. Sometimes there were flashes of light and rumbling thunder seeping around the door cracks.

Twice he had gotten the nerve to charge inside and rescue his little sister, only to find the room perfectly calm and Luna playing dolls or feeding her goldfish. She looked at him curiously each time, but said nothing as he slunk awkwardly back out.

Tonight, there were lights beneath the door and sounds, too--not rumblings, but whisperings of words he didn't know. Marshall kept walking, more fearful of his younger sister's pitying look than of any ghosts inside. Her ageless gaze made him feel small.

The next test was the twenty-three pictures hanging on either side of the wall, none of them his blood relatives. He felt the eyes of every stranger along the way. *Imposter! This isn't your house. You don't belong here.*

After the pictures, and just before the stairs, was the final obstacle: the library, which was off-limits by order of both parents. He had secretly gone inside once when his curiosity overcame him. It seemed an ordinary room, with nothing inside but books and two chairs, but the energy felt different from the rest of the house. Unwelcoming. And cold. When he was halfway in, lured by the possibility of a new history book, he heard a loud repeated rapping from behind the shelves. He bolted out and closed the door, not telling a soul. That was enough to keep him out of the room for good. And though the door was always closed, he still went by quickly, covering his ears so he wouldn't hear that horrible knocking again.

Finally, he reached the stairs, letting out the breath he didn't know he was holding, practically skipping all the way down to the living room. He smelled Auntie Ruth Anne's woodsy scent before he even saw her. She reminded him of one of those trees that hung from rearview mirrors. He liked Ruth Anne and felt a kinship with her--they both appreciated books, cheese sandwiches, maps, and plaid.

His aunt was in the living room with Luna, who was randomly stabbing a plastic screwdriver into a flattened sheet of orange play-dough. *Wasn't Luna just in the bedroom?*

"Like?" Luna asked Ruth Anne.

"Finest piece of art I've seen all day," Ruth Anne said, snapping photos of Luna's clay project. "This should be in a museum."

Luna hugged Ruth Anne's leg and continued with her work.

Marshall coughed to announce himself. Though he'd lived here a year, he still felt like a guest most of the time. "Hi." He waved awkwardly, wondering if he should give Ruth Anne a hug but decided against it. She wasn't his real aunt, like she was Luna's.

"Hey handsome," Ruth Anne walked over and gave him a playful slug in the arm. "Read any good books lately?"

"Yes!" Marshall grinned. "Aunt Merry dropped off a 1960's Spider-Man comic after my trip to the...uh..."

"A great era for Spidey," she agreed, saving him from having to say the word hospital out loud. "Are you ready?"

"Ready for what?" Montana appeared on the stairs. "I thought you were going to Grandma Jillian's?"

"Aunt Ruth Anne is taking me," Marshall explained, proudly. All the kids adored their funny aunt, and he was getting special time with her.

"But Grandma lives behind the house." Montana pointed backward. "You can walk there with your eyes closed."

It was true. Jillian lived in the old carriage house, and he could get their in the count of thirty. But Montana had already lost interest and was instead trying to steal the screwdriver away from Luna, who fought him off with squeals and snot bubbles.

They went through the kitchen, hugging goodbye to Daddy and Maggie, who were cleaning up. Jillian's cottage was at the edge of the property, surrounded by pretty elm trees that she claimed were even older than she was.

Marshall stopped before the front door, tugging on his ear.

"What's wrong, sport?" Ruth Anne asked.

"I'm scared," he admitted.

"Why are you scared, kiddo? It's just Jillian."

He shrugged, not knowing either. Didn't he want the visions to go away? And to stop wetting the bed and being teased?

He looked down at his feet. "Because if she can't help me, then I'm going to be a freak forever."

CHAPTER 15
RUTH ANNE

Ruth Anne straightened the collar of her jacket, as if straightening a tie, then patted Marshall's head. She'd never actually been inside Jillian's home, not since Shane had converted the old carriage house into a mother-in-law suite. Jillian had a small housewarming party at move-in, where everyone ate cake on unpacked boxes. Was that an entire year ago? Since then, she'd only met with Jillian in town, or at Sister House and Harvest Home. *I don't think she's ever invited me inside.*

"Do you visit your grandma here often?" Ruth Anne asked Marshall.

Marshall shook his head. "No. Mommy Maggie says grandma needs her privacy. Grandma Jillian comes to our house instead."

"Does Maggie visit Jillian much?" Ruth Anne asked, suddenly curious.

"Not much. She drops things off at the door but doesn't go in." He shrugged, but Ruth Anne saw a stirring in his eyes. He was as curious as she was. She squeezed his hand and he blushed. *Poor little guy. So shy.* But Ruth Anne understood. She was prone to shyness herself.

"Welp, it was nice knowing you," Ruth Anne teased him, stuffing her hands into her pant pockets. Marshall smiled. Ruth Anne smiled back.

"Why are you here, too?" he asked.

She shrugged, forgetting how smart and self-aware he was. "It's important to document things," was all she could truthfully answer.

"I understand. My mom wrote down everything. My first words. My first shoe size." He sniffled, wiping his nose with the cuff of his sleeve.

"She's still alive, right?" Ruth Anne asked. "Writing stuff down somewhere?"

"I don't know," he admitted. "Daddy says she is, but I can't feel her. I can't..."

Ruth Anne braced herself for his wave of grief to follow. She knew the wave, had felt its unexpected grip clench her chest, whenever she remembered someone she lost. He sucked in a breath, catching himself before there were any tears, then let it go. She liked that he was able to hold it back—not that she would tell him that. Merry and Maggie were teaching the kids to express their emotions, but Ruth Anne had made an entire life of keeping hers bottled up. And it had worked so far.

She drew the boy into her side. "It's weird, huh? When you have this really cool gift like yours, but you can't control it?"

Marshall nodded. "Yes."

"That's pretty much how all the superheroes started out, right? You think Spiderman was slinging his web on the first day? No way. It took at least a whole semester. And Superman probably tried flapping his arms before he thought to hold them straight out, right? But they kept at it, and look, they have their very own comic books now."

Marshall laughed, his shoulders dropping away from his ears. "Yeah..."

"Maybe Jillian can teach you how to hone your gift. All superheroes have a mentor."

Ruth Anne felt the vials of elderberry juice she had brought to

Jillian inside her pockets. Not the sacred elderberries, but an online version, with great reviews. Of course, none of the reviewers had been bitten by Hellhounds.

"Knock, knock!" she called, jiggling the locked doorknob when Jillian didn't answer the first two times. *Is she okay?* First, they heard her footsteps. Then they heard her coughing, for an uncomfortably long amount of time. When Jillian finally opened the door, she was wearing fresh lipstick and a smile, which worried Ruth Anne even more.

"Hello," Jillian said, overly bubbly as she greeted them. "Come in. Sorry I didn't hear you right away. I was making tea."

Ruth Anne wandered around the living room while Marshall hung out near the door. She'd presumed the place would be modern, clean, minimalist, and practical—like Jillian herself. But in reality, it was like stepping back into a 1970's time capsule. An old record player sat on the ground in the corner, a stack of albums beside it, Paul McCartney and Wings at the very top. The walls were adorned with macramé weavings and classic movie posters, unframed. A lava lamp bubbled on a set of cylinder block shelves.

"Nice collection." Ruth Anne said, smiling as she poked through the record stack. "And all in great condition. I'm surprised Merry hasn't tried to put these up for sale in her shop."

"Merry doesn't know." Jillian returned with a tea tray she set on the coffee table, in front of two oversized bean bag chairs. *This is not what I expected at all.* Still, she could see why Jillian liked the place. It felt very comfortable, in a groovy, hookah-puffing, kind of way. "Ruth Anne, join me for tea. Marshall, there's chocolate milk and a banana on the counter for you."

Marshall ran into the kitchen and Ruth Anne poured her tea. "I'm feeling a little bad about listening in on your session," Ruth Anne whispered. "But I can't help feeling this is tied to the missing school. I know it's a long shot, but if it leads us to a book on how to cure this thing, it's worth it, right?

"Always follow your intuition," Jillian said, seeming just as regal sitting cross-legged in a bean bag as a queen on her throne. "Your presence here won't disturb either of us."

Once the formality of tea was over, Jillian called for Marshall, and Ruth Anne brought in chairs from the kitchen. He sat down, nervously clicking his heels together. Ruth Anne moved the coffee table just to the side, setting her audio recorder on top, and Jillian sat in front of Marshall. "You'll do great," Jillian said to him. "You always do."

Ruth Anne loved watching Jillian interact with the kiddos. She was gentle and loving, unlike Ruth Anne's own mother. Though she loved Sasha, no one would ever call the woman affectionate.

Marshall closed his eyes, pressing his arms against his sides, stiff as a toy soldier. Jillian covered his lap with a small blanket. "Marshall, follow my voice. I'm going to count you back to Tuesday morning, okay?"

"Okay," he nodded.

Within a minute, Marshall's head flopped to the side and he was under.

"Marshall, I'm going to help you with your visions, but we need to learn all about them first. When they happen. What you see. How you feel. But I need you to trust me, okay Marshall?"

"Yes."

"Tell me how these usually begin. Can you do that for me?"

He wrinkled his nose. "If I smell something, or hear a weird noise, or touch something, it can make them come. I can't feel my body and a movie runs in my head. Except it's not a movie, it's real."

"Thank you, Marshall. Now, what can you tell me about Tuesday morning, when you kept repeating those words? Did something prompt the event?"

"I heard Mommy Maggie... said the word... school."

Ruth Anne flashed Jillian a look. *School?*

"And then the movie started in your head?"

"Just words at first."

"Did you see someone say those words?"

"No. Yes. It wasn't me who made the sounds. Someone was speaking through me."

Ruth Anne felt the hairs rise on her arms, but Jillian remained calm, so she tried not to panic.

"Like a radio?" Jillian asked.

"Uh-huh."

"Was it a man or a woman's voice?"

"Neither. A kid. A little girl." He scrunched up his face. "The words wouldn't stop. I couldn't turn them off. They just kept coming!" He covered his ears and kicked his feet.

"It's going to be okay. I'm here, Marshall. You are safe." She touched his knee. He immediately relaxed, his feet back on the ground.

"Let's try and view the girl from a safe distance. You can look through a window and see her, but she won't see you. Understand?"

"It's Mommy Maggie...when she was a kid."

Jillian's face paled. She looked at Ruth Anne, then returned to Marshall. "Do you understand what Mommy Maggie was saying now?"

"No... I don't understand those words."

"Can you repeat them back?" Ruth Anne interrupted, holding up her recorder. Jillian gave her a sharp look. Ruth Anne stepped back, mouthing 'sorry.'

"I don't want to. The words make the shadows come." He whimpered, one eye twitching.

Shadows?

"We won't make you say the words," Jillian promised. "But can you tell us where Maggie is when she's saying these words?"

"She's with her sisters, but not Daddy. Daddy's in Montana. He's safe." Marshall exhaled with relief.

"That's good. But where is Maggie?"

"She's in a building. Big... white stones... spooky."

Mother of Hercules, I knew it! Ruth Anne inched closer.

"There's a chalkboard and long tables. Science stuff. There's an iron gate around the building and a cemetery next to it. Sasha doesn't like the cemetery. She wants to move it. And she wants to shut the school down."

"Why does she want to move the cemetery and shut the school down?" Jillian asked, anxiously.

"Because Mommy Maggie accidentally let out the darklings. Some got loose. They'll bring back more, and even worse things. And the ring..."

"What ring?"

"I don't know. I don't know." Marshall began weeping and Jillian could no longer get through to him. She broke the trance, and Marshall didn't remember a thing.

Ruth Anne clicked off her recorder, looking first at Marshall and then Jillian. *What ring?*

~

"Welp, that was a trip," Ruth Anne said, after seeing Marshall home and returning to Jillian's porch. "But he left smiling, so you must have helped him."

"I find that when you have something bottled up, it's best to set it loose."

"Tell that to Aladdin," Ruth Anne said. "Speaking of things in bottles..." She handed Jillian the elderberry vials. "I'm not sure of the potency, but if we have to take twice as much, so be it."

Jillian nodded, then coughed so hard she doubled over.

"Are you okay?" Ruth Anne asked, reaching out.

"Yes. Just allergies."

"Gotcha." Ruth Anne said, hiding the skepticism in her voice. They were each experiencing the Hellhound effects differently, so she couldn't be certain how sick Jillian really was, especially since she wasn't any more forthcoming about her inner world than she was. Ruth Anne had lost her mom, and wasn't sure her heart could handle losing Jillian, as well?

Ruth Anne pushed those thoughts away. This was Jillian. And Jillian was a goddess. And goddesses were immortal.

Too restless to sleep—*who needed sleep anyway*—Ruth Anne drove the backroads, telling herself repeatedly that she would *not* go to the Old Dune House. "There's nothing there," she said, turning up a country radio station to drown out her inner voice:

Memories...schoolyard days...
seeing you for the first time,
in the second grade...
I won't forget,
that first day dress,
or the way you didn't run from me,
when we played kiss and catch...

Ruth Anne grimaced and turned it back off, only then noticing her hands had turned onto one particular side road while her mind was preoccupied with song lyrics.

She pulled to a stop, tucking the Jeep in a cluster of trees, where she could watch the house and decide what to do. Peter Dune was supposedly staying out of town, but there was something inside that house. Whether it was the Murlough ghosts, or someone else, she didn't know. But pictures didn't lie. Strangely, she cared very little for seeing ghosts at the moment, more concerned that if she didn't act soon she might be joining them.

"But why exactly am I here?" she asked herself, massaging the steering wheel. The gold book wasn't there. She had made a pretty thorough investigation of the library on her last visit. And that shaft, she had seen it once, but then it was gone. Did she really think the school would reappear through it?

She had checked her camera photos that night after taking pics of the shaft--luckily backing them up on her tablet, too, before Maggie blew up everyone's phone chips in *Dip Stix*. She had looked at both versions: There was nothing there. Just wilderness. If nothing else, maybe she could figure out the mechanics of the shaft—to discern if it was creating optical illusions or projections, or if it had really given them a glimpse of the building.

Ruth Anne was surprised to see a man in slacks and a cardigan stepping outside. He leaned against one of the columns as he smoked on a cigarette. He took only three long inhalations before stamping it out on the cement porch. He waved to her, beckoning for her to join him.

"Busted..." she whispered, rolling up her window and locking the doors. *I thought Merry said he was in Linsburg this weekend?*

Walking across the long yard, she smiled as she tromped up the steps. "I'm Ruth Anne," she said, shuffling the keys in her pocket. "You must be Peter Dune."

"My reputation precedes me," he said, giving her a tight-lipped smile.

"Well, you're the talk of the town. You and *Java Juicer*. One of the *perks* of living in a small town—ooh, that's a good pun." She took her pen and notebook out of her inner jacket pocket. "Gotta remember that when I write the article on the coffee shop."

"You're a journalist?" he asked, tilting his head, looking slightly more intrigued.

"Uh, yes. Trying to get the town paper going on a regular basis." Mostly true, she figured it would act as her cover and hopefully help her gather information. "Actually, I was hoping to interview you. Learn a little more about you, and your plans for the house."

"You're an insomniac, too?" He took a flask from inside his sweater, swigged a drink, and then handed it over. "I find this helps."

Ruth Anne took the flask, thinking she had little to lose, no matter what she drank. Whiskey. It was the good stuff, smooth as melted caramel. "Ah!" she said, wiping the back of her mouth and returning the flask. "Hair of the dog that bit me."

"But that wasn't a dog that bit you, was it?" Peter smiled cryptically, and Ruth Anne's face heated. Was he alluding to her Hellhound mark? The elderberry juice? Her budding alcoholism? "It was the bookworm that bit you if I remember right. You're here to see our library. For your story, of course."

"Oh..." She gritted her teeth. "Yes?"

"Always reading. You were my favorite, way back then."

Ruth Anne tilted her head, the whiskey cutting both her pain and her inhibitions. "Merry said we went to school with you, but I have no memory of that. Of course, I don't remember a lot of things so please don't take it personally."

Peter laughed, took another drink, and narrowed his eyes. He stepped close enough for her to smell the whiskey on his breath. He'd obviously been drinking for hours. Ruth Anne curled her hand around the bear spray in her pocket, just in case.

"We both attended *Miss Sasha's School of Magick*. There were only a few of us, outside of you and your sisters, selected by the great Miss Sasha herself, invited by a hand-delivered note. I think I still have mine somewhere."

He went to the missing school?! "I'd love to see that note," she said, standing up straight.

"It's back in Baltimore. And don't be upset that you can't remember."

He waved his hand. "There was the forget spell. I've only been remembering recently, myself. My sister seems to have forgotten altogether."

He knew about the forget spell! "Isabella, right?"

"Yes. She was the one who received the invitation, but was insistent that I attend, too. Though your mother had a disdain for..." his lip curled beneath his mustache.

"Warlocks? Yes. We've heard." Ruth Anne laughed darkly. *Warlock* was another term for a male witch who used powers for his own gain, also called an oath-breaker. "We're a little more progressive these days. We don't look at all guys as warlocks anymore."

It surprised Ruth Anne, and at the same time didn't surprise her, that they were talking about schools, forget spells, and magick. She felt oddly comfortable with Peter Dune, despite his odd appearance and demeanor. But it could have been the alcohol. "Why are you back, now?" she asked.

"Officially, to sell the house. You can write that in your story. But unofficially...something that belonged to my sister was left behind in that school—something precious to her. An heirloom, if you will. I am going to find it, and then convince her to come live with me in this house. Along with her two kids."

"So you're not selling the house?"

"Not if I find what I've come for."

"Your sister can't come back without it?"

"No. It's a talisman, if you will. She wore it around her neck every day she went to school here, because the magick here was too rich for her delicate nature. She removed it at Sasha's urging, to *trust in her own protection*, only to have it taken when the school disappeared. She refuses to return to Dark Root without it."

"Not trying to pry—okay, yes I am—but why do you want her to move back here if she's opposed to it?"

Peter stared up at the stars, and Ruth Anne followed his gaze. The three stars making up Orion's Belt were threaded together between two ominous clouds. "She's gravely ill, straddling two worlds really. She has two daughters, who share our family's gifts. I thought their talents could be nurtured here in Dark Root, and I could help look after them if we lived together in our ancestral home. I left her back in Baltimore, and my teaching job as well, to come and scope it out."

He said Baltimore again. Merry must have confused it with Boston. "Does Merry know you're intending to stay in the house?" Ruth Anne asked, feeling protective of her sister. "She thinks she's going to help you fix this house up and list it. She's a single mom. You can't play games with her."

His eyes shifted from Orion to the Seven Sisters constellation.

"My original plan was to sell it," he said carefully. "But plans change, as I'm sure you know?"

Though Ruth Anne didn't have Merry's innate ability to detect lies, her journalism skills were useful in discerning truthful information. She believed that Peter had always planned to keep the house. So why involve Merry?

Never trust a warlock. Sasha's words filled her head.

"What do you think happened to the school?" She asked, wanting to keep the questioning going. She would sort out truth from lies later. "And do you know how we can bring it back? I need a book that was inside and belonged to my mother, and you need an heirloom. Maybe we can work together?"

"Your mother didn't just cloak the school, Ruth Anne," he laughed, with a hint of bitterness. "She sent it into another dimension. And the only way to bring it back is with a spell—a spell found only in that book that was also taken away, the same book you're looking for.

"Nooooo." Ruth Anne tapped her head on the column. So, they couldn't find the school until they found the spell... and they couldn't find the spell until they found the school. No wonder the building didn't register on any of her equipment. "There's nowhere else to get that spell? Or it's counterspell?"

"It is an ancient incantation, birthed in Mesopotamia, when children of the old gods walked the earth. The only one of its kind, as far as I know. But then again, that book contained many spells that were one of a kind."

Over Peter's shoulder, Ruth Anne detected movement in the front window. It was just a flash, but she was certain she'd seen a female silhouette in a wide skirt hurry by. Her mind immediately went to the ghost of Mrs. Murlough.

"Everything...okay here?" she asked.

"With the house?" he looked behind him, smirking. "Just a few bad memories; other than that, no complaints."

"I'll do some research," Ruth Anne promised. "We'll find that school. I'll get the book and you'll get the *bracelet.*"

Peter lifted his chin, nodding. "With your help, her talisman will be fitted back on Isabella's wrist very soon, where it belongs. And perhaps that alone can heal her."

CHAPTER 16

MAGGIE

The witching hour had come. I could feel it in my fingers and toes, even without looking at the clock. That time of night when the *Veil* was thinnest, magick most potent, and spirits traveled more freely. I had always been attuned to this hour—often awake, usually alert, sometimes visited. And tonight, as I was sipping tea alone in the kitchen, I was visited again.

"Hello, Juliana," I whispered, feeling her familiar presence behind me. I had known that she would come—had seen it in my dream only an hour before, and had crept out of bed and down into the kitchen in only my robe to wait for her. I turned my head, just a little so that I could see her in my peripheral vision. Juliana's shimmering ethereal form was close enough to touch. She smelled of roses and gardenias and nothing like winter.

Slowly, I turned my body all the way, taking her in, a little at a time. Our eyes locked, and for a moment she was no longer a spirit, but a live woman again. With feelings, emotions, awareness. Her eyes were trying to communicate something to me, but when she opened her mouth to speak, nothing came out.

"Show me," I said, rising to my feet.

I followed Juliana Benbridge as she drifted out of the kitchen, already knowing where she was leading me. I didn't dare turn on any lights. *They all need some sleep,* I told myself, my heart racing as we entered the supply closet, the lock no longer locked.

The rug over the hidden hatch door was pulled back, and dim light shone around the cracks. *Had Shane gone down there while I was in the kitchen?*

As quietly as I could, I lowered myself into my workshop, landing beside the table, next to the alchemy book I'd pushed aside when I attempted to seduce Shane, now set precisely back in place.

The gas lamp burned on the table, pointedly illuminating the open book, like the beam of a lighthouse cast over a dark sea. I studied the page, one I'd not seen before--a charcoal drawing of shadow beasts, with black holes for mouths and blood-red eyes. They towered over a small man holding a staff, standing inside a pentagram, his arms raised high. The caption read: *Solomon Binds Demon Army.*

A faint thumping sound, which at first I mistook for my heartbeat, spun me in the direction of the eye chart, just in time to witness it collapse down to the floor and curl up on itself. The thumping sound grew louder, clearly coming from the exposed tunnel. It was a frantic sound. Full of fear and dread.

I realized that it didn't matter if we sealed up the secret room and the mirror inside it. Even if we bricked the whole corridor, the entire basement, something wanted our attention and was not going to rest until it got it. Nor would Juliana, it seemed.

There were no dead bodies in there, I reminded myself, taking the lamp and the salt canister. Just a creepy old mirror.

Shane was not going to be happy, I thought, pressing salt over the chalk line and mortar grouting. The wall opened again, and I entered before losing my courage. The thumping stopped immediately when I entered the chamber, its source seemingly satisfied.

Blue glowing symbols danced across the obsidian glass before me, as if being typed out, then traded for another. I looked around for Juliana, but she was nowhere to be seen, or felt. *Is this what she wanted to show me?* "You could help me out here," I said to Juliana, if she were still lingering about.

The closer I drew to the mirror, the more I sensed its power. Its magick was strong yet tainted, touched by too many hands over too much time, before finding its way into my basement.

Careful not to touch it, I leaned forward to observe the cyphers, forming and reforming on the silvery glass, fading in and out like puffs of breath. Some lingered longer than others, but each was meaningless to me.

It was some form of communication; I was certain of that. But whether it was a song, poem, historical account or instruction, I had no idea. Nor in what language it was composed.

In a sudden flash of insight, I knew why Juliana had brought me here. She didn't just want me to see the symbols, she wanted me to decode them!

"I'll be back," I promised to Juliana, to the mirror, to the room, to whoever was listening.

I moved as fast as I dared, careful to douse the lamp before pulling myself up into the closet. I locked the door behind me, praying the thumping wouldn't return and wake up the house.

Grabbing Shane's pickup keys from the hook on the wall, and one of his jackets, I snuck out of the house and jumped in his truck. I cringed as the engine roared to life, breaking up the silence of the night.

To decode the message in the mirror, I needed the proper implement. The same implement I'd used to decode Juliana's journals. The *Deciphering Stone.*

Locked away in the secret cubby, behind Juliana's portrait, I had promised to use it only when necessary. Well, if this wasn't necessary, I wasn't sure what was.

CHAPTER 17
DORA

Dora had lived a very long life, longer than most ordinary people could imagine. And still, the memories of her life were vivid, and could be pulled up and examined at will. Which was why it was troubling that Sasha had wiped a good chunk of them clean.

She never doubted the woman. Sasha always knew what she was doing, but sometimes forgot to fully explain why. Or just didn't bother.

The two had met in the old country, near Dora's village, in those exciting years after adolescence but before she was a full-grown adult. Sasha was barely a woman herself, though she was poised and sharp and formidable—already skilled in the ways of magick, and filled with a sense of adventure and longing. Yet Sasha was always compelled by duty—an oath born from her birthright.

The two had both been invited to an old manor, where the lady of the house was conducting a séance—popular in those days before the war. They were the guests of honor. Dora should have been intimidated by the pretty young woman with fashionable boots and an aura of superiority, and she in her homespun dress and unruly hair. But there was an instant spark between them—an awareness of shared gifts. Kindreds, they were, right from the start.

The séance was a bust, when the lady's dead lover came through instead of her dead mother, in front of her still-quite-alive-husband. But the bond between Dora and Sasha was formed, and the former followed the latter around the world, seeking out lost artifacts together in old buildings and street markets. These then ended up in Dark Root for safe-keeping. Both women had seen the prophecies—Dora in her tea leaves and Sasha in her scrying mirror. *The Second Great Trial* was upon them. There were dark forces also looking for sacred objects, to elevate their power, and it was imperative to keep those sacred artifacts out of such hands.

When *The Second Great Trial* passed—two world wars and millions and millions dead--they were both saddened and grateful. Saddened by the senseless destruction, and what they personally missed out on searching for those artifacts: love, family, friendship; grateful that the world was still intact. Brittle, but intact.

After that tumultuous period, Sasha and Dora decided to return to Dark Root for good. Their aim was to create a Council to ensure the protection of these artifacts from the darkness of the world, and train those who could wield aether, in preparation for *The Final Trial,* which could come in a day, or a millennium. The trial where *The Dark One* was said to return after his long sleep.

Sitting at her kitchen table, Dora cupped her chin into her palm, watching the Felix the Cat clock on the wall. Its oscillating eyes counted down the seconds until the witching hour arrived.

Tick. Tick. Tick.

Magick was fullest during certain times of day, just as it was during certain phases of the moon or seasons. Transferring scenes from the tapestry into her globes required energies from the hours of midnight to 3 a.m., when the *Veil* was thinnest.

She wasn't certain she wanted to remember everything from that timeline. It was an era of betrayal, when the last remnants of the Council fell apart and Armand staged his mutiny with Larinda.

Those moments she remembered, with keen clarity. Having to hide the girls away, lest they be used for their magick, like artifacts themselves. Like objects.

But Dora knew the girls deserved to learn the full truth of those days. *Needed* to learn. Recent omens were too numerous to ignore. She'd seen *The Dark One* rising, in her tea leaves, and her dreams. It began shortly after Herman arrived in town, wearing the fabled *Ring of Malchezdiach.* The rings were collecting, as well as the darklings that hungered for them. Whoever wielded them in those final hours would have near-absolute power—even more, if they also found the most sacred of all relics, the *Stone.*

"Sasha, give me a sign." Dora sat up in her kitchen chair, alert. As if she'd just said the word *Abracadabra* out loud, there seemed a change in the movement of the tapestry before her, in the scene depicting the final night of the school. Dora put on her reading glasses, marveling at the detailed story unfolding before her on the woven strands, though still too small to see clearly.

"Thanks," she said, carefully draping the section of tapestry over the memory globe, rubbing it into the glass bulb with a wooden coin, like one would transfer an Easter decal onto an egg. She paused after every pass, for extracting memories was taxing, on her body and her spirit.

Once she felt the transfer was completed, she leaned in, her nose close to the glass. She was back in the school with Sasha, after the girls had been sent home and the mirror sealed shut. The image appeared so fresh, as if she were right there again. She could smell it too--the remnants of cabbage soup simmering over the hearth, mixing with smells of chalk, old books, and potent magick. She felt the chill in the air from the storm outside, and sensed Sasha's worry as she frantically collected things into baskets and piled them by the front door.

"Faster, Dora," Sasha said, as lightning flashed outside the window. "Whatever we don't save by midnight will disappear with the school .I'm

leaving the book here. It's safer on the other side, and it lessens the chance that someone will reverse the spell."

"Are ya sure there's nothin' else we can do?" the phantom Dora asked, gathering a stack of very old cookbooks in her arms.

"If we had more time, perhaps we could come up with something. But whatever was set loose tonight will return. It hungers for the ring and knows where it is now. Or where it should be, anyway. It will bring other darklings with it, or worse."

"But the cemetery..." That part really didn't sit well with Dora. You didn't banish a cemetery like you did a building, even if its occupants weren't attached to their discarded bodies anymore. The dead remembered their resting places, and it would leave them confused.

"It cannot be helped. It's too close to the school and the spell will engulf it. Although, the consequences may actually be beneficial, once we bury the Ring of Resurrection there. The Ring of Life will not satisfy those inside the mirror forever, and they will hunger for the more powerful ring. So will the vile soul trapped inside the bottle, not to mention those still in physical form who wish to find the ring."

"Ya mean Armand?" Dora asked, packing up mason jars containing plants and herbs collected from around the world, some extremely rare.

"Possibly. Armand's powers are great, and as we both know, he is not to be trusted. He is the perfect pawn for The Dark One. And no matter how clever the pawn thinks it is, it is still just a pawn."

"All this work, all this training... fer nothin'!"

"Nothing is ever for nothing." Sasha gathered a fistful of wands and tucked them under her cape. "These spells, powerful as they are, will not hold indefinitely. There will come a day when this school will be found. If the fates be with us, our girls will find it first."

"An' if the girls' don' find it?"

"We trust in the Fates, Dora." Sasha went to the gold book, sighing heavily as her fingers flipped through its ancient pages of thick parchment. "Goodbye, old friend," she said lovingly. The book, whatever it truly was and wherever it truly came from, was in Sasha's possession even before Dora met her.

Rushing around the building, they gathered all that they could before the clock struck twelve. They tucked their belongings into a wheeled cart outside the door, stacked high and covered by a tarpaulin. It was a somber moment, as they stood outside the iron gate, knowing they were about to forget. Forget not only knowledge but more intimate parts of their lives, as well. Dora shed a tear for the memories the girls would not have, and then one for the memories she was also going to lose.

Sasha raised her hands, drawing magick down from the moon as she recited the incantation she memorized from the gold book, commanding the school to disappear. It was a language Dora did not understand, nor was it pleasant on the ears. In a sudden fiery blaze, the entire school was engulfed, along with the adjoining garden, playground, and cemetery. Not even the iron gate remained. The image before her imploded into a pinprick of light, which then itself popped out of existence.

"Dear Gods, what did we do?" Sasha stumbled, drained by the powerful spell, and Dora helped her to stand. Her friend's normally steel eyes were distressed. "It's like losing the Library of Alexandria all over again," Sasha said.

"Where did it go?" Dora asked.

"A place outside of time, where it will be hidden from both man and monster."

"I'm ready fer the forget spell," Dora said stoically.

"Let's have one last cup of tea first," Sasha said, as they stood side-by-side and pulled the cart through the storm back to Sister House. "This isn't the ending, Dora," Sasha promised, placing her arm around her old friend. "Just another turning of the wheel."

CHAPTER 18

RUTH ANNE

Ruth Anne left the Dune house just as it began to rain, turning into a torrent within minutes. Her busted windshield wipers did little to cut through the storm. But she wasn't going home. Not yet.

She leaned forward to make out the road ahead of her. Even with her high beams, it was a dark and stormy night; and as a writer, Ruth Anne knew that nothing good ever happened on dark and stormy nights. *Just ask Snoopy*. Even so, she pressed her foot to the gas pedal, taking a back road into the woods behind the Dune house, to where the school should technically be, according to the shaft and her calculations.

There was nothing but wilderness. Trees and brush and sporadic fields of tall grass. She parked, letting the Jeep idle as she tapped on the steering wheel while the rain poured around her.

Peter was lying to me, but why?

First, he'd said Isabella wore a talisman around her neck. But later, prompted by her lead, he went along with her misdirection, saying that it was a bracelet.

Is his sister really in Baltimore? Or Boston? And what about the shadows in the windows? Was that her?

She would have thought Peter lying about the school too, he knew so many things about their past, including her love of books and Sasha's disdain of warlocks. And most importantly, he knew that the school had been vanished by a spell, and its students were placed under a forget enchantment.

Perhaps Merry had misheard about Isabella's residence? Maybe she did live in Baltimore. But what of the talisman? Ruth Anne could have dismissed it, because he was a man and might not know a bracelet from a necklace. But his sense of fashion suggested otherwise. Not to mention, even men knew that a bracelet is worn on the wrist while a necklace is worn around the neck.

What talisman could be so powerful that he came here to find it for Isabella? Ruth Anne wouldn't be trying to find the school, intentionally hidden by her mother, if the book inside was not so necessary.

Maybe there was no Isabella? They only had Peter's word on it, for now. And they only had his word that his name was Peter Dune, for that matter.

Ruth Anne's hands tightened around the steering wheel as a new concern stepped up to the plate: What if Peter wasn't really looking for an amulet at all, but the same magick book that Ruth Anne sought? He obviously loved books, and if he had been at the school, he was also a student of magick. What a treasure the gold book would be to his collection. She couldn't trust a word he said, since he had already proven himself a liar.

Didn't you lie to him, too?

She could almost hear Sophie's voice in her head, always trying to make her a better person. *Yes, I told some minor lies, and yes, I omitted a few things, but it was to protect the book, not use it for nefarious purposes.*

Like Sasha says: never trust a warlock.

Just because he's a man, doesn't mean he's a warlock, phantom Sophie reminded her.

Then again, it didn't not make him one, either.

"I'm right. I feel it in my gut," she said to herself, steaming up the windshield. He wanted the book. Either to use it or to sell it. There was a profitable black market for such things. "I'm going to find that book. It belongs to my family," she said, resolutely.

Wriggling in her seat, she managed to put on her rain poncho. Shutting off the ignition, she grabbed her pack out of the back seat and set off into the woods. She didn't stop until she came to a winding creek. "Where is it?" she asked, pulling out every instrument she had to measure radio frequency, thermal heat, electromagnetic pulses, voices from the gods...

Through the rain, she caught the faint hint of sulphur. Another thought then occurred to her: *What if Peter is setting me up? He knew I'd come out here after that conversation. What if he knows the Hellhounds are out here, too?*

"I'm being paranoid," she told herself, tromping through the mud, her flashlight and compass now her main tools. "Peter can't possibly know about the Hellhounds." *Can he?* She searched her pockets for the small iron stake she kept with her at all times now. Its smell was ward enough, but she'd happily plunge it through the heart of one of the beasts if given a chance. The scarred wound on her arm burned, as if in response to her thoughts.

She needed that book. That little bird-man was not going to get it.

Ruth Anne stood under a clump of trees for shelter, taking her tablet from her pack to review the photos of the school again—or rather, what should be photos of the school. As before, there was nothing there but forest.

"What's this...?" She enlarged the last picture with her fingertips, zooming into where she thought she saw a length of an iron bar, but it was only a thin tree branch. But it drew her attention to something she'd not caught when looking through her camera photos--a dozen or so blue and silver bubbles hovering above a low bush. Ruth Anne had seen these bubbles in her investigations. They were Spirit Orbs. A concentration like this suggested that many people had died in that area... or that many people were buried there.

A cemetery.

"Holy guacamole! Mother didn't just vanish a school, she took a cemetery, too." Ruth Anne pulled back her hood, letting the rain fall from the boughs onto her face. "But why, Mama?"

She sloshed around in the mud, kicking aside bramble and weeds, searching where she thought the cemetery might be. Eventually, she found a piece of cut wood that had once been nailed through the center. *Perhaps part of a headstone cross?* There was nothing more.

"If you hadn't erased our memories, we could probably have understood your eccentricities a little better," she said, both angry and awed. Had Sasha designed some grand strategy that unfolded with time? Or had she simply covered up a messy plot, to be dealt with later?

After scouring the area, she returned to her Jeep, her poncho covered in muck, her hair soaking wet, her tablet battery dead. She pulled out her phone to take photos of the cemetery, to review back home. When she opened the camera app she was greeted by the picture of Luna, looking up from her sheet of clay. Ruth Anne smiled at the sight of her adorable niece. But looking closer, there seemed a unique look in Luna's eyes in the photo. A perceptive gleam. Almost smug.

Ruth Anne was struck by a thought. Enlarging the photo, she looked at the clay that Luna had been poking holes into. The flattened sheet was lined with cut grooves, formed by the edge of her screwdriver into the dough. There was almost an order to it, the marks in straight lines, quite symmetrical. The picture looked very much like an old tablet from the ancient world. Looking closer, she was almost certain of it. *This is... cuneiform!* One of the earliest forms of writing, fashioned through a series of wedge shapes cut into clay.

No, it can't be!

Yes?

Ruth Anne squinted, running her hands along the lines, trying to make out any meaning. Sumerian. She knew some Sumerian words, having studied the ancient civilization for an archeology credit. She recognized one symbol immediately—*banish.*

Ruth Anne shivered as she zoomed and scrolled the picture. She copied each symbol she could read into her notebook, hoping to translate them. What she couldn't do herself, she'd look up online.

By dawn, fevered and sneezing, Ruth Anne had decoded most of the words. She arranged and rearranged them many times, finally coming up with what she thought was the best order.

It was a Mesopotamian spell.

A spell to remove something, not only from view, but from this entire plane of existence.

CHAPTER 19
MERRY

Merry had a full schedule, with not a second to dilly-dally. She frowned as she watched June Bug braid and unbraid her hair, at least a dozen times. And they hadn't even packed their lunches yet!

"Mae Maddock, we need to go," Merry said, tapping her watch, using her daughter's birth name to show she meant business.

June Bug furrowed her brows, tossing her barrettes onto her vanity. "Fine. I'll be ugly," she said.

"I can braid your hair if you want?" Merry offered.

"No, you never get the part right."

"Someone slept on the wrong side of the bed," Merry said, as June Bug grabbed her sweater and bounded down the stairs, three steps ahead of Merry. Aunt Dora awaited them in the kitchen, already removing apple pies from the oven to deliver to *Dip Stix*.

"I don't like this school," June Bug said. "The kids make fun of my cousins. I want to cast on them—I want to cast on them so bad."

June Bug's cheeks reddened and her finger swiped through the air as if it were a wand.

"I know it's difficult," Merry said, getting cheese and bread out for their lunches. "But we have to accept everyone where they are at. Be patient and things will turn around." She packed each of their brown paper sacks, handing one to her daughter and keeping the other.

"You just don't want to admit that this school was a bad idea," June Bug said.

"If ya wanna learn ta cast, I can help," Aunt Dora said, turning from the oven. "Been meanin' ta break out the old wand again."

"No casting!" Merry said firmly. "Not today, anyway."

"Grr...what good is being a witch, if I can't cast spells?" June Bug took a Pepsi from the fridge and headed out the back door. "I'll meet up with you in town," she huffed, marching off on her own.

"We're starting promptly at eight, on the corner of..." Merry called after, but June Bug had already put in her earbuds and was marching away. Merry folded her arms and leaned against the counter, watching her aunt box up the pies. "At what age do they start acting normal again?" she asked.

"I'll let ya know when I find out."

Merry laughed, then sniffed the air. The sweet fragrance coming off Aunt Dora was neither apple nor arthritis cream. "Is that perfume I'm smelling?" she grinned.

"Jus' cream fer my spider veins."

"Well, I'm off. It's *Good Citizen's Day*. We have several stops lined up. Those children should be whipped into a sense of morality, and a sugar frenzy, by day's end," she said.

"Jillian called—Maggie's sick. She won't be able to do her letter."

Merry frowned. "Maggie hasn't been sick since she was pregnant."

"Well, maybe her and Shane are all made up then," Dora chuckled.

"Should I look in on her?"

"Nay. She said she jus' needed rest."

"Okay...I can rearrange some things." Merry tapped her pen against her clipboard. No solution, no problem. That was her motto.

"Maybe Herman can go a little longer..."

She looked at her chart. Shane had *D*...Erin *L*... The pie shop lady--what was her name? —had *P*. She added in her own name and business, *Merry's Mentionables (Now on Main!)*, coupling it with the letter *M*. There. Fixed.

As Merry packed her tote bag, Dora put a gentle hand on her shoulder. "Be careful today, okay? There's somethin' different in the air. An' I'm not sure it's good."

Aunt Dora's predictions were usually accurate, though not always in the manner she indicated. "I think you're just sensing Maggie's bug. You'll feel better once she's up and about again." She kissed Dora's cheek. "But I promise, I'll be extra careful today," she added, seeing the still-troubled look in her aunt's eyes.

"Mind the rain," Dora said, as Merry left.

"What rain?" Merry smiled, upturning her hands. "It's all sunshine today. It's been dry for hours."

CHAPTER 20

RUTH ANNE

"I'm gonna say it. No, I'm not gonna say it."

Ruth Anne paced in front of her Jeep, the cuneiform spell now deciphered and written in her notebook, bouncing between her hands as she went back and forth on her decision. If she'd had any doubts before, she was certain now that it was meant for her to find the spell. She also believed it possible that, by having changed out a few key words, she could reverse the spell and bring back the school from wherever Sasha sent it. How the spell came to Luna, and how she could possibly write in cuneiform, was another mystery altogether—one that would have to wait.

Unlike her sisters, Ruth Anne had no real magick of her own. The incantation would have to do the work alone. What if it was a one-time-use spell? If she botched it up, it might not work again. *Should I go get the others?*

No. Merry would want to wait. Debate about it. Go through a list of 'Pros and Cons'. Put it on an agenda. It might take three election cycles for Merry to make a decision.

What if I just get Eve and Maggie? Three was a good number for a spell, and they probably wouldn't react as strongly against the idea as Merry. Maggie might even be onboard. She started to text Eve, but stopped. What could she say in a text or a call? *Hey guys, uh, Luna somehow channeled in a spell from 4,000 years ago. Wanna see if it conjures back our old school?*

She would need to ask them in person, and that would take longer than Ruth Anne wanted to wait. Especially with Peter Dune looking for the school, too, and her arm on fire. *The school is here somewhere, and so is the book.*

"I'm gonna say it," Ruth Anne proclaimed, facing the direction of the missing school.

She looked up, squinting, noticing that it wasn't raining anymore and her hair was starting to dry. Was the sunshine a good sign? She took it as a yes. Or at least a maybe.

Wiping off her glasses and clearing her throat, Ruth Anne held the notebook out before her, as if declaring an official proclamation. The language was hard to pronounce and tickled the back of her throat when she'd audibly deciphered the words. She knew that spells, especially the ancient ones, had to be articulated exactly and precisely. One small mispronounced syllable could change everything. The time/space continuum, even. The magick and vibration had to align completely—

Shut up, before you talk yourself out of it.

She spoke the old words loudly and clearly, her knees trembling with every syllable. She wasn't quite finished when the ground jolted sharply, sending her stumbling backwards. The whole area lurched around her. Trees tilted in conflicting directions, one leaning almost onto the hood of her Jeep.

Ah, crap!

She looked around, at the shaking world, as she scrambled back up to her feet. It was too late to go back now. She could only pray that her hunch had been right. If not... she wouldn't think of that yet.

She finished the recitation, her voice booming with authority, while trying her best to keep standing as the earth shifted beneath her.

Then followed an ear-splitting roar, erupting up from underground.

Ruth Anne watched, with horror and fascination, as the earth before her pushed together and upwards, like it was trying to form a new mountain. Rocks and chunks of dirt were thrown into the sky, obscuring her view and forcing her to cover her head for fear of getting hit.

As the air cleared and ground calmed, an imposing structure built of thick white stones phased into view, enclosed by a black iron fence, and a blanket of fog. The gate read: *MSSM Est 1981.*

Ruth Anne gawked at the structure for a long time. "No way," she whispered. Then her look of disbelief was exchanged for a victorious grin. "Heck, yeah!" She punched one arm upward, wishing her sisters could see this feat she'd just performed, with nothing more than her intellect and determination. And Dark Root's inherent magick. And Luna's... whatever that was. "Look at me," she jigged about, hopping on one foot, then the other. "I'm a witch, too," she said, wriggling her fingers like her sisters did.

She went to the front gate, half-expecting to touch air, but the iron was both cold and real. "I'm gonna buy Luna the biggest ice cream I can find," she thought, jogging towards the door, wondering if it would open, or if that would require a key or another spell. She'd find out soon enough!

Her elation was short-lived. On the North side of the building, the earth had not yet settled. It was still regurgitating, spitting up white rocks, some of them crumbling as soon as they appeared.

No, not rocks. Headstones. *The old cemetery!*

Ruth Anne froze—silently processing the implications of bringing back the dead, from another dimension... Had their souls followed their bodies, to the other side and back? Or were body and soul reunited here? She hadn't considered this when she cast the spell.

The wound on her arm began to flare with heightened pain, and she felt fevered once again. The stench of sulphur grew thick in the air. The sun dropped behind the clouds. And the earth continued to belch up stones.

It was like The Book of Revelations, playing out in one schoolyard.

She swallowed, backing away through the iron gate. She wasn't attuned to the spirit world like Maggie—but she had the distinct sensation of being watched. And not by human eyes. Something had changed—and it wasn't just the landscape.

Racing for her Jeep, Ruth Anne set off for town, fighting to ignore the biting pain pulsing from her festering Hellhound bite.

I'll bring back the others. We'll handle this together.

CHAPTER 21
MERRY

"The first stop on our Good Citizens tour is..." Merry bit her lip, looking at the very elderly woman standing in front of the group, holding up a lemon pie with a smiling but confused face. She turned to the side so Merry could read her name tag. *Peggy. Peggy the Pie Lady*. "... is with Peggy." Merry continued. "Peggy, would you like to talk about how you make your pies?"

The school kids and their parents standing on the sidewalk before *Peggy's Pies—of course!*—then gave a polite clap, then listened attentively as Peggy explained, in her strong German accent, how she created each and every pie on her menu.

Merry's mind drifted off, her eyes tracking the emerging gray clouds. She looked along the sidewalks, hoping to see her daughter. June Bug said she would meet her in town but hadn't specified where. And the girl wasn't answering her texts!

"You haven't seen June Bug recently, have you?" she whispered to Eve, who shook her head. "Nova? Have you?"

"No. sorry."

Just great.

“And what does being a good citizen mean to you?” Merry asked when Peggy reached the bottom of her menu.

Peggy shrugged her thin shoulders. “It means not invading someone else’s country.” There were a few uncomfortable laughs, and Merry quickly ushered the kids forward to the folding table, where pecan pie samples awaited in small paper cups.

Merry blew her hair out of her eyes, determined to forge on, feeling the first sprinkle of rain tap her forehead. “We won’t be going into the magick shop today,” she said, as they passed the darkened storefront and crossed the street. “But we’ll be making a quick stop at *Dip Stix Cafe*, for some hometown hospitality. The owner treats every guest like they are not only friends, but family. We could all learn a lesson about community from Mr. Shane Doler.”

“My daddy works here,” Marshall announced, as they stopped in front of the café.

“He owns it,” Montana said.

“Owns,” Luna repeated.

“Well, he better have good cookies,” Susie said.

“He’s not making cookies. He got letter ‘D’. He’s making donuts.”

“Well, they better be good.”

Oh, dear gods, why isn’t Shane coming out? Merry looked at her watch as the kids and parents milled about restlessly along the curb. She poked her head inside the door, catching him as he delivered a glass of milk to a table.

“Ah, sorry,” he apologized, wiping his hands on his apron and stepping outside to greet them. “We had a bit of a grease fire, so I’m afraid we don’t have any donuts today. I’ve got leftover deviled eggs from lunch yesterday, if that helps.”

“Yuck,” said Susie. All the other kids agreed, making faces and boo’ing.

Merry scratched her cheek, trying to keep it together. “Mr. Doler, can you tell us how we can improve our community?

Shane wrung his hands together. “Vet your new employees,” he said, running back inside towards the screeching sound of a smoke detector going off.

There is still *Charmed, Merry's Mentionables,* and *The Imaginarium,* Merry reminded herself, ushering the crowd down the sidewalk. It was starting to get chilly and windy, and the raindrops were more frequent.

Charmed, at least, was entertaining, if not slightly too adult. Erin, in a very form-fitting blouse, talked about her Love charms, for the letter 'L'. She then gave everyone a lucky charm in the shape of a clover, strung on a silk ribbon. When asked what she thought made communities great, she said, "handsome men and hot coffee".

Isn't anyone getting the point of this? Merry asked herself, as the students and parents made their way down the street to *Merry's Mentionables,* pulling up their hoods and popping their umbrellas as they walked. Once there, Merry talked about 'management' for the letter M, and gave them all sugar-free marshmallows from the hot cocoa display.

"So, what do you think makes a good citizen?" Merry mock interviewed herself, using her pen as a fake microphone.

"Well, children," she answered herself, to a group that just wanted to get out of the rain. "I think...I think..."

She scrunched her brow, realizing she hadn't thought it through, either. It should be easy enough to answer, right? Kindness, sure. Compassion, obviously. Doing what's right. Caring for your neighbor. Discounts for locals. But what could she say, in just a few words, to encapsulate what she was trying to teach them? Something that would hopefully carry over into their own lives?

Merry looked up and down Main street. All the shops, and the shopkeepers, all very different from one another. Yet they all worked alongside one another, in spit of these differences. *Dip Stix* and *Peggy's Pies* coexisted, despite the fact that Aunt Dora sometimes supplied pies to both restaurants. Merry and Herman took turns watching each other's stores. For the most part, Erin and Maggie usually managed a somewhat professional relationship. Even *Java Juicer* had its place.

"Respect," Merry said. "That's what it really all boils down to. When we can all live together, mindful of our differences, yet accepting of them, then we have built a true community."

"Boring," said Montana, who was standing beside her. To which Merry accidentally stepped on his toe.

"Let's get to our last stop. If we finish up early, maybe we'll spend the rest of the day playing games," she promised, ushering them over to *The Imaginarium,* where Herman stood outside, before the drawn curtains of his shop window. The rain had even stopped.

I wish Maggie was here. She had just given a lecture on respect, and it occurred to her that by silencing her sister, insisting she knew better for her children than Maggie did, that she hadn't given her the same respect she'd just preached about. She quietly texted her:

'I hope you're feeling better. I'll bring you pie. Xoxoxo.'

Now, if only she could find her own daughter.

CHAPTER 22
MAGGIE

I stood before the mirror, the brick entrance behind me braced open with a length of 2x4 board I found under a workbench. My eyes were glazed from hours of staring into the obsidian. It might have even been days. There was no time inside the mirror, only the urgency of now. Even so, I was firmly grounded by the presence of the *Deciphering Stone,* pulsating in my palm like a heartbeat.

Using the stone was instinctive, though I had never translated in this way before. Slowly, laboriously, I locked onto each flashing blue symbol, pulling it into my mind's eye as I ran my fingers along the rough edges of the ancient relic. I eventually received back a series of sounds—high pitch, low bass, up and down in octave, bouncing staccato and steamy hum. A language, all its own.

It was a song, and I'd heard it before. Not once, but twice--in *Dip Stix,* when Marshall was rolling on the floor... and when I was a young girl in Sasha's school.

Someone had whispered that song in my ear then, over and over, until I had no choice but to scream it out.

I remembered now. I didn't even need to finish with the symbols. I lowered my hand, remembering every word.

Was this the spell that hid the school? Or something else?

Though nothing happened when Marshall spoke it, I had the sense it would be different for me.

I was a witch. And Juliana had led me here.

I said a quick protective spell, then began to recite the words:

Oh-h-men-irsirsi,
no-ma-na-num,
lo-osh-oo...

The mirror began to shimmer.

CHAPTER 23
MERRY

The *Imaginarium* was greeted with more enthusiasm from the families than the other shops, and Merry was glad she'd saved it for last.

Herman waited for them right outside the window display. His long gray-red beard was knotted into a single braid, with beads woven throughout. His golden eyes looked intently over the crowd. He was wearing a gown, purplish and regal, too big for his small frame.

Merry was excited about Herman's presentation. He claimed to have traveled the world three times, and was the only one smarter than Ruth Anne that she knew. He had been given the letter A, and she wondered what he chose to speak on, relating to his store: Astronomy? Aerodynamics? Animals? His shop constantly shifted merchandise, having a little of everything, so it was hard to guess.

Without acknowledging anyone, in particular, Herman clasped his hands together and the deep blue curtains covering the window drew open. The cemetery scene and ravens were no more. Now, the display was stacked high with gold coins and gold bars.

"Alchemy..." he began, with a flourish of his hands, "...the quest to turn lead into gold."

"Well, this is about as interesting as those fake luck charms," Eve whispered.

"Mmm..." Merry said, checking her phone again for word from June Bug, her worry escalating by the minute. Maybe she went to see her sick Aunt Maggie, perhaps to try and 'heal' her? Merry texted Maggie again. *Is my daughter there?* As before, there was no response.

"Have you seen June Bug?" she asked her daughter's friend, Trevor.

"Not today." He looked worried, too, his man-grin now a little boy's frown.

"Ahem." Herman cleared his throat, looking Merry's way. She mimed zipping her lips and he continued. "But there was more to alchemy than turning lead to gold." He clapped his hands and the coins and bars all disappeared, much to the astonishment of the crowd.

In their place were metallic, three-dimensional shapes, suspended from thin ribbons that twisted and twirled. "The alchemists sought perfection in all things, and believed that just as lead could become gold, the human body could be made whole again--not just healthy, but youthful and undying."

He clapped his hands again and the 3-d shapes were drawn upward like puppets, replaced by a large, egg-shaped crystal, suspended by nothing that Merry could see. The families oohed and awed as it slowly spun before them. "But in order to achieve immortality, they needed one thing--the *Philosopher's Stone*. Those privileged few who accomplished its creation were granted eternal life, and mastery over time itself."

"Herman..." Merry interrupted, edging up beside him, sensing he was going off track.

"Almost done," he said from the side of his mouth. "I just need to show them the homunculus."

"The what?"

"The small, fully formed human being in the bottle..." He readied his hands to clap.

"I think we need to wrap this up!" she said quickly, directing everyone's attention to the small card table set up beside him. "Thank you, Herman, that was fascinating. And he is sending everyone home with...antacids?"

"Modern magick," he nodded.

"That's uh, great. But before we leave you, can you tell us what it means to be a good citizen?"

Herman's eyebrows crested down over his eyes. He stood with his hands clasped before him so long Merry feared he had fallen asleep on his feet. Then he answered. "Seek to perfect yourself, not others."

Merry did a double-take. "Wow. That's actually...perfect." Merry patted his shoulder. People never ceased to surprise her.

Nor did Mother Nature. Without warning, the rain began again, dumping down on them in sheets. Merry lifted her clipboard over her head. "Everyone, let's all move towards the... hey, there's June Bug!" She felt a rush of relief as she spotted her daughter, coming out of *Merry's Mentionables* on the other side of the street. *Was she in there the entire time?*

"June Bug!" Merry called, waving her hand.

"I'll get her!" Trevor said, rushing off the sidewalk.

Merry reached out to grab his arm, but he was too fast. The next moments occurred in separate frames, one tick at a time.

Brakes squealing in the rain. A cry out of warning from the crowd. The skidding and slipping of tires in the water.

Ruth Anne's Jeep, rushing into town along Main Street, skidded to avoid the boy as he ran out before her. Merry could see her sister's panicked face as she yanked on her steering wheel.

June Bug, her attention on Trevor crossing to greet her, stepped into the street from the other side. As Ruth Anne swerved to avoid Trevor ahead of her, the Jeep skidded directly at her niece.

In that frozen moment, Merry understood that Ruth Anne was

going to hit her daughter. *No!!!!* Full panic and dread seized every ounce of her being, instantly and completely.

Merry went to scream, but it was Montana's cry that pierced through the rain. "Stop!" He stepped forward, thrusting out his hand. The Jeep popped up into the air, flipping over June Bug and landing upright on the other side. The rear end clipped Trevor as the vehicle came to a stop against the curb, sending him flying backwards and landing hard on the asphalt.

"Trevor!" June Bug ran to her friend.

Merry was beside her daughter in a flash. "Herman, keep everyone on the sidewalk! Eve, check on Ruth Anne!" she called behind her.

Trevor's leg was bent the wrong way. He writhed on the ground, whimpering, as Merry called out for his mother.

"She's not here," June Bug said, with a quivering lip. "She never comes to school things." She touched Trevor's wet face, trying to reassure him.

The other families huddled in the doorways and under the awnings, whispering and calling on their phones. Merry overheard snippets of their conversation. Did they really just witness what they thought they witnessed? Some backed away from Montana, as if he was afflicted with a plague. "Told you that family is weird," Susie's mother said.

Trevor's face was ghost-white, his eyes rolling back into his head with pain. June Bug tapped his cheek, repeatedly, to keep him conscious. "Don't worry—" she said, her eyes betraying her own worry as she inspected his twisted leg.

Eve and Ruth Anne joined them around Trevor. "Ah, Geez! I'm so sorry. The brakes, they... is he okay?" Ruth Anne asked, dropping to the ground beside the boy.

"No, but he's going to be." Merry locked eyes with June Bug. They would have the talks they needed to have later. But in this moment, it was time to respect her daughter, and herself. And that meant using their given gifts. “Let’s do this,” she said to June Bug. “Together. On the count of three...”

“Really? In front of everyone?” June Bug asked, through a mat of wet hair, her eyes scanning the families bunched together on the sidewalk.

“What good is magick if you can’t use it? Especially for a good cause.”

Mother and daughter lay their hands over Trevor, flooding him with warm energy from either side. Healing had always been Merry’s strength, a gift she had passed down to her daughter. The rain poured down, but neither felt it. Everything felt like sunshine.

“What happened? The pain’s gone.” Trevor blinked several times and sat up, slowly straightening his leg to normal again. There wouldn’t even be a bruise. “But... it was all crooked.”

“And now it’s not.” Merry squeezed his shoulder, ignoring the louder whispers coming from the sidelines. As June Bug helped Trevor to his feet, Merry pushed back her wet hair and looked at her sisters. “Everyone saw what we did,” she said, looking around through the pouring rain.

“Yep,” Eve agreed. “It will be hard to come back from this one. Unless we can turn back time.”

“Not to worry,” Ruth Anne said. “I can fix this.”

“How?” Eve asked, as they made their way to the nearest awning for cover.

“I’m bringing back the ‘Dark Root Press’, once and for all. A few key words in the Sunday edition and poof—the whole event becomes an entirely new story. Eventually, truth is buried and reality shifts.” Ruth Anne wriggled her fingers, not like she were casting, but typing. “My special brand of magick.”

“You really think that will work?” Eve asked, returning a glare from one of the onlookers. “I mean, practically everyone in town witnessed this.”

Ruth Anne smiled. “Of course it will work. Happens with every politician’s speech and every episode of the nightly news. People are eager to believe what they want to believe, and they want to believe their world is safe, ordered, under their control. Magick has no place in that world."

"Words do have power," Merry agreed.

"Let's hope." Eve shrugged. "If that doesn't work, Merry can always conjure up another festival, and give them something new to focus on."

Merry sighed, finally ready to accept defeat. *Not defeat*, she reminded herself. *Progress*. "I guess it's time to find that school. Our kids do need more training before we set them loose on society. I guess I didn't have everything as under control as I thought I did."

"Then today might be your lucky day." Ruth Anne said, cryptically. Then she looked around. "But we're gonna need Maggie."

CHAPTER 24
MAGGIE

The obsidian glass splintered as I repeated the words, over and over, and I was powerless to stop them. The voice speaking through me was not my own, but foreign and guttural. Commanding. *Ancient.*

The mirror itself expanded and contracted, it's cracks growing with each recitation. After an unknown amount of time, and the spell repeated an unknown number of times--my eyes glazed and head heavy--the glass in the undulating frame finally exploded like a burst lung. Shards sprayed out in a wide arc, miraculously landing all around me, but not touching me, except for a few stray bits in my hair.

With the explosion, I felt a deep release. Exhaustion and relief. But relief turned to dread as I surveyed the shattered glass all around me, and the ruined mirror. I touched my throat. *What took hold of me?*

It was storming outside—I sensed it. Dark Root would be a sheet of rain. My doing. The invocation had chased the sun away.

The empty mirror frame continued to pulse. To breathe. *In and out. In and out.* In the center of its blackness, a silver spiral formed. It spun outward, dawdling at first, then quickening--churning out a host of serpentine black mists with fiery red eyes.

My own heart momentarily stopped, as I realized what was happening.

Darklings.

I knew them from both experience and study. Lesser demons, but demons nonetheless. The souls of soulless men. Had Juliana meant for me to release them? Or had something gone wrong?

They whizzed about the cavernous room, seemingly oblivious to me, swooshing like bats as I helplessly watched. *How many?* More than a handful. Maybe a dozen. *I should have brought my wand.*

Before the spiral closed in on itself, it ejected a gold ring that rolled and spun to a stop before my feet.

"Ring..." A darkling whispered, swooping to take the band. My crystal bracelet flared, momentarily illuminating the room and repelling the creature into the wall. It hissed out its irritation, blinking its eyes against the flash of light.

I snatched up the ring as the darklings all turned their attention to me. Their greedy eyes bounced from the stone in my one hand to the ring in the other. They all drew nearer, surrounding me tightly on all sides, the air turning glacially cold. "Riiiing," they whispered together in raspy harmony.

I chanced a glance at the ring in my palm. A simple gold band embossed with a seal: two snakes twining around a tree. I'd seen it before. It belonged to Sasha, once upon a time. How did it end up inside the mirror?

"Stay back!" I ordered, spreading my arms wide. I drew in the energy around me, from the house, the workshop, the pieces of the broken mirror, even the ring and the stone. My fingers crackled with electricity. My bracelet came alive. I wasn't certain I could hold enough magick to bind them, but I was going to try. "By the power of my ancestral line," I began with authority, weaving my hands together, in preparation to cast.

But their attention had shifted away from me, their red eyes all turning towards the opening in the brick wall. “Riiiiiing,” they hissed, swooping towards the opening, one by one. “Riiiiiii-innnnnnnnnggggg....”

“No! Fight me!” I commanded. *Where are they going? What are they after?* “Fight me! I have the ring!”

I lifted the ring to lure them back, but they paid no heed.

I watched, powerless to stop them, as they poured out into the tunnel, disappearing out into the world.

“Uh-oh.”

EPILOGUE: MERRY

LATER THAT EVENING...

The fire pit in the side yard of Harvest Home blazed, as Ruth Anne and Marshall added kindling, logs, and copies of *The Linsburg Sun*. The rest of the family gathered nearby, enjoying the warmth on a chilly night.

"There," Ruth Anne said, stepping back and rubbing her hands, once the fire was up to her standards. "Better."

Marshall mimicked his aunt, smiling up at her now and again, as the orange glow illuminated their faces like Jack-o-lanterns.

"Is it time for s'mores?" Nova asked, bouncing on the heels of her sneakers.

"Not yet," Eve said. "Aunt Merry's gotta make a speech first."

"A speech about s'mores?" Montana asked, looking both gleeful and confused.

"You'll see," Eve promised.

Merry watched her family, gathered around the fire pit--some with hot cocoa in their hands, others with rum and cider. She frequently glanced at the back door, and then craned her neck to get a view of the front yard, checking for headlights.

Where are Maggie and Shane? Shane had texted that they'd be there shortly. *I hope Maggie isn't too sick to join?* She looked at her phone, nervous when she still didn't see a text or call come through. The kids were growing restless and she wasn't sure how much longer she could keep their attention. Was it okay to assume Maggie and Shane were still on board? She swallowed. As the head of the Dark Root Education Department, it was her job to make these calls.

I guess we start without them.

She clinked her mug with a spoon to get everyone's attention. They turned to her, standing before the frosty garden filled with Dora's underdeveloped pumpkins. She couldn't help but smile at the family they had cobbled together. Three generations of witches—maidens, mothers and crones – along with their husbands and sons. Who were also witches, Merry reminded herself. Or magicians, as the boys liked to call themselves. Plus a stray or two—she looked at Trevor, sitting on a folding metal chair next to June Bug, too close for her liking.

"Thank you all for coming tonight on such short notice, and after such a...busy day," she said, winking. "As most of you know, my *Good Citizens' Day* didn't go exactly as planned..."

To which everyone laughed.

"...but fortunately, everything turned out okay."

June Bug beamed at Trevor and he grinned back.

"Trevor, shouldn't you be heading home about now?" Merry asked, uncomfortable with not only discussing magick around the boy, but also by the way he looked at her daughter.

"Nope. Mom had to work a double shift. She said I could hang out with Mae."

Mae? June Bug didn't let anyone call her that, though she seemed pleased as punch to hear her given name coming from him. With the boy staying, Merry realized she would have to choose her words carefully.

"We've had a meeting and decided that the new school is not quite large enough for everyone. In fact, we might even be breaking some fire codes," she said. "So...we are going to be opening a second school, not too far from here, just for you guys."

"Huh?" Marshall asked, dropping his empty paper cup into the fire."Just for us?" He motioned to his siblings and cousins.

"Yes. A place where your individual talents can be fostered. Nurtured. Molded. The curriculum will be focused on... the arts, and science."

"We get a new school!" Montana said, whooping about."Hurray! Wait, do we have to sit at desks still? Will the recesses be longer?"

"We will work all that out in the coming weeks," Merry assured him, slipping on her reading glasses and picking up a clipboard from her lawn chair. Though there was nothing attached to the clipboard other than blank pages, none of the others needed to know.

"I liked our old school," Nova frowned. "I made some friends there."

"That's just because you don't have magick," Marshall said, then immediately shut his mouth, his eyes sliding to Trevor.

But Trevor's mind was elsewhere, namely on June Bug. He didn't seem to hear.

"I'm now turning the meeting over to Ruth Anne, to explain in more detail." Her eldest sister was buried in a quiet conversation with Jillian and didn't hear her cue. Merry cleared her throat. "Ruth Anne, would you like to give out the plans for the new school?"

"Roger that." Ruth Anne bounded forward. She crouched low, opening her arms wide, really selling her vision. "When me and my sisters were kids, we got to go to this really cool school. I mean, it was huge. With a yard to run in and labs to play in and a library---that library!" She whistled. "Oh, the things you could read about..." Merry tapped her arm, to keep her on track. "But the school closed down, because of...because of..."

"Bugs?" Luna proffered.

"Bugs! Yes, the 'Great Bug invasion of 1996'. But not to worry--the place is going to be cleaned up, fixed up, exterminated..."

Exterminated. Merry's eyes slid to the pack still slung across Ruth

Anne's shoulders, containing her ghost hunting equipment. The sisters—minus Maggie—had gone to the school right after Ruth Anne excitedly filled them in about cracking the Mesopotamian spell, and the subsequent appearance of the school and cemetery.

When they approached the school, Merry almost couldn't believe her eyes. She sat in the Jeep with Ruth Anne and Eve, taking in the grandeur of the building. Patches of her childhood returned--hopscotch, gardening, lab experiments. And rabbit stew. The last she could have left in the past, being a bunny-loving vegetarian. But the memories that came back were good ones, mostly. She was more convinced than ever that they needed to reopen the school and give their own kids a taste of their own magickal childhood.

Of course, there were things to do first, but structurally at least, the school seemed fine. A coat of paint. A thorough cleaning. A few spirits they needed to send to the light.

"...and we'll build a greenhouse," Ruth Anne continued, explaining to the kids, "filled with herbs and flowers and elderberry bushes."

Merry cocked her head. Elderberry bushes? "Okay, any questions?" she interrupted, looking again for headlights.

"When do we start?" Marshall asked, hand raised.

"Excellent question. You start next week. Although we don't anticipate that the school will be open until October. In the meantime, your Uncle Paul and Auntie Eve have donated their café to meet in, since it won't launch until the new year."

"Who's going to be our teacher?" June Bug asked.

"Well...me...and Ruth Anne, and Paul has a degree in music and art!" she pointed to her handsome, soon-to-be-brother-in-law, standing beside Eve. "He's agreed to teach a day or two a week. And Jillian and Eve can assist from time to time." She looked at her clipboard, pretending to read. "As for the other school, Peter Dune has graciously agreed to take my old position."

"How'd you swing that?" Ruth Anne asked out of the side of her mouth.

"I confronted him about selling his house. I agreed to terminate our contract if he agreed to teach for a year," Merry said, from the side of her own mouth.

"Ruthless! I love it."

"Will Trevor get to come, too?" June Bug asked, folding her hand protectively over Trevor's.

"No, I'm sorry. Not yet." Merry had already come up with an excuse, to deter anyone else wanting to enroll. "We are using the state's home-schooling curriculum, and can only 'teach' members of our own family. I'm so sorry, Trevor."

"That's not fair!" June Bug pulled Trevor to the other side of the fire. He obliged like a puppy. Maybe it was better separating the two, Merry thought. They seemed a little too attached.

"Does anyone have any other questions, concerns, comments?" she asked the kids.

"Not... kill... bugs?" Luna asked, with worried eyes.

"We'll do our best to relocate any lingering bugs we find to the woods," Merry said. "Anything else?"

"Can we go play now?" Montana asked.

"Well, yes--"

Immediately upon hearing the "Y" word, the kids scattered about the yard. Montana zoomed up beside her. "Thanks! Grandpa says the ring is here somewhere and I need to go find it."

Grandpa? Ring? Merry watched him run off. *Children and their imaginations.*

"Well, that didn't go as terribly as I thought," Ruth Anne said.

There was only one other obstacle left--the elder witches hadn't voiced their opinion yet, and this was a family decision.

Aunt Dora had been sitting quietly on the concrete bench, her hands stitched together over her lap. "Aunt Dora, would you like to say something?" Merry asked. "I know you had your misgivings."

Aunt Dora shook her head. "That school was meant ta be found. Better by our family than another."

Merry smiled. She had braced for Dora's opposition, after their conversation in the pie shop.

"I agree with Dora," Jillian said, from her spot beside the fire. "Sasha was smart. I think she knew this day would come, and that it would be her daughters who found it. I'm in."

"Woot! I'll start inspecting the building more thoroughly tomorrow," Ruth Anne said, jigging about. "Anyone wanna come along?"

"I think we need some permits first," Merry said, making a mental note.

"Is there a separate form for ghost schools?" Eve asked.

"Mommy and Daddy are here!" Montana called on his next dash around the yard, as Shane's bright headlights flooded the side yard, then died with the engine.

Shane popped out of the cab and ran to the passenger side, opening the door. When Maggie stepped out, she was wearing her ceremonial blue cloak and hood. *What, why?* Shane took his wife's hand and helped her across the lawn. She seemed to be limping.

"Aunt Dora, you still have some of that soup left?" Merry asked, seeing her sister's pale face beneath her hood.

"In the fridge," Dora said, already standing up and making for the kitchen. "I'll heat some up."

The drawn look on Maggie's face, and the worried look on Shane's, told Merry that whatever ailed her sister might require more than soup. "How are you doing, Maggie?" She reached out to touch her sister's hand and was immediately shocked back.

"Be careful," Shane warned. "She's fully charged right now, hence the cloak." He escorted Maggie to the concrete bench.

"You look like a ghost," Eve commented. "What did you get yourself into?"

"She's not sick," Merry said, reading Maggie's aura. It was strong but gray, and she sensed tainted magick. "Maggie, were you cursed?"

Eve, who specialized in curse removal, looked her over closely, stepping beside her. "She's not cursed. But there is something here..." She ran her hands through the air around Maggie.

Maggie shook her head and stood up, pulling back her hood. Her lips were parched, her skin like linen. Her eyelashes almost white. The sisters collectively gasped when they saw a shock of white hair, an inch wide, ribbon through her natural red locks.

"What happened?" Jillian asked, concern on her face as she pressed in close.

Maggie looked between them as they fired off questions. Finally, she answered. "I may have done something really reckless, even for me." She pulled back her right sleeve and extended her hand, showing them a new ring on her finger--a ring Merry thought she recognized but couldn't place.

"Where did you get that?" Merry asked, stepping in to inspect it.

Aunt Dora rejoined them, a coffee mug between her hands. "Soup's heatin'," she announced. When she saw Maggie's new white hair, and the ring on her finger, she dropped the cup.

"Ya found the mirror! How? Sasha said she'd hid it so no one would e'er find it again."

Jillian took Maggie's hand, inspecting the ring closer. "I remember that! The *Ring of Life*! Sasha used to wear it all the time, until one day she just stopped."

"She sacrificed it, ta hold back the—" Dora's eyes shifted.

"Demons?" Maggie ventured. "Apparently, Sasha hid the mirror, the ring, and the demons in a secret cavern in Sister House. And I unwittingly opened their portal."

"They brought the ring back to this realm with them," Shane said. "But Maggie sensed they are after something even more precious to them than *The Ring of Life*."

"They were impatient to escape—hungry," Maggie agreed, gravely.

Merry swallowed, looking up at the sky, as if she might see the swarm fly overhead.

"I suggest everyone hang garlic from your rafters until we know what they're after," Ruth Anne advised. "We'll find the demons and bind them."

"I know what they want," Dora said, her eyes both far away and tactically present. "They're after a ring e'en more powerful than Sasha's. A ring that also returned from the other side, when Ruth Anne raised the school and the cemetery. That's what I feared."

"The *Ring of Resurrection*?" Jillian asked, and Dora nodded. "A ring that returns the dead to life," Jillian explained to the others. "We must find it first. Those demons won't be the only ones looking for it. Wars have been fought over that ring. It will come known that it resurfaced, and no matter how many wards we put up, it will never be enough."

Demons. Portals. The Ring of Resurrection? Merry's mind couldn't process it all. *How had everything changed so suddenly?*

Merry shivered. They all shivered--the night suddenly colder and darker--even as the bonfire burned bright beside them.

The End

Order Book Two: Bloodlines and Bindings here (available May, 2022)

Continue reading for bonus material from The Witches of Dark Root, and check out other April Aasheim books.

BONUS MATERIAL:

EXCERPT FROM THE WITCHES OF DARK ROOT:

The house was cold, a down-in-your-bones cold, and I wrapped my arms around myself, trying to fight off the freeze. I found one of Mother's old fur coats in the entry closet and put it on. It was itchy and musty, but it was warm.

"Where are the cats?" I asked. Aunt Dora had been coming by to feed them, but the house was uncannily quiet and I had no idea where they were caged.

"Probably hiding, afraid they will be turned into another coat." Eve laughed, inspecting me.

"Aunt Dora let them loose in the basement," Merry said.

Eve and I turned our attention to our older sister, watching as she sprinkled a white powder in the shape of a five-pointed star onto the floor. A pentagram. Next, she formed a powdery circle around it. "The star must be inside the circle but the two shapes must not touch," she said.

I nodded, remembering from Mother's book that this was the symbol for protection.

"Maggie," Merry said, not looking up. "Can you sprinkle sea salt around the outside of the house? It will keep your 'thing' from escaping."

I swallowed hard, peeking out the front window. Small black shapes twisted in the night.

"I'm on it," Eve said, and I mouthed a grateful 'thank you' to her.

"What can I do?" I asked, watching Eve through the curtains. She had no awareness of the small creatures that slid into the shadows as she approached.

"Find more candles. The shop was out. Light as many as you can. Mostly whites, but the other colors are okay, too. Just no black ones."

"Got it."

Mother's shop might be devoid of candles, but her house had dozens. I found them tucked into drawers and baskets, and scattered across shelves. Once they were lit, I put them in holders and teacups around the living room. I then took five white tapers and placed them in the spokes of the pentagram—something else I had learned from Mother's book.

Finally, I placed the crystal owl in the center of the pentagram, though I wasn't sure why. It just felt right. When I was done, I tapped Merry on the shoulder.

She inspected the room, smiling. "Just like old times," she said, cocking her head to the side. "I kinda missed this."

"No ritual Magick with Frank, I take it?" I reached inside my purse, pulling out Mother's book and the sage stick. I passed the bundle of sticks to Merry, who nodded approvingly then lit it from a purple candle on the dining room table.

"No magic of any kind, I'm afraid. You know," Merry said, fanning the smoke from the burning sage towards the kitchen. "I sometimes wonder what life would have been like, if we hadn't all moved away. I mean, it wasn't so bad here, was it?"

"Well..." I hesitated, not wanting to dredge up bad memories. "Ruth Anne left and we never talked about it. Some people might say that's pretty bad."

"Yes, but..."

"And Mom was going nuts. You know, the last year that Eve and I were here together, I can't remember her saying more than a handful of words to either of us." I recalled my mother, sitting in her rocking chair, staring vacantly out the window. "It was like she had given up on everything."

"Oh, Mags, I had no idea." Merry draped her free arm around my shoulder, squeezing me. "I shouldn't have left you girls. I'm sorry." She sniffed, rubbing her nose with the back of her hand. "...And I didn't mean what I said about leaving because of you and Eve. That was my excuse. The real reason was..."

She paused, looking around the house we had grown up in.

"It's okay," I said, my own nose beginning to run from the bitter aroma of the sage. I was half-tempted to wipe it on Mother's fur coat but found an old Kleenex in the pocket instead. "We all had to go."

"And some good things came of it," Merry said, brightening. "You got to see the country. I had June Bug. Eve got to live as a glamorous actress in New York."

"Yeah, about that..."

"Yes?"

I stopped. Only a few hours earlier, I would have killed for the chance to tell her about Eve's real life in New York. But things were different now.

"I didn't travel around the country so much as the West Coast."

Merry smiled. "It's all good."

"All done!" Eve returned through the front door, showing us an empty cellophane wrapper. "Now let's get rid of Maggie's monster."

**

"We need to keep the lights off," Merry said, as we moved single-file through the ground floor of the house. Merry braved the front of the line, waving the smoke from the sage stick before us. Eve held the middle, plunging her candle into the shadows around us.

I lingered behind, clutching Mother's book and glancing over my shoulder to ensure that we were alone.

"Spirit of Sister House," we called out. "We demand that you to make your presence known!"

We repeated the phrase in each of the lower rooms: the living room, the dining room, the kitchen.

"It's not really a spirit," I reminded Merry when we had cleared the floor.

"I don't have a word for what it is," she said. "Spirit will have to do."

"What about that room?" Eve nodded towards a door that had always been locked—Mother's secret room. It had been forbidden for so long I had almost forgotten it was there.

Merry nodded and I gave her a quizzical look. Unless she had a key, that door was not going to open. We stood before it. Merry said something under her breath, then tried the handle.

"Crap!" she said, stamping her foot. "I thought it would work."

"Thought what would work?" I asked.

"The incantation, *Door of steel, door that's locked, let me in with just a knock."*

"Where did you learn that?" Eve and I asked.

"Well," Merry admitted. "When I was a kid and couldn't sleep, I'd sneak out here and hide on the staircase watching Mama and her friends. Twice I saw her go into this room after reciting the incantation but I never tried it myself."

"Maybe we should hold hands," I suggested, feeling foolish as I put the book down on the floor. Merry reached for one of my hands and I grabbed Eve by the wrist so that she could still hold onto the candle.

"Let's say it together," Merry said.

"Door of steel, door that's locked, let us in with just a knock."

We said the incantation, our voices one. The candle in Eve's hand flickered.

Merry tried the door again, but it wouldn't budge.

"We forgot to knock," Eve reminded us, rapping on the door. We heard the soft click of the lock and Eve twisted the knob.

We were in.

Eve pushed the candle inside and our heads followed. The space was the size of a small bedroom and was just as crammed with stuff as the rest of the house. But instead of boxes and bins, there were chests and picture frames and books and things that sparkled—a tiny dragon's lair. Something in the far corner glimmered and if I hadn't had to climb a small mountain to get there, I would have retrieved it.

"Mother's hoarding. The early years," Eve said.

Merry passed the sage stick inside as we asked the spirit once again to show itself, with no luck.

"We will come back," Merry promised, shutting the door. "There are secrets in there, I'm sure. But we have other things to deal with now."

She glided towards the staircase and we obediently followed.

"This floor is clean. Now let's go upstairs."

***

Download The Witches of Dark Root Here

ALSO BY APRIL AASHEIM

Want More?

All My Series are in KINDLE UNLIMITED!

Get the next book in the Miss Sasha's School of Magick Series:

Bloodlines and Bindings

The Daughters of Dark Root Series

Read the series that started it all. Four sisters try their hands at life, love, and witchcraft, in this beloved, multi-genational witchy saga.

Magick. Mystery. Romance. Sisterhood.

***Jane Austin meets Charmed.**—Amazon Reviewer**

Get the first book in the series:

The Witches of Dark Root

Or grab the entire collection in one box set here!

The Children of Dark Root Series

(Bridge Series between Daughters of Dark Root and Miss Sashas School of Magick Series)

Get the first book here:

Inherited Magick

Alchemy of a Witch Series.

A Stand alone series featuring lore from current Dark Root books

A young woman fearing for her life, flees her village, and the nefarious witch hunter stalking her.

Along the way, she gathers wisdom and artifacts, meets other magickal people, and learns the ways of magick.

An enchanting witchy saga, filled with mysticism, lore, and romance.

Get the four book collection here:

Alchemy of a Witch Box Set or Paperback

Or get just the first book here:

Alchemy of a Witch Series Page

The Baylee Scott Mystery Series:

A psychic with a penchant for scones solves mysteries from her families tea house.

- Touch of Light
- Touch of Darkness

Other Dark Root Books and Short Stories:

- The Good Girl's Guide to being a Demon
- The Universe is a Very Big Place
- A Dark Root Christmas: Merry's Gift
- The Council of Dark Root: Armand
- A Dark Root Halloween: The Witching Hour
- A Dark Root Solstice: Dora's Dilemma
- A Dark Root Solstice: Magick Mistletoe
- A Dark Root Halloween: The Mystery of Ice Pond Road

About the Author

April Aasheim is a writer living in Portland, Oregon. She is a mother and a wife, and enjoys spending time with her family, and her familiar: Boots the cat.

When not writing, April enjoys reading, dancing, research, and Macaroni and Cheese. And donuts. Mostly donuts. She also reads Tarot cards and plays video games.

Get updates on her current work, and sign up for her newsletter at: www.aprilaasheimwriter.com

Follow her on social media.

www.ingramcontent.com/pod-product-compliance
Ingram Content Group UK Ltd.
Pitfield, Milton Keynes, MK11 3LW, UK
UKHW041637190726
13854UKWH00006B/2545

9 798786 088787